RAVES FOR JAMES PATTERSON

"PATTERSON KNOWS WHERE OUR DEEPEST FEARS ARE BURIED…THERE'S NO STOPPING HIS IMAGINATION."
—*New York Times Book Review*

"JAMES PATTERSON WRITES HIS THRILLERS AS IF HE WERE BUILDING ROLLER COASTERS." —Associated Press

"NO ONE GETS THIS BIG WITHOUT NATURAL STORYTELLING TALENT—WHICH IS WHAT JAMES PATTERSON HAS, IN SPADES."
—Lee Child, #1 *New York Times* bestselling author of the Jack Reacher series

"JAMES PATTERSON KNOWS HOW TO SELL THRILLS AND SUSPENSE IN CLEAR, UNWAVERING PROSE." —*People*

GRAND
CENTRAL

**LARGE
PRINT**

For a complete list of books,
visit JamesPatterson.com.

MISSING PERSONS:
A PRIVATE NOVEL

JAMES PATTERSON
& ADAM HAMDY

GRAND
CENTRAL

LARGE PRINT

Grand Central Publishing
Hachette Book Group
1290 Avenue of the Americas, New York, NY 10104
grandcentralpublishing.com
twitter.com/grandcentralpub

Originally published as *Private Rogue* in hardcover in the UK by Century in 2021, Penguin Random House. First paperback edition published in the UK by Penguin Books in 2022, Penguin Random House.

First North American Edition: January 2024

Grand Central Publishing is a division of Hachette Book Group, Inc. The Grand Central Publishing name and logo is a trademark of Hachette Book Group, Inc.

The publisher is not responsible for websites (or their content) that are not owned by the publisher.

The Hachette Speakers Bureau provides a wide range of authors for speaking events. To find out more, go to hachettespeakersbureau.com or email HachetteSpeakers@hbgusa.com.

Grand Central Publishing books may be purchased in bulk for business, educational, or promotional use. For information, please contact your local bookseller or the Hachette Book Group Special Markets Department at special.markets@hbgusa.com.

LCCN: 2023946033

ISBNs: 9781538754528 (trade paperback), 9781538754535 (hardcover library edition), 9781538766484 (large print paperback), 9781538754498 (ebook)

Printed in the United States of America

LSC-C

Printing 1, 2023

For those who face adversity so others stay safe

CHAPTER 1

"OVERLORD, THIS IS Sabre. We are three clicks from the target."

"Copy that, Sabre. All eyes show a clear run. Maintain your current heading."

"Copy," Captain Joshua Floyd replied.

Command saw no threats, but Floyd knew better than to relax. He had been on missions that had gone from still water to a Category-5 hurricane in the blink of an eye. He checked his radar display and confirmed what he'd been told: no obvious threats.

The engines of his MV-22B Osprey hummed reassuringly as he guided the aircraft low over the pitch-black mountainous terrain. They were flying dark with low infrared in the cabin and cockpit. Floyd used the contours of the illuminated heads-up display to pick out his flight path. He'd rehearsed the mission endlessly. Cross the Pakistan border near Sham Shah, drop low into the Mangwal Valley, and fly north over the mountains of Nuristan, deep into Afghan territory, toward Nangalam and their target. Floyd knew every crease and wrinkle in the rugged terrain, and guided the Osprey with a deftness of touch that meant the Green Beret unit in the main cabin were hardly stirred.

"Looking good," said Nat Porter, Floyd's co-pilot.

"Give them the sixty," Floyd responded.

Nat had the winning smile of a college quarterback. He flashed it now, flipping the cabin ready light from red to green.

"Colonel Elmore, sixty seconds to target," Nat said over the radio, and turned to give Elmore the ready signal—an index finger wound rapidly through the air.

Floyd glanced over his shoulder and saw sixteen heavily armed men in black tactical uniforms run through their final equipment and weapons checks. Colonel Sam Elmore, a grizzled veteran who was used to wrestling death into submission, gave Floyd a thumbs-up.

He pulled the Osprey into a gentle climb, tracking the gradient of the final hill, about two hundred feet above ground level. As they neared the apex of the ridge, he throttled back to reduce airspeed. There was a moment of inertia as the aircraft leveled out. Then came a stomach-churning change of direction as Floyd allowed gravity to take hold and pull them into the valley on the other side.

"Thirty seconds," he said into the radio.

Floyd slowed further, and began the rotor tilt. The propellers, which had been configured as a plane, shifted as the motors on each wing ground them out of position, turning the aircraft into a dual-rotor helicopter, capable of a pinpoint landing. Floyd looked ahead to see their target, a compound of four low rectangular buildings, each about the size of two school buses.

"Ten seconds," he said.

"Ten seconds," Elmore repeated over the radio.

"Sabre, you are a go mission," Command informed them.

"Copy that, Overlord," Floyd acknowledged.

Intelligence reports suggested their mission objective was located in the building that lay to the east of the compound, and Floyd had rehearsed setting the bird down within twenty yards of the structure. He banked slightly, dropped to within fifty feet of the deck, and lowered the landing gear.

"Five seconds," he said.

"Five," Elmore confirmed.

The simple concrete buildings stood like gray teeth against the black sky, and seemed to grow larger as the Osprey swept in.

Floyd's heart started racing when he saw a flash of light off to his left. For the briefest moment the silhouette of a man was illuminated against the southernmost building. Floyd recognized the unmistakable shape of a shoulder-mounted rocket launcher, and watched with horror as the projectile traced a line through the sky, heading directly for them.

"Brace, brace, brace!" he yelled, as he banked starboard. "Brace for impact!"

He knew any attempt to outmaneuver the projectile at this range was futile, so he dropped the bird down and killed engine power. If they were going to get hit, being closer to the ground would increase their chances of survival.

Floyd could see the rocket approaching fast, and quickly elevated the port wing in an attempt to keep the impact away from the fuselage. The rocket hit the port engine, and the explosion sent the aircraft spinning. Floyd felt the landing gear snap as the aircraft thudded onto the ground. He was blinded by bright flames, and the cockpit erupted with a barrage of alarms.

"Sabre is down, I repeat, Sabre is down!" he shouted into his radio. "We have taken hostile fire. Sabre is down!"

"Bravo Nine, sound off!" Elmore yelled, and his unit responded with their condition.

Shielding his eyes against the flames, Floyd made sure the automatic fuel shutoff had killed the feed to both engines. He could see the extinguishers were working, but they weren't enough to put out the inferno that was raging from the port engine, and spreading fast.

"We need to evac," Nat said, eying the flames nervously.

"Agreed," Floyd replied.

"Sabre, this is Overlord. What's your situation?" The operator's voice was calm, but Floyd sensed a panicked edge.

"Port engine is on fire," he replied. "We've got to evacuate."

"Copy that," the operator replied. "Any casualties?"

Floyd looked at Elmore, who was on the same radio channel. He held up two fingers and shook his head somberly.

"We have two KIA," Floyd responded, feeling a familiar lurch deep in his gut.

"Copy," the operator replied. "Do you have eyes on hostiles?"

Floyd peered through the cracked windshield, but saw nothing in the darkness. The glare of the fire was making it impossible to pick out anything further than a few yards away.

"Negative," he replied.

"You are to abort and withdraw to secondary RV," the operator said.

They were being told to abandon the mission and move to a secondary rendezvous point for extraction.

"This is Sabre leader," Elmore cut in. "Negative. We're still on mission."

"You have your orders, Sabre," another voice responded over the radio. Floyd didn't recognize it, but he could identify the confident tone of authority.

He glanced back to see Elmore shake his head in frustration. "Copy that, Overlord."

"Charges," Floyd said to Nat.

His co-pilot immediately reached for a safe beneath the instrument panel.

"We're moving out," Elmore told his unit. "Secondary RV. Let's go."

Floyd unclipped his harness and hauled himself up, while Nat touched his finger to a scanner that opened the safe. Inside was a keypad linked to a series of strategically placed charges concealed throughout the aircraft.

"Do it," Floyd commanded.

Behind him, Elmore's men opened the cargo bay, and the hull ground against rock as the pneumatic jacks forced the door.

Nat input two codes and a digital display was illuminated. It started counting down from five minutes.

"Colonel, we have five," Floyd said.

"Copy," Elmore replied. "Let's move. Weapons hot, eyes sharp."

Elmore's men lowered their night-vision scopes and the two nearest the cargo door ran out in fire formation. The others followed, including two teams of three, who hauled the bodies of their fallen comrades.

Floyd checked the navigation display and made his final radio call. "Overlord, estimated time to RV is two hours."

"Copy that, Sabre. Good luck."

"There's nothing we could have done," Nat said.

Floyd nodded, removed his headset, and ushered his co-pilot ahead of him.

"Contact on my nine!" a voice yelled. There was a sudden flash and a blast of gunfire as one of Elmore's men shot into the night.

Others joined him and a reply came almost immediately, bullets zipping through the air. The plane's nose was pointing north; the enemy seemed to be located to the west, hidden behind a line of rocks that ran between their location and the compound.

"We're sitting ducks in this position!" Elmore yelled. "Bravo nine, double time to those rocks on our three."

He pointed to some jagged shapes about a hundred yards to the east.

Floyd drew his side arm and sprinted as the bullets continued to fly around him. Elmore and his men were laying down covering fire in alternating waves as they fell back to the rock formation. Floyd saw one of the men go down with a leg wound, another was hit in the shoulder, and a third took a head shot that cracked through his helmet.

Floyd and Nat were almost at the formation. More gunfire crackled to their rear, followed by shouts and curses from Elmore's men as they tracked back to help the fallen. Nat scrambled up a large granite slab and Floyd followed.

Suddenly, a man with a black headscarf wrapped around his face reared up from behind the rock, leveled an AK-47 at Nat's chest, and fired. The volley of bullets sent him shuddering backward and tumbling down the slab.

Floyd instinctively raised his gun and pulled the trigger. The man in the black headscarf cried out and fell back. Another quickly appeared from behind the rock and rushed forward, but Floyd was too quick. Two shots in the chest put him down.

Floyd hurried down to Nat and tried to find a pulse that wasn't there. He felt a wave of nausea and wanted to be sick, but his training kept him going. He glanced back toward Elmore and saw the colonel alone in a field of fallen. All his men were either dead or injured. Their mission had become a scene of slaughter.

"Go!" Elmore yelled. "Get out of here!"

He fired a volley at targets Floyd couldn't see. Muzzle flashes flared on the horizon and Elmore was caught by a bullet. Then another. Then another. He cried out in pain and bucked violently as he hit the ground.

Floyd turned away from the horrific scene and climbed up the slab to the first man he'd shot. He grabbed the AK-47 from the dead man's hands and ran. Behind him, there was a violent dawn as the charges on the Osprey detonated, creating a fireball that reached to the heavens. Floyd felt the searing heat and soft push of the blast wave, pressing him forward into the night.

CHAPTER 2

SOME OF THE other parents were gathered beneath the gnarly, bare branches of the old oak tree, but Beth wanted as much sun as possible. It was brutally cold and the air had a razor-sharp bite. The sunlight seemed as faint and unwarming as a refrigerator bulb and would soon be gone, but it was better than nothing. Beth patted her sides and shuffled on the spot, willing the sun to slow its descent behind the roof of Garrison Elementary School. She watched some younger kids running around the basketball court, skipping and skidding across the ice, laughing as they waited for their older siblings. She remembered when Daniel and Marianne had been that age, and while toddlers were cute, they were also exhausting. She preferred her kids at their current ages, still cute, but a little older and a lot more independent. Now seven years old, Danny had all the confidence and charisma of a future president, and Beth sometimes felt he already believed he'd attained that high office. Maria was two years older and was blossoming from a quiet, thoughtful little girl into an assured, intelligent child.

Some of the other parents obsessed over grades, but Beth and her husband didn't care how the kids did at school, as long as they were happy. Maybe that's why she didn't click with the other moms. She glanced over at Laura Fox-Ryan and her little gang of five, who were part of the group huddled under the tree, and got a couple of polite nods in reply. *We're not going to ignore you, because that might be awkward, but we're not inviting you into the circle.*

It reminded Beth of high school. Boasting, envy, and competitiveness were the game there, and her casual indifference to the things others considered measures of success threw them off.

She was almost certain they considered her a bad parent, and she knew there were whispers about the apparent lack of a man in her life.

If they knew the truth, Beth wondered how eager they'd be to make friends. *Better a true enemy than a false friend,* she thought, recalling her father's sound advice.

Her eyes were drawn toward the daily ritual of kids being unleashed on the world. After the first flurry of youngsters surged out in a melee of bags and coats, she saw Danny and Maria walking out together.

"Hey, guys," Beth said. "What news?"

"He's talking Lego again," Maria replied.

"Is there any other subject?" Beth asked.

"No," Danny chuckled. "Where would we be without Lego?"

"Come on," Beth said, ushering them toward the parking lot.

Minutes later, they were heading north along Bear Mountain Highway, past high mounds of blackened snow. Beth engaged in the daily interrogation of her children, while they acted like mobsters on a witness stand, divulging as little information as possible.

"Stuff," Danny replied after Beth asked him to clarify what he had done that day.

She rolled her eyes and glanced at Maria, who sat in the passenger seat of their white GMC Yukon.

"What about you?"

"Other stuff," Maria replied with a smile.

Beth couldn't help but grin.

She switched on the radio as she made a right on Indian Brook Road. Maria immediately started singing along to Ariana Grande as Beth followed the winding route into the pine forest that surrounded Garrison.

As they passed the Mullers' house, Beth noticed a black-and-gold police cruiser parked on a track to their right. She wondered what the State Police were doing out here and glanced in her rearview to see the car pull onto the road behind them.

A moment later, there was a flash of blue and red. Beth glanced back to see the officer in the passenger seat was signaling for her to pull over.

Beth was religious about vehicle maintenance, but had one of her brake lights blown?

"What do they want, Mom?" Danny asked, craning around to see the cop car.

"Probably nothing," Beth replied, but her stomach was tightening into a knot.

She turned off the radio and pulled to the side of the road.

"Are we in trouble?" Maria asked.

"No, honey," Beth assured her as the police car rolled up behind them.

Suspicion kicked in the moment the two men stepped out of the car. They didn't move like cops, and the driver, a tall man with paper-white skin and a thick black goatee, kept glancing up and down the otherwise deserted road. His passenger, a blond-haired man, had his hand on his holstered gun, which was nickel, like an old Smith & Wesson or maybe a Walther P88—both extremely powerful firearms, and neither permitted for state troopers' use.

Beth's mind conjured up her darkest fears. She had lived in dread of this day ever since she and her husband had first planned for it.

"Have you got your seat belts on, guys?" she asked.

The men were a few yards from her vehicle.

Danny and Maria nodded.

"I'm going to need you to switch off the engine, ma'am," the blond man said loudly, drawing his pistol.

Beth threw the Yukon into drive and stepped on the gas. She watched in the rearview mirror as the two uniformed men ran back to their car. Beth turned her eyes on the road as she built speed.

"Mommy!" Danny cried as the Yukon flew around a bend.

Beth glanced at Maria, who gripped her seat belt fearfully.

"It's OK, kids," Beth said. "We're going to be OK."

She glanced in the rearview mirror and saw the police car gaining, but speed wasn't the only advantage out here.

The first gunshot startled her, but it sailed harmlessly past. Danny started crying, and Beth glanced back to see her son's bright eyes shedding tears.

She swerved across the road, aiming at a gap between the trees. It marked a logging trail they'd walked a few times in summer. Beth didn't slow as the road gave way to rutted track, and she kept her foot on the gas as the Yukon hit frozen mud. The big SUV bounced around violently as it climbed the steep track and threw chewed-up mud and slush into the air behind it.

Maria yelped and squealed but Beth kept going, pushing the Yukon to the limit. The suspension crunched and groaned, and the engine growled, but the large car roared on. Beth checked behind her to see their pursuers weren't so lucky. The patrol car made it about ten yards before getting stuck on the steep slope.

They soon crested a rise that took them out of sight of their pursuers, and Beth eased off the accelerator.

"It's OK," she said, reaching around her seat to squeeze Danny's leg. "It's over. We're safe. Is anyone hurt?"

"No," Maria replied.

Danny shook his head.

"Those weren't real police, were they?" Maria asked. Her face was rigid with worry.

"No, honey, I don't think so," Beth replied. She kept stroking Danny's leg and his crying turned to shuddering, uneven gasps. "But it's OK. We're prepared for this, remember?"

Beth hoped the children wouldn't connect the dots and realize what this meant for their father. She could hardly bring herself to think about it either.

Maria nodded uncertainly, and when Beth glanced back she saw Danny doing the same. She was so proud of her kids. Their father would be too.

CHAPTER 3

THE SUN WAS touching the horizon by the time they reached Lake Waramaug. Beth turned left off Preston Hill Road onto the track that led toward Mount Bushnell. The snow was thick up here, and the Yukon growled and grunted its way through deep drifts. The mountain was covered in pines that were so tightly packed they were like bristles on a toothbrush.

The track was kept in good condition by the folks who lived at Marks Hollow, but it didn't look as though it had been plowed for a while. Beth climbed a steep turn. When she looked to her left she saw the lake a mile or so away, shimmering gold in the sunset. Danny had fallen asleep, but Maria's eyes were on the water.

"Isn't it beautiful?" Beth remarked, and her daughter nodded.

About half a mile further on, Beth turned right down a trail that was covered in packed snow. The SUV's wheels spun and slid around, but the snow tires found enough purchase to make slow progress and propel the vehicle forward in uncertain bursts. They turned west, the red sun flickering through the trees, blinding them both. Beth glanced in the rearview and saw Danny's eyelids tremble in the bright light.

"Nearly there," Beth told Maria, who smiled wanly.

The Yukon skated and spun its way along the trail for a little over half a mile until the dense forest thinned and then fell away. Beth drove into a half-acre clearing. A small cabin stood in the center, its tiled roof covered with sparkling snow that was tinted pink in the dying light.

"Here we are," she said, and sensed Maria's relief.

The kids knew and loved this place. Maria called it Gray Havens, which Beth didn't particularly like, but if it helped her daughter process the idea of a sanctuary, she was prepared to put up with the nickname.

Beth stopped the SUV in front of the cabin, and Danny stirred at the sudden loss of momentum. Beth turned to look at her son and saw the familiar bewilderment that marked the transition from sleep to waking. He took in their surroundings, and after a moment, Beth sensed him relax.

"I'm hungry," he said, and she smiled with relief. Hunger was a run-of-the-mill problem that could be solved by her snack-making skills.

"We've got food in the cabin," she said. "Lots of it."

"How long will we have to stay here?" Maria asked.

"Until we figure out what's happening."

"Will we get in trouble at school?" Her daughter frowned.

"No. I don't want you to worry about anything like that," Beth replied.

"Is Dad OK?" Danny asked.

Beth bit her lip. She never lied to her kids. "I hope so. He's never not been OK."

That seemed to satisfy them, and Beth didn't expand on the subject. She stepped out of the car and opened the rear door to help Danny down, but he brushed her hand away with "I'm not a baby, Mom," and jumped into the crisp snow.

He followed his sister, who skipped toward the cabin. The two of them made little puffball clouds of hot breath in the icy air, like a pair of steam engines.

Beth went after them, but she hesitated as she neared the wooden deck that ran around the cabin. She sensed something wasn't right, and froze.

"What is it, Mom?" Maria asked.

"Shush!"

Danny glanced fearfully from his mom to his sister, and the three of them stood still as Beth strained to listen. She heard the rush of wind through the trees, the creak of branches, the brush of pine needles. Then there was something else—an insectoid sound, like a swarm of bees.

Beth felt a wave of nausea as she looked up and saw a drone hovering above the trees near the track.

"Move!" she told the children, and ran across

the deck to the tiny key locker beside the front door. She punched in the code, grabbed the key from inside, and opened the door. She hustled the children into the rustic living room and ran to the window box. She pulled the cushion off, lifted the hinged lid, and took a fabric cover off the gun safe concealed inside. She spun the combination lock to the correct sequence of numbers and turned the thick metal handle. Inside were a couple of pump-action shotguns and an AR-15. She grabbed the rifle and a box of ammunition.

"Stay here," she told the children breathlessly, loading the rifle as she strode through the living room.

Beth opened the front door, pressed the rifle stock to her shoulder, and sighted the target. A hundred, maybe a hundred and twenty feet. Light wind. She squeezed the trigger and the crack of the shot echoed through the cabin. The bullet struck true, sending the drone spiraling into the trees.

Beth knew what was coming next and didn't waste a moment. She ran inside, slamming the door shut.

"Mom?" Maria said uncertainly.

Danny was crying again.

"We've got to go," Beth told them. "Grab our winter coats."

Maria nodded and ran to the rack beneath the stairs. She got coats for all three of them as Beth watched the track through the living room window.

Maria froze first. A moment later, Beth heard it too. First one, then multiple car engines.

Beth ran to Danny and crouched down. She held his shoulders gently. "Dan. Danny," she said, and her heart broke when she saw her son trying to be brave and fight to control his sobs. He was desperate not to let her down. "It's OK," she assured him. "I'm scared too. But we're going to have to leave, and we've got to do it quietly. Do you think you can be quiet?"

Danny took a long, shuddering breath and nodded.

"Good boy," Beth said. She stood up and turned to Maria. "Let's go."

Beth grabbed a long down coat from her daughter, picked up the rifle, and put the box of ammunition in her coat pocket. She led the children through the kitchen and out the back door.

They pulled on their coats as they crossed the clearing to the treeline, hurrying through thick forest until Beth was confident they couldn't be seen.

"OK," she whispered, pulling the children to a halt. "We should be safe here."

Maria and Danny looked petrified, but Beth couldn't console them yet.

"Wait here," she said.

Danny whimpered and Beth stroked his hair. "I promise I'll come back."

She crept toward the cabin. As she neared the edge of the forest she was able to peer through the thickly laden branches and see three black Cadillac Escalades emerge from the mouth of the track and stop in front of the building.

The two men who'd pulled her over jumped out of the lead vehicle. They had ditched their police uniforms and were now dressed all in black. They were joined by five others who emerged from the cars behind.

Beth took her phone from her pocket and checked to see whether she had a signal: nothing, meaning she couldn't send anyone any pictures, which was a disappointment because she knew she couldn't take the device with her either. There was too much risk they'd be able to track it. So she dropped it in the snow, and when the men had all congregated on the other side of the cabin, she hurried back toward the children. She stopped at the sound of the front door being kicked in, and glanced back to catch a glimpse of the men through the cabin's rear windows. They were turning the place over, searching for them.

She reached the children, who were stiff with fear. They breathed sighs of relief when they saw her. Beth ushered them forward, leading them deeper into the forest.

CHAPTER 4

RECENT EVENTS IN Moscow had a huge impact on Private. The organization I'd founded had been labeled a Russian front, and I'd been branded a traitor, but we'd come through it to universal acclaim—it had been a swift and life-changing turnaround. Since then, business had boomed, but Moscow hadn't only changed things for me professionally. Justine and I had started seeing each other again. I knew there were risks in having a relationship with a colleague, but we were good together. My experiences in Moscow had reminded me of the fragility of life, and the need to value the things that are truly important.

Justine and I weren't living together, but we were spending a few nights a week at each other's homes. I wasn't sure she was ready for a serious commitment. We'd hurt each other before and were taking our time so we could avoid making the same mistakes.

Justine had gone to see some friends last night, so I'd spent the evening alone, reviewing case reports from around the world. With numerous offices on five continents, I had to rely on the heads of those branches to manage their own caseloads, but I still liked to be kept well-informed. I ran Private like an intelligence agency, and each office had a great deal of autonomy. Success had temporarily taken me away from frontline detective work in order to focus more on overarching strategy. At least I thought it was success...maybe it was fear? Perhaps Moscow had left me with more than superficial physical scars? I dismissed the thought. The Moscow investigation had led to a degree of infamy that would fade with time. That and the growth of the business were the real reasons I hadn't been doing any genuine detective work recently.

I'd been spending more time in Los Angeles

than I had for a long while, and I was enjoying it. Private Los Angeles was where everything had started, and for that reason it would always be special to me. I would always think of it as home.

I slowed my Mercedes SLS, an extravagant gift from a grateful client, and turned into the entrance to the parking garage beneath our building on Wilshire Boulevard. I stopped at the bottom of the ramp to give the sensor time to recognize my license plate, and the gate rose to allow me inside.

A brief minute later, after sliding the Mercedes into my parking space, I took the elevator up to Private's offices on the fifth floor and emerged into the lobby, where Michelle and Dewayne, Private's two receptionists, sat at their shared desk. Both were on the phone, but they smiled and waved when they saw me. Michelle, a bright young woman in her twenties, signaled something behind me, and I turned to see a tall, muscular man in his early fifties rising from one of the seats in our waiting area. He wore a navy blue suit and had salt-and-pepper hair and a matching beard. He was deeply tanned, his wrinkled skin covered in blemishes and liver spots—the marks of prolonged sun exposure.

"Mr. Morgan?" he said. "I'm sorry to intrude on your day, but I need your help."

His accent was Southern: Georgia or Louisiana.

"I tried to tell him to make an appointment," Michelle said, shielding the receiver.

"This can't wait," the man said.

He drew closer and offered his hand.

"My name is Donald Singer and I need your help finding my daughter. She and my grandchildren disappeared yesterday."

"I don't..." I began.

Singer cut me off. "I know who you are, Mr. Morgan, and I know what you're capable of. I'll pay whatever it costs. I need you to bring my daughter home."

CHAPTER 5

MY WORK MEANS I've made a lot of enemies over the years. I've taken on the Mob, former Soviet spies, assassins, and a great many more dangerous individuals and organizations besides. I knew better than to take walk-ins, so, after listening to the basics, I left Donald Singer in reception and retreated to my office, where I did some background research on the guy. I was coming to the end when Justine knocked and entered. She was always elegant, even when casually dressed as she was now, in jeans and a thick turtleneck sweater. Her eyes shone with intelligence and as ever her smile brightened my day. As Private's resident psychologist and profiler, she supported a wide range of investigations, but always started and ended every day in my office.

I got up and crossed the room to kiss her. I ran my fingers through her jasmine-scented wavy brown hair.

"Jack," she whispered. "This is definitely blurring the line."

We'd made a deal to try to maintain professional boundaries in the office.

"So step away," I suggested.

Instead, she pulled me close and kissed me.

"Now who's blurring the line?" I asked.

She pushed me away playfully.

"How was last night?"

"Fun. Sarah had too much to drink and I had to drive her home," Justine replied. "Did you survive without me?"

"Just about."

"Michelle said the guy in the lobby is waiting for you."

She missed nothing.

"His name's Donald Singer. I was just running background. He's the founder and CEO of Singer Investments, an East Coast property fund. Wife died twenty years ago, leaving him to raise their only child, Elizabeth Singer. She lives in upstate New York with her two children, Daniel and Marianne. They went missing yesterday and he wants me to find them."

"Why you?" Justine asked.

I feigned offense. "He wants the best, of course."

"Well, he can't have you. You're mine."

There was a slight edge to her teasing tone. Things had been great between us while I'd been in LA these past months. Justine wanted to keep it that way, and so did I.

"We do have a New York office," she said.

Justine was right, of course. Our New York office was one of our largest, and the team there were more than capable of handling this case.

"OK," I said. "But if I have to let him down, you're sticking around to help me do it."

I returned to my desk, called Michelle, and asked her to bring in Donald Singer. Minutes later, she showed him into my office.

"Mr. Singer, this is Justine Smith, our chief psychological profiler," I introduced them.

They exchanged greetings and we made ourselves comfortable in the seating area by the windows. Los Angeles spread toward the green hills north of the city. White buildings shone and cars gleamed in the morning sunshine.

"Well?" Singer asked.

"We'll be happy to take your case, Mr. Singer," I said. "I'm afraid I won't be able to handle the investigation myself, but we have a fantastic team in our New York office who I'll assign this to."

Singer nodded slowly and reached into his jacket pocket. He produced a photograph, which he showed us. It was a picture of himself with a young woman and two children.

"Mr. Morgan, I don't want a team. I don't want the second best. I want the best." He handed Justine the photograph. "That's my daughter, Ms. Smith. Her name is Elizabeth. Those are my grandkids, Danny and Maria. I think they're in trouble and I believe Mr. Morgan can find them and bring them back to me."

I glanced at Justine and saw her resolve wavering. It was one thing to have abstract conversations about which cases to take, but when a father pleaded desperation in the face of loss, it was hard to refuse.

"I'm prepared to pay any price." Singer thought for a moment. "Two hundred and fifty thousand, with a half-million-dollar bonus when you find them. How's that sound?"

"That's a very generous offer, Mr. Singer," I replied. "But I can't do it. I have obligations here. And, as I said, we have a highly skilled and experienced team in New York who I trust implicitly. They have the time and the resources to give your case the attention it deserves."

"I understand," Singer replied sadly.

Justine handed him back the photograph. He looked at it fondly before returning it to his breast pocket. There was moment of awkward silence.

"Well, thank you for your time," Singer said, getting to his feet. He looked like a broken man.

Justine shot me a look that communicated exasperation and defeat. I smiled.

"Mr. Singer," she said, "I think I might be able to cover Jack's duties here."

He turned to face me, his expression hopeful. "You mean..."

I nodded. "I'll take the investigation and do my best to find your daughter and grandchildren."

"Thank you, Mr. Morgan," Singer responded gratefully, and for a moment I thought he might cry with relief. "You're a good man. Thank you."

CHAPTER 6

JOSHUA FLOYD HAD spent the night and most of the following day hunkered down in a small cave about two miles from the crash site. He was higher up, on the side of a mountain, at the start of an expansive cedar forest. It was cold, but his flight suit and jacket kept him insulated from the worst of the chill. He'd heard voices around midday and had peered out of the cave mouth to see men creeping through the trees, searching for him. He'd spent the afternoon cleaning the AK-47 until he was certain every component was in the best possible shape. He tried to do the same with his personal locator, but the beacon had been damaged beyond repair, either during the crash or the ensuing escape.

As he looked at the wrecked locator in the dim light of the cave, he thought of Nat and Elmore, and the last time he'd seen them. He couldn't help but picture their families back home, broken by the news of their deaths. Floyd was determined that his own family would never receive such a heartbreaking message.

Exhausted, he had finally fallen asleep in the late afternoon and woke when the light inside the cave was deep purple. He got to his feet, grabbed the machine gun, and crept outside. He paused to scan the area. The air was infused with the scent of cedarwood, and the spicy aroma reminded him of Sunday mornings spent in church at his grandmother's side. Floyd invoked her protection with a brief, silent prayer. Satisfied the men hunting him were not close, he set off, tracking south, retracing the path he'd taken the night of the attack.

He believed his pursuers had gone west, and the border with Pakistan was to the north, but he wasn't about to leave Afghanistan without something to show for all the lives that had been lost. And if any of his comrades had survived, his plan might facilitate a rescue. Floyd hurried through the trees, descending the steep slope to the bottom of the mountain, which would take him back to the crash site and the compound that had been their original target.

Floyd fought gravity for half a mile, and by the time he reached the rocky foot of the mountain, he was breathless and sweaty. The smell of cedar was much fainter here, and there was a smoky hint of distant fire, but when he scanned the rocky horizon, he saw no telltale lights. He continued onward.

In the distance, he heard a dog bark; it was swiftly answered by the cry of a fox. Twenty minutes after he'd left the cave, Floyd slowed and climbed the steep rise near where he'd killed two men the previous night. Their bodies were gone, but Floyd's memory of their anguished expressions haunted him as he dropped to his belly and crawled across the granite slab.

He saw the burned-out wreckage of his Osprey, and to its right the compound that had been their target. There was no sign of any bodies, and the buildings looked to be completely deserted. There were no lights, no vehicles, and the only sound to break the still night was the distant barking of the dog.

Floyd got to his feet and ran toward the nearest structure, which stood to the east of the compound. He skirted the blackened wreckage of the Osprey, trying to avoid looking at pieces of body armor and charred fragments of clothing as he closed the gap to the building.

He pressed himself against the cold concrete wall and crept around the structure. He craned his neck to peer around the corner, but saw no sign of life. He hurried on, staying close to the building. The noise of his boots on frozen rocks sounded like crunching thunder, and he scanned the horizon nervously in case there was anyone around to hear.

The building had a few small windows. When he came to the first, he peered inside and saw nothing but darkness. The same was true of the second window, and when he reached the steel double doors that formed the main entrance, he found them open.

Floyd pushed one wide and immediately recognized the smell that met him: the sweet, acrid stench of death. He stepped into a large hallway to see the bodies of his comrades laid out in rows. They'd been stripped of their uniforms and gear, and were positioned on their backs in their underwear. Floyd gagged and couldn't hold back his tears as he registered so many faces he recognized. Elmore, Nat, and at the back of the hallway, caught by the moonlight coming through a small window, in a more advanced state of decomposition, Said Masry, the CIA spy they had been sent to rescue.

An Al-Qaeda cell had said they were holding him for ransom, but it looked as though he'd been killed long before they'd arrived. Floyd couldn't understand why they would execute such a high-value asset, but inquisitiveness took second place to anger and he hurried from the building. There was nothing for him here.

He ran outside and turned north, heading back up the mountain, the way he'd just come. Shock and grief were quickly giving way to fury. He had to avenge the fallen, and the best way of doing that was to get home and tell people the truth about what had happened here. America would make the perpetrators answer for their crimes.

CHAPTER 7

"I'M SO TIRED, Mom," Danny said as they trudged along the single-lane road.

The sun was falling and night's chill nipped at Beth's cheeks.

"We're nearly there," she replied. "You OK?" she asked Maria, who was a few yards behind them.

The girl had withdrawn into her own world. It took a moment for her to register her mom had spoken, but finally she nodded.

After they'd fled the cabin, they'd made their way through the forest toward the edge of Oscawana Lake. It had been night by the time they were within sight of the placid water. By then the temperature had dropped rapidly, so they'd needed to find shelter quickly. Beth had surveyed the properties that edged the lake, and found a huge mansion being built on the east shore. She'd helped the children over the wire fence, and found some shards of metal, which she'd used to pick the padlock on the foreman's office. It had been years since she'd been taught how to roll a tumbler, but it came back to her soon enough. Inside, they'd found a couple of couches, some snacks, water, and a coffee machine. More importantly there was a heater, which had kept them warm as they'd slept.

In the morning, Beth had risen before the children and spent a few calm moments considering her options. Local motels were out; their pursuers would be looking for any recent arrivals. They could go to the few friends she had in Garrison, but she wasn't sufficiently close to any of them and her presence might put them in harm's way. So she'd settled on the only man she felt she could trust who lived within reasonable walking distance. Once the kids had woken and feasted on a terrible breakfast of Cheetos and Hershey bars, they'd set out for Pleasant Valley, which was about a ten-hour walk cross-country.

The kids hadn't complained much in the morning, but after a lunch made up of the remains of the snacks Beth had taken from the site office, hunger had frayed tempers, and there had been a couple of difficult hours marching along quiet rural roads, bickering in the freezing cold. Beth had thought about hitching a ride, but every contact was a potential lead for their would-be abductors, and the level of sophistication they'd demonstrated in tracking her to the cabin suggested she was dealing with professionals. Finally, late in the afternoon, the kids had stopped arguing and lapsed into exhausted silence.

As they finally approached the outskirts of Pleasant Valley, a car roared by at speed and the driver sounded his horn. Was it a warning? Or a loud question: *What the hell are you doing walking out here?* The car disappeared around a bend, and Beth and the children followed at a slow, steady, and fairly miserable pace. A few minutes later, she caught sight of what she was looking for: a narrow driveway that ran north off Freedom Road.

"That's it," she told her children, and saw a glimmer of hope light up both faces.

They turned right and followed the trail

through rough scrubland that had been seasoned with a scattering of icy snow. The trail bent right before straightening up, and there at the end, Beth saw the single-story home of an old friend.

He emerged from the house as they approached. Beth glanced around to see if she could spot the motion sensors that were likely to have announced their arrival. She wasn't surprised not to see anything; he'd be too conscientious to leave such things anywhere they could be seen. Apart from grayer hair, wrinkles, and the fact he wasn't in uniform, her former instructor, Ted Eisner, looked the same. He still had that ramrod posture that made him seem even taller than his six feet two inches. He was broad with a barrel chest, and wore a US Army branded T-shirt and green cargo pants.

"I'll be damned," he said, stepping off the porch in front of the house. "Elizabeth Singer. And these must be your kids."

"Sergeant Eisner," Beth responded.

"It's just Ted now," he said, stopping near the children. "And you are?"

"Danny and Maria," Beth replied.

"Pleased to meet you, Danny and Maria. I

used to work with your mom, until she decided she had better things to do with her life."

The remark was delivered with a smile, but it was clearly intended to hurt. He was obviously still smarting.

"Not better," Beth replied. "Just different."

"I guess you could say that," Ted said, looking her up and down. "So what brings you here, on foot and all bedraggled?"

Beth took a moment to think about how best to answer.

"Never mind," he said, before she could. "It's too cold to wait out here for you to figure out a lie. You'd better come inside and do it."

He started back toward the house, and Maria and Danny looked at their mother uncertainly.

"You know Mom doesn't lie," Beth said. "He's just being grumpy because we had an argument a while back."

Ted glanced over his shoulder. "Come on, Singer. I might not feel the light of forgiveness much longer."

Beth nodded at her children and the three of them followed the old man inside.

CHAPTER 8

I'D SPENT THE day learning everything I could about Elizabeth Singer. Public records and internet research told me very little, other than that she was the daughter of Donald and Mary Singer. Donald had filled in the rest for me. Mary had died twenty years ago, and he'd dealt with his grief by devoting himself to his property empire. Elizabeth, or Beth, as Singer told me she preferred to be called, lived outside Garrison, New York, and had two young children, who attended the local elementary school. I couldn't find anything about their father, and Singer had said that he wasn't in the picture.

Beth didn't have any social media presence, and her finances were unremarkable, except for one thing; as far as I could tell, she had no sources of income. Singer said he didn't support her. He offered to regularly, but she always turned him down.

It was a little after six when I wandered down to Maureen Roth's computer lab on the fourth floor. I'd recognized the importance of computer crime early on, and had ensured Private had the very best people and technology at its disposal. Maureen Roth, known to everyone at Private as Mo-bot, was a computer geek extraordinaire. Fifty-something, she was a salutary lesson in the unexpected. Her tattoos and spiky hair suggested a cold, hard rebel, but she had the warmest heart and was thought of by many at Private as their second mom, someone they could go to with any problems. The only thing that hinted at a softer side, and spoke to her age, were the bifocals she wore, which I always said looked as though she'd lifted them from a Boca Raton grandmother. She managed a team of six tech specialists in the LA office, and oversaw dozens of others in Private's international units.

When I stepped into the super-cooled lab, I found her with Private's chief criminalist, Seymour Kloppenberg, nicknamed Dr. Science—or Sci for short. He ran a team of twelve forensic scientists who worked out of a lab in the basement of the building. He was an international expert on criminology, and when time allowed, would consult for law enforcement agencies all over the world, ensuring Private stayed current with the very latest scientific thinking. A slight, bookish man, Sci dressed like a Hells Angel, which was where I think his heart lay because he was always restoring old muscle bikes.

These two had been with me since the early days of Private, and were often the first people in the office and the last to leave. Diligent and brilliant, I'd known them long enough to consider them good friends.

"Better stand up straight. The boss is here," Mo-bot joked. She nudged Sci, who was leaning against her desk.

I smiled as I walked deeper into her lair. Computer servers, routers, and black boxes whose purpose I didn't know filled the racks that lined the walls. I could not help but imagine them as her minions, watching me. Judging me.

"I hear someone got you out of retirement," Sci said.

"Time you stopped moping around like an old geezer," Mo-bot added.

"That hurt," I replied. "It's true that I'm working a case, though, and I need your team to run a full background, but since they've clocked off for the day, you'll have to do it."

Sci laughed and Mo-bot pursed her lips. She was about to reply when my phone rang.

"Elizabeth Singer. These are her details." I handed her a piece of paper, and answered my phone.

"Where are you?"

It was Justine calling me.

"In the reprobate's lair," I replied, and earned myself a withering look from Mo-bot.

"Which one—Sci or Mo?" Justine asked.

"The digital enchantress," I said.

"You still want that ride to the airport?"

"Sure," I replied. "I'll meet you downstairs in ten."

"How are you both?" I asked Mo-bot and Sci as I hung up.

"Hurt and offended," Mo-bot replied. "Reprobate?"

"Pretty good," Sci chimed in.

"Staff satisfaction at fifty percent," I responded. "I'll take it."

"I don't know why I put up with you," Mo-bot said.

"Because you love me. Give me a call if you find anything on Beth Singer," I replied.

"Will do," Mo-bot said. "Have a safe flight."

I headed back upstairs to my office to grab my ready bag, an emergency carryall I kept for just such unexpected trips, and then down to the basement parking garage. Justine was in her black Mercedes S65, and the engine was running. I was greeted by a blast of warm air when I opened the passenger door and slid my bag onto the tiny back seat. I got in and kissed her.

"You sure you want to do this?" she asked as she put the car in drive and we started our journey.

"This isn't just about Donald Singer," I confessed. "I need to get back out there." We hadn't discussed it much, but she knew recent events in Moscow had taken their toll on me. "And this feels like a good case to ease me back in."

Justine nodded. "I just don't want to lose what we've built over the past few months."

I squeezed her leg reassuringly. "Nor do I, believe me. I'll find this woman and her kids and be back before you know it. You probably won't even notice I'm gone."

"Now that's impossible," she replied as she pulled onto Wilshire Boulevard and joined the rush-hour traffic heading west.

CHAPTER 9

"YOU GONNA TELL me what's going on?" Ted asked as Beth returned to the living room.

The place was a museum. *The Edward Eisner Museum of Military Excellence,* Beth thought, and couldn't help but smile. There were medals on display and photos of him with senior brass, one with President Obama, others on deployment, and about a dozen of him giving instruction. There was a glass case that contained fragments of shrapnel taken from his leg, along with trophies he'd plundered from Afghan and Iraqi enemies—shell casings, medals, watches with photos of Osama bin Laden and Saddam Hussein, and other strange keepsakes.

The furniture was old but well cared for, but the television was new and enormous, and Beth guessed it was a source of company. Ted Eisner was a naturally abrasive man. People often thought a heart of gold lay beneath the rough exterior, but she knew his heart was made of steel and was locked away in an icebox. He had been a great instructor, but eventually he fell out with everyone who crossed his path, including Beth. She hadn't spoken to him for more than ten years, despite living less than fifty miles away.

Danny and Maria had taken ages to settle in the strange house, but were now asleep in Ted's spare room, Danny on the floor because he didn't want to share the queen bed with his "stinky" sister.

"Is it your husband?" Ted pressed. Even now, Ted refused to say his name. To begin with, Beth had suspected there was a racial element to Ted's dislike of her husband, but she came to realize the animosity wasn't motivated by the fact he was Black; Ted simply resented the choices she had made after getting married.

Beth had tried not to think about her husband too much since the men posing as cops had pulled her over. Getting her kids to safety was her primary focus; she didn't have time to worry about him at the moment. And she definitely couldn't allow Maria and Danny to see she that she was worried—they wouldn't be able to cope if they thought anything had happened to their father. But what else could it be? Beth hadn't been in the field for more than ten years, and the chances of an old enemy targeting her after all this time were remote.

"I think so," she conceded, taking a seat on a brown leather couch.

Ted was in an easy chair, nursing a bottle of beer.

"I told you he'd be trouble."

That was Ted. No empathy, just a dogged belief he was always right. If she hadn't been so worn down by events, Beth might have risen to the provocation, but instead she stayed silent.

"I'm sorry," he said in a moment of uncharacteristic reflection, "but you were one of my best. If you hadn't been a damned woman, and fallen in love, you could have gone all the way. Pentagon material, dammit."

"Even your apologies stink, Sarge," Beth replied.

"It wasn't a real apology. I still think you were a damned fool letting yourself get trapped by life's baggage. Kids? Damned kids? You were a warrior. You had a great thing going, and you ruined it."

"Thanks. Raking over my perceived failings is exactly what I need right now."

"Face the truth, soldier," he snapped. "If you had anywhere else to go, you'd already be there."

Beth got to her feet. "You're as exhausting as ever. I'm going to crash." She was furious with the old man, but she didn't want a fight. She wouldn't put it past him to kick them out if things turned sour.

"I'm sorry for my bluntness," he said at last. "And that's a genuine apology. Sometimes, I... well... this damned mouth of mine has killed far too many friendships. You threw it away, Beth. All of it. I find it frustrating, that's all."

"I get that," she said. "Goodnight."

She left the room quickly, keen not to give him a chance to reply. Within minutes, she was in bed beside Maria. She lay listening to her children, who breathed deeply in a peaceful sleep, something Beth knew she wouldn't get tonight while her mind fizzed with anxiety and anger.

CHAPTER 10

I WAS IN the frozen landscape north of Moscow with Dinara Orlova and Leonid Boykov, studying the ancient wreckage of an accident. Two cars protruded from a thick drift of pristine snow, their twisted shells mangled together, jagged shards of rusted metal spearing the night. Behind them, a snow-covered forest faded into darkness. As I looked at the shadows between distant trees, I felt a primeval fear building within me. There was something stalking me. Something merciless...

"Mr. Morgan?" A voice roused me from my dream, and I woke to see one of the flight attendants at my shoulder. "We're starting our descent."

I rubbed my eyes and looked around the cabin to see my fellow passengers stretching and preparing for landing. Bright sunlight flooded the compartment as blinds were raised.

The plane touched down at JFK, and I grabbed my bag from the overhead bin. After a short delay waiting for the jetway, I disembarked and hurried through the terminal. Red-eye flights from all along the West Coast were arriving. The building was full of sleepy people grasping cups of coffee. I went into the arrivals hall and was about to head for the cab stand when I saw a face I recognized.

"Justine gave me your flight number," Jessie Fleming said as she approached.

Jessie was the head of Private New York. Now in her mid-thirties, she was a former FBI agent I'd hired straight out of the New York field office's Counterintelligence Unit. It was one of my very best decisions.

"You come to my town without telling me?" she asked mockingly.

"I didn't want to distract you," I said. "It's just a missing persons case. Something I can handle alone."

"OK. Well, even if you don't need a partner, the very least I can do is give my boss a ride."

"That would be great," I said. "Thanks, Jessie."

"Where we heading?" she asked.

"Garrison. Upstate. I'll give you the details on the way."

"It's good to see you," she said. "In person, I mean."

We had a video conference call every week, something I did with all the managers of our offices.

"I was beginning to wonder if you'd gotten stuck behind your desk," she went on.

"Not stuck," I replied. "Just comfortable."

"Well, we wouldn't want that." She flashed a smile. "My car's this way."

I followed her outside and ice-cold air stung my lungs. We crossed the street and went into the terminal garage. She led me to her car, one of Private's staff vehicles—a black Nissan Rogue SUV. We got in, and started our journey north.

CHAPTER 11

DANNY WAS SNORING gently when Beth put her hand over his mouth. His eyes opened instantly and filled with a wild look of fear. Beth rubbed his arm to soothe him, and signaled for him to be quiet. Maria was already up and putting on her shoes.

"We need to go," Beth whispered.

Danny nodded.

Ted's spare room was much like his living room, full of old furniture and military memorabilia. His life in the Army was all he had, and he clung to it like a desperate lover who refused to move on from a broken relationship. Beth had been glad to leave her old life behind, but then she had her family. Ted had no one.

"I need the bathroom," Danny said as Beth helped him on with his shoes.

"We'll stop on the way," she told him. "Come on."

She gently ushered the children out of the room and they crept along the corridor through to the kitchen, which was a small, sad place. There was no stove, just a two-hob countertop camping cooker, a small table with a single chair, and some ancient cabinets that had been transplanted from the seventies. Beth pictured Ted eating here alone, suddenly feeling a pang of pity for the difficult old man.

She unlocked the door to the garage and led Maria and Danny inside. She eased the door shut behind them and switched on the light, illuminating Ted's ten-year-old black Buick Enclave. He might not have been a government employee anymore, but he certainly bought cars like one. It was the kind of sensible SUV favored by G-men all over the country, and Beth wondered whether her former instructor had purchased it at a federal auction.

She found the keys hanging in a tiny cabinet by the kitchen door, and unlocked the car.

"Is this stealing?" Danny asked as Beth opened the back door.

"No, honey," she replied. "We're just borrowing it."

He nodded thoughtfully, but Maria gave her mother a skeptical look as the kids climbed in the back. Beth slid into the driver's seat. She found the remote for the garage door in a cubby in the center console and pushed the button. The door started rising and Beth put the key in the ignition, but when she tried the engine, she was greeted with silence. She tried it again. Nothing happened.

"Mom," Maria said, and Beth turned to see Ted standing in the kitchen doorway, a look of disappointment clouding his face.

There was a time when Beth would have been afraid of the man, but now, dressed in yellow and black pajamas that made him look like an angry bee, she was only annoyed at having been caught.

"Well, well, well," he said, shuffling through the obsessively tidy garage in a pair of open-back slippers. "Looks like we've got ourselves a family of thieves."

Beth glanced back at her children. Danny seemed on the verge of tears, but Maria was defiant.

"It's going to be OK," she assured them.

Ted opened the passenger door and sat down next to Beth. He stared directly ahead, and for a moment she watched him in silence.

"I can't believe you were just going to steal my car," he said at last, and she felt the children hold their breath, ready for a scolding. "Without even saying goodbye," he added, and turned to face Beth with a palpable expression of hurt.

He hesitated. Beth sensed he had more to say, but his mouth snapped shut, and he leaned forward and opened the glove compartment to reveal a bundle of crisp twenties and a holstered pistol.

"I don't know what kind of trouble you're in, but it's rare that money can't help," he said. "And I'll trade you this pistol for that Kalashnikov you brought with you. This is more discreet."

Beth smiled, overcome by his generosity. Tears sprang to her eyes. "Thank you, Sarge."

"Don't go getting soft on me," Ted said. "I thought I drilled that kind of nonsense out of you."

He leaned under the dash and signaled for Beth to bend down. She did so and saw his finger against a tiny lever.

"Immobilizer," he said. "Just flip it."

He pressed the switch and, when Beth tried the ignition, the engine came to life.

"Ted, I can't say what this means to me. To my family."

"That's Sarge to you, grunt," he responded, heaving himself out of the car. When he turned to face her, he sported a heavy frown. "I warned you about that soppy stuff. Just make sure you stay alive so you can come visit again," he said without any change of expression.

Beth smiled and put the gearshift in reverse.

"Yes, Sarge," she said as she backed the Buick out of the garage.

CHAPTER 12

IT TOOK US a little over an hour and a half to reach Elizabeth Singer's house on Avery Road in Garrison. I used the time to bring Jessie up to speed, and she asked many of the searching questions I'd put to Donald Singer: Did Beth have any connections to organized crime? Strange new friendships? Had there been any ransom requests? The answers to these questions were no, and neither Jessie nor I could figure out why a seemingly law-abiding mother of two would simply disappear with her children.

Three missing persons reports had been filed, and Jessie suggested we check in with the local police as a courtesy, but first I wanted to visit Elizabeth's house.

Avery Road was located in a quiet residential area north of Garrison. The street cut through a thick forest, and houses nestled in large lots between long runs of densely packed pine trees. Mounds of blackened snow were piled everywhere, and ice crystals sparkled on roofs and treetops.

"This is it," Jessie said, indicating number 1085, Beth's address.

Jessie swung the Nissan onto a graveled driveway and took us up to a single-story, red-brick bungalow. Elizabeth's house stood at the heart of a one-acre garden. The brickwork was pristine, the slate roof covered in a thick layer of snow. An ice-crusted swing set and slide formed a play area near the trees.

I grabbed my Arc'teryx winter coat from the back seat while Jessie parked in front of the house. We both got out and approached the front door. She rang the bell and I searched the plant pots for any sign of a spare key but found nothing. Jessie produced a set of lock-picking tools and opened the door in under sixty seconds.

"Hello?" I said, as we went inside, but the place was as still as a museum.

"You take the bedrooms," I suggested, indicating a corridor that led off to the left.

Jessie nodded and headed that way. I pressed along the entrance hall and went through a doorway on my right, into the living room. There was nothing immediately remarkable about the house. A few toys were scattered here and there, and the living room was clearly set up for a young family. A handful of Lego models were clustered in one corner, near a Captain America beanbag. A fabric-covered sofa faced a large TV and the bookshelf beside it was packed with children's books. Framed photos of Elizabeth and her two children, Daniel and Marianne, covered every surface, and larger pictures of the children hung on the walls. There was no doubt about Elizabeth's priorities in life—their smiles could be seen everywhere I looked.

I checked the drawers in the TV stand and found spare batteries for the remote, a couple of kids' card games.

I moved into the kitchen, which was a large open-plan space at the back of the house, with floor-to-ceiling windows that overlooked the backyard and the forest beyond. The fridge was covered in magnets that secured reminders and school papers against its surface. The magnets looked like a historical trail of places the family had visited: the Empire State Building, Disney World, Busch Gardens. There were dozens, but a couple of odd ones popped out at me—Kabul Bird Market and the Great Mosque of Kufa in Iraq. Not the sort of places I imagined this family touring. I searched the cupboards and drawers, but found nothing else out of the ordinary.

"You got anything?" Jessie asked as she entered.

I shook my head. "You?"

"Nothing," she replied. "They're vanilla."

"I wouldn't say that," I said, pointing out the unusual fridge magnets.

"Might be from friends," Jessie suggested.

I pulled open the only drawer I hadn't searched and found it full of spatulas, large serving spoons, and an assortment of odd kitchen tools. I rifled through, and near the bottom discovered a bottle opener with an emblem on the handle. I recognized it immediately—the three lightning strikes crossing a raised gladius sword, the emblem of Third Special Forces Group, a Green Beret unit.

"She might have a military connection," I said, showing it to Jessie. "They don't sell these in gift shops. It's a trophy given to members of the unit who've seen action."

"Boyfriend? Family member?" Jessie asked.

"Maybe," I replied. "I'll ask Mo-bot to run a contact check. See if Beth Singer has a connection to anyone who served in this unit. It's not much of a lead, but it's the best we've got."

CHAPTER 13

FLOYD FELT AS though a rodent was gnawing his innards. This was a deep and profound hunger, the likes of which he hadn't experienced since his escape and interrogation course, when he'd had to survive in the Rockies for ten days as part of his training for Third Group. And even that had not been as bad. He'd been climbing into the Hindu Kush mountains for hours, using the map in his flight suit to guide him toward the border with Pakistan. It was cold, and the snow-covered cedar forests yielded no sign of food. It was February, and any animals were either hibernating or had the good sense to keep well away from the desperate American pilot. He'd managed to find a stream with clear water, and had purified it using one of the tablets from his emergency kit, but the chill liquid only served to make his stomach feel even emptier.

Floyd pulled his flight jacket tight and pressed forward, following a rutted track that wound up the steep mountainside. As he walked around the bend, he spotted some marks in the snow in the center of the trail. They looked like the tracks of a small, cloven-hoofed animal—perhaps a goat? The thought of such a creature set Floyd's mouth watering, but he pushed images of hot stew from his mind and focused on the task at hand. According to the map, he wasn't far from Kamdesh, a town located on the slopes of the Bashgal Valley. The CIA briefing he'd read before the mission said the village was the ancestral home of the Kom people. It had seen heavy fighting when the War on Terror had been at its peak. There would be food, and possibly even a phone, when he reached it.

Floyd followed the rutted track east. After a short while the forest to his right thinned and then fell away to be replaced by a sheer drop. It was too dark to see the valley floor, and when Floyd threw a stone over the edge, he didn't hear it hit the bottom. The track turned west, and as he followed it, he saw lights dotting the mountainside ahead. Some of the closest were flickering—fires, Floyd assumed—and he immediately began walking faster, drawn instinctively to their warmth.

The town was built on the steep mountainside. Its two-story homes were clustered in tiered terraces, arranged so that the roof of one house would act as a prop to its higher neighbor. Made of cedarwood and red and brown mud bricks, with concrete supports, the houses were simple and functional. Floyd guessed there were perhaps two or three thousand homes ranged across the mountain, and most of them were in darkness.

He hugged the treeline to his left as he approached the foot of the settlement. Narrow paths ran through the town, cleared of snow to reveal rough stone or gravel beneath. Not great surfaces for moving silently, but Floyd hoped the sound of televisions coming from some of the homes would cover his approach. His plan was simple: break into one of the homes, grab some food and any useful supplies, and move on as quickly as possible.

He was twenty yards from the first house, which was completely dark. It looked a little more run-down than some of its brightly lit neighbors, and as Floyd got closer, he noticed some of the brickwork was missing and had been replaced with matted straw. He heard the movement of animals and the lowing and calling of goats as he approached the building. He pushed through one of the straw in-fills and saw that the first floor was a stable.

He glanced up at the terrace that was built on the roof of the first floor, and spied irregularities in the brickwork that would make good hand- and footholds. As he reached for the first hold, Floyd sensed movement behind him and turned to see a figure in a heavy Russian Army issue winter coat. The figure stepped forward out of shadow and Floyd saw it was a wide-eyed teenage boy.

"Don't be afraid," Floyd said, but he got no further.

A sudden blow to the back of his skull sent him crashing to the ground. As he was swept out of the conscious world, he saw a second, much older man, loom over him, his face disfigured by the jagged scars of violence.

Floyd cursed his own carelessness as everything went black.

CHAPTER 14

"WHO ARE YOU again?"

Steve Shaw, the ruddy-faced local police chief, was either in need of a neurological examination or he was trying to make a point. I'd already told him who we were and why we were there, before he'd invited us into his corner office in the Highland Falls Police Department, a tiny red-brick station he shared with the local ambulance service. Shaw was most definitely trying to be a big fish in a little pond, the walls of his office lined with medals, certificates, and photos of him with local dignitaries. When I looked a little closer, I saw some of the medals had been won at high school swim meets. Every photo featured him oozing self-satisfied pomposity, which was exactly the expression he wore now as I once again introduced myself and Jessica to him. I glanced at her as I did and she flashed me a smile.

"And why should I tell you anything, Mr. Morgan?"

"Our client filed the missing persons report with you, correct?" I asked.

"Indeed. And when he filed it, he didn't ask whether we would assist an overpriced glory hunter with free information."

"Is Greg Chandler still overseeing this department?" Jessie asked. "He and I used to throw back beers every now and then when I was with the Bureau."

Shaw grinned arrogantly. "Chandler moved up to the Capitol. I'm on the shortlist for his job, but I don't like to throw back too many beers."

"We just want some background on Ms. Singer," I said. "Anything you can tell us about friends, local contacts, people she might have gone to in time of need."

Shaw was impassive.

"We'll reciprocate. Bring you in on anything

we find. We'll give you additional investigative resources. Private is one of the world's leading detective agencies."

"So you say, Mr. Morgan," Shaw replied. "And while I appreciate your generous offer, we do everything by the book here, and the book says: Don't share information with third parties. So I'm sorry, I can't help you."

I shook my head and shrugged. It was time to admit defeat. Some people were obstinate for the sake of it. Others thought they were doing the right thing. I suspected Shaw was the former.

"Thanks for your time, Chief," I said, getting to my feet and leading Jessie out.

We stepped into a small open-plan office at the front of the building. A couple of uniform cops were at their desks, and the chief's assistant was on the phone. She waved at us and signaled the exit.

"Talk about making us feel welcome," Jessie remarked.

"Places like this are good for keeping our feet on the ground," I replied as we headed for the door.

As we crossed the threshold I reached into my

pocket to answer my ringing phone. The display showed Mo-bot's smiling face.

"Go ahead," I said.

"No 'hello'?" she replied. "No 'how are you'?"

"How are you?" I asked as we stepped into the New York winter. A storm was coming in from the north, and the first flurries had started.

"We don't have time to waste on pleasantries," Mo-bot shot back, and I laughed. "I've found a nearby unit contact. Former instructor with the Third called Ted Eisner. He lives about an hour from Garrison. Might be nothing, but he's the only former member of that unit within a hundred miles."

"Thanks," I replied. "We'll check it out."

"Anytime," Mo-bot said. "And I'm fine. Thanks for asking, Jack."

I hung up and crossed the parking lot. "That was Mo. She found an instructor from the Third Special Forces Group who lives upstate. It's tenuous, but it's the best we've got right now."

"A lead is a lead," Jessie replied as she unlocked the car. "A good detective chases them all down, right?"

"Right," I agreed.

CHAPTER 15

THE WEATHER HAD turned, and heavy snow tumbled in a swirling, blinding cascade as Beth steered Ted's Buick west along I-80. She was crawling behind a long and steady stream of traffic. Two lanes of red lights stretched into the distance before being lost to the white storm. Beth squinted, but it was getting increasingly difficult to see. There had been an accident on the other side of the interstate. Two lines of vehicles were at a standstill behind the wreckage of a pileup. Police and paramedics were on the scene, and the flashing lights of their vehicles gave everything an ethereal, purple tint.

Beth and the children had been on the road for hours but had only traveled a hundred and fifty miles. Their slow progress had taken its toll on the children, and Danny had been complaining about feeling carsick for the past forty-five minutes.

"How much longer, Mom?" Maria asked.

"My tummy hurts," Danny added.

"Why don't you swap with your sister?" Beth suggested.

"I don't want to go in the back," Maria protested. "I'll feel sick."

"But it's OK for me to," Danny snapped back.

"How much farther?" Maria pressed.

The journey from Garrison to Chicago should have taken twelve hours, but at this rate they'd be on the road for days. Beth was trying to reach Connor Reid, one of her oldest friends, but she knew it was foolish to think she could push through this weather.

"Mom, I really think I'm going to be sick," Danny said, and when she glanced in the rearview mirror, Beth saw he'd turned a grim shade of green.

She opened the windows to swap some of the

stuffy heater air for an icy blast. She signaled, and forced her way onto the shoulder. The car slid and slipped as it came into contact with the icy slush massing at the edge of the highway. She steered into the skid and brought the vehicle to a halt.

Danny jumped out and leaned against the car, gulping in deep breaths. Beth got out and grabbed his coat from the back seat. She threw it over his shoulders and stroked his shoulder.

"Don't fight it," she said, and then realized he was sobbing. "It's OK, Danny. It's OK." She stroked his hair. "We're going to stop for the day."

Beth glanced around and over the tops of the passing cars. Through the thick flurries she saw a brightly lit sign for the Relax Inn, Bloomsburg.

Danny looked up with wild fear in his eyes. "I don't want to stop. I want to get to Uncle Connor's."

"It's OK," Beth assured him. "We'll find somewhere safe and wait out the storm. How are you feeling?"

"A little better."

"Think you can handle a short drive?"

Danny nodded and wiped his eyes.

"That's my little soldier," she said, crouching to give him a hug.

He turned to climb in the back, but found his sister grinning at him.

"If I'd known you were going to make such a fuss, I would have let you have the front seat in the first place."

Beth grinned at her. Maria loved her little brother, but made a real effort not to let him know that.

"What do you say, Danny?" Beth asked, but before he could reply, Maria cut in.

"Oh, it's OK, Mom. I don't want his thanks. I'm only doing this so I don't have to listen to his whining."

Beth shook her head, and Danny frowned as he clambered in the front seat. He buckled himself in while Beth jogged around the car and got in.

"We're going to stop until the storm passes," she told Maria.

Beth started the car and eased back into the line of traffic heading for the next exit.

CHAPTER 16

WE MADE SLOW progress to Pleasant Valley. Powder was being dumped by thick gunship-gray clouds that hung low over the mountains. Jessie drove carefully—our journey was interspersed with glimpses of others who hadn't been so cautious and had come off the roads. We'd always stop and ask if they needed help, but most already had all the aid they needed from other passing motorists, and those who didn't were waiting for roadside assistance to tow them out of trouble.

"I'll never understand people who don't want to help," Jessie said as we reached the outskirts of

Pleasant Valley. A roadside sign told us it had a population of 9,608.

"It's cold. Maybe people don't want to risk catching a chill," I replied.

Jessie shook her head. "No, I was talking about the chief of police. Why be such a stickler?"

I shrugged. I'd encountered plenty of sticklers over the years and it was impossible to say why they were so inflexible. They were generally almost impossible to reason with, and yet utterly convinced they were right.

"I think it's a sign of a lack of confidence," Jessie declared. "They can't think creatively, so anything that requires them to step outside the rules is scary."

"Maybe," I replied. "Or maybe they just enjoy making life difficult for everyone else."

Jessie smiled, and took a right onto a narrow drive that ran between two stretches of woodland. A set of fresh tire tracks had been carved in the new snow, and we followed them around a gentle bend to a parking area that lay in front of a single-story house. The tire tracks ran up to the adjacent double garage.

Jessie parked and we got out. I grabbed my coat

from the back seat. Jessie did likewise and we started toward the house as we pulled them on. The snow fell so thick and fast I could already feel it beginning to soak through my clothes in the short time it took me to zip up my coat. The swirling storm muffled all sound, and even the crunch of our footsteps took on a muted quality as we approached the front door.

It opened before we reached it and a tall, gray-haired man with a muscular physique filled the frame. He wore a checked shirt, faded jeans, and a pair of black socks. The glint in his eye and ramrod posture said ex-military.

"Mr. Eisner?" I guessed. "Edward Eisner?"

"That's right. But only my dad called me Edward. It's Ted," he replied. "Whatever it is you're selling, I'm not interested. I want you off my land."

"We want to ask you about Elizabeth Singer," I said.

"Haven't seen her for years," Ted replied, a little too quickly for my liking. "She left the army back when I had a lot less gray hair. I thought she was wasting her life and I told her so. We haven't spoken since."

I looked at Jessie and could tell she was picking up the same dishonesty.

"Now I already asked you to leave," Ted said.

"We're sorry to have troubled you, Mr. Eisner," I said.

Jessie and I returned to the Nissan and jumped in. She started the engine. I watched Ted Eisner eyeball us as Jessie turned us around and drove away from his house.

"He was lying," she noted.

I nodded. "Pull over once we're out of sight."

Jessie continued along the drive until we were almost at the intersection with the road. We were shielded from the house now by a thick screen of pine trees, so she pulled over and killed the engine and we jumped out.

We picked our way back through the trees. I was grateful for the snow, which enabled us to move silently. We followed the treeline around the edge of the parking area until we were level with the house. There was a yard, maybe twenty feet or so, separating the trees from the side of the building.

"Ready?" I asked.

Jessie nodded and we set off, crossing the gap in a matter of moments. We pressed against the wall of the house and worked our way along. We moved to the nearest window, and I glanced in to see a living room full of framed photographs of Ted Eisner in uniform, and caught the polished shine of medals and trophies everywhere. These weren't for swimming. There was no mistaking this was the home of a decorated veteran.

I signaled Jessie and we crept toward the rear of the house. We passed another couple of windows that gave us views of a bedroom and a corridor. I could see shadows moving against the corridor wall. Ted Eisner was not alone.

We went around the back of the house, past another bedroom, until we came to a window beside the back door. I approached it carefully and glanced in to see Ted Eisner sitting in a chair by his kitchen table. He was facing me, but didn't register my presence. His attention was on the two men in black tactical gear, standing directly in front of him. Both had pistols drawn, and the taller of the two used his to strike Ted's shoulder. I could almost feel the force of the blow. The veteran groaned as it knocked him out of his chair.

"Tell us where she is," his assailant demanded. The man had a thick Russian accent.

Ted looked up at the man with steel in his eyes. "Do your worst. I ain't saying nothing."

CHAPTER 17

JESSIE AND I stepped away from the window and moved back along the side of the house. She took out her phone and indicated she was going to make a call, before moving toward the woods. I gave her the "eyes on" signal and returned to the kitchen window. I crouched down and peered through the misty glass.

"Tell me where she is," the taller of the two men growled. His accomplice punched Ted in the ribs.

The veteran groaned, but said nothing. I heard a phone ring. The tall man answered it. He spoke in Russian, and listened for a moment before hanging up. His mood seemed to have shifted and my hackles rose when I saw him check his pistol.

He said something in Russian, and his accomplice backed away from Ted. I knew what was coming next, and cast around desperately. I caught sight of a woodpile by the back door; buried in one of the logs was a snow-covered hand ax. It would have to do.

I ran to the woodpile, grabbed the ax, pulled it free, and barreled toward the back door. Through the glass panel, I saw Ted raise his hands instinctively as the Russian aimed the pistol at his head.

The shorter man registered my presence first, but he wasn't the immediate threat. I saw him glance at me as I rushed onto the porch and smashed through the back door. Glass sprayed everywhere, and my loud crashing entrance had the desired effect. As the gunman turned in my direction, I threw the ax and it hit him heel first on the forehead, knocking him off his feet and sending his gun clattering across the floor.

His short accomplice, a man with a rough beard and a dirty face, reached inside his jacket, but I was on him immediately, throwing a couple of jabs that knocked him back. He managed to draw his gun, but I blocked him when he tried to bring it around, and it went off by my ear, deafening me on my left side. Silence was suddenly replaced by terrible ringing, but I ignored it and grabbed his arm, twisting it around, causing him to drop the gun. I kicked it away, but immediately sensed movement behind me.

I turned just in time to see the tall Russian getting to his feet. I dived for his gun before he could reach it and turned it on him. He upended the kitchen table, shielding himself from my aim, and both he and the shorter assailant ran through a door into the garage, slamming it behind them.

I checked on Ted, who was alive but dazed, and ran to the door to the garage as I heard the rumble of an engine. The door was locked, so I stepped back and fired three rounds by the handle. The lock popped and I burst into the garage to see a large black Escalade smash through the double doors, taking part of the brickwork with it.

Through the wrecked doors, I saw Jessie reverse the Nissan into the Escalade's path. She was trying to block the driveway, but the driver of the Escalade swerved and struck the rear of the Nissan, sending Jessie into a violent spin. The Nissan skidded on the icy snow, twirling like a carousel, until it came to a crashing halt when it collided with a tree. I ran out and fired a couple of wild shots at the Escalade, which was already speeding into the distance, then raced across to the wrecked Nissan, desperate to see if Jessie was OK.

CHAPTER 18

THE FIRST THING Floyd registered was the smell. Sweet, ripe and rotten, an almost overpowering stench of manure and livestock. He opened his eyes and saw straw and droppings, and heard the bray of a nearby animal. He raised his head to see a horned goat poking its muzzle through the wooden struts of an interior partition—its lips working the air as it strained to reach the sleeve of his flight suit. Behind the creature were others, gnawing on some kind of meal heaped in a clay trough.

Floyd moved his arm and the goat snorted and joined its fellow inmates. Floyd looked up and saw wooden beams supporting rough boards, a ceiling of sorts, the lines of light that fell between them broken by the movement of people over-head. He could hear their footsteps. Lots of foot-steps.

He sat up and looked over his shoulder to see two short stern-faced men in gray *shalwar kameez* tunics and trousers, standing beyond a wooden gate. Both of them held bolt-action rifles and had pistols holstered in gun belts slung across their chests.

One of them yelled something in Kamviri—the local language, which Floyd was aware of but not enough to understand—and there came an almost immediate reply from someone he couldn't see.

The more dangerous of the two—Floyd had characterized him so because his face was a criss-cross patchwork of old scars—stepped forward and opened the gate, while his companion kept his rifle aimed at Floyd's chest. Scarface said something and gestured with his long-barreled gun. Floyd didn't need a translator. He shuffled toward the two men. He was tempted to disarm Scarface, but there was every chance he'd catch a bullet in the gut for his troubles. And besides, he had no idea what lay outside this building. The people of Nuristan weren't to be underestimated. They'd been at war with one enemy or another for an almost unbroken period of more than a century. Combat was a way of life, and the CIA briefing on the region had left Floyd with a sense of awe at the ability of these people to structure their lives and society around almost ceaseless war.

When he stepped out of the stall, Floyd saw an exterior door, and another man, about the same height as the first two, but older, with narrow, cruel eyes. He was armed in similar fashion, and when he opened the door, Floyd caught a blast of bitter air. He longed for his flight jacket, but it was nowhere to be seen. Scarface jostled him forward, then directed him through the door leading outside. He was pushed up a flight of stone steps that ran off to the right and was almost blinded by a powerful flashlight shone by a figure at the top of the stairs.

The ice-cold air chilled his lungs and his head swam from the exertion of climbing the stairs. Whoever had hit him had cracked his head good.

He paused for a moment, but a rifle barrel in the small of his back told him to keep moving. When he got closer to the top of the steps and the flashlight being shone on him, he saw it was being held by a teenage boy with a scraggly beard. He wasn't sure, but thought it was probably the kid who'd surprised him when he'd first come to the village. The teenager urged Floyd through a doorway that led into a small antechamber full of shoes and coats. The boy opened an interior door and ushered Floyd into a large, well-lit hall.

There were fifty or sixty people in a space about the size of a tennis court. The floor was bare cedarwood, but the walls were hung with ornate woven rugs and a large fire burned in a central hearth. A brick chimney rose into the steeply angled roof. The people were nearly all men and had clustered before the fire. The only two women Floyd could see in the throng were both in their sixties and were seated in heavy armchairs covered in the chipped remains of old gilding. Next to these women were three older men in similar, once grand chairs. These five seemed to command reverence from the assembled crowd.

"*Amrikani*," a gray-haired man in a brown *shalwar kameez* said, looking at Floyd. He was seated in the armchair at the center of the line of elders.

"You are accused of being a spy and a thief," the man said in English.

He turned to the crowd and said something in Kamviri.

"I'm neither of those things," Floyd protested.

The elder continued as though he hadn't spoken, "The punishment for these crimes is death."

CHAPTER 19

THE ELDER BARKED a command in Kam-
viri, and a man stepped forward from the crowd.
He was dressed in black, a red sash tied around
his waist. He held a long sword in his right hand.
Reflected flames danced along its polished blade.
Floyd's stomach lurched as he realized he was
looking at his executioner.

"I'm not a thief or a spy," he protested, back-
ing away. "I'm an American soldier who was shot
down. You can hold me as a prisoner of war, but
you cannot execute me."

The elder said something Floyd didn't understand. Scarface and his other jailer grabbed hold

of Floyd's arms and pushed him forward. He tried to resist, but they held fast and forced him on. The executioner's gaze did not waver. Floyd could tell from the thin half-smile on his face that this was a man who enjoyed his work.

After a few steps, Scarface and his companion forced Floyd to his knees.

"No!" he cried, trying to push himself up.

He was rewarded with a punch, which dazed him.

"Don't struggle and it will be quick," the elder advised.

Floyd fought and bucked against the two men holding him, but they dragged him to the right of the fireplace, where the crowd parted to reveal a wooden block stained black and marred by deep scores. Two metal eyelets and a long leather strap left no doubt as to the block's purpose.

"You can't do this," Floyd protested as he was hauled over to the block.

He tried to force himself up, but someone threw the leather strap over his shoulders and a moment later he was pinned in position. His legs kicked at the floor, to no effect.

"No!" Floyd yelled as he saw the executioner approach.

The man raised his sword and muttered something under his breath. Reflected flames danced across the blade, and the edge glinted in the golden light.

Floyd felt a lump form in his throat and his stomach churned with nausea as he faced reality: he was about to die. He would never see his wife or children again. Never hold his son or hug his daughter. He felt tears spring to his eyes.

"Please," he begged.

There was a sudden crash and the clatter of wood hitting something solid. Someone yelled something in Kamviri, and there was commotion in the crowd. The elder replied and was challenged by a new voice. Floyd tried to turn, but he was held fast. He heard footsteps behind him, and another exchange with the elder.

A moment later, a man came into view. Although he wore a navy blue *shalwar kameez* beneath a thick woolen coat, there was no mistaking his Western features. He reached out and began to pull the leather strap from Floyd's shoulders. He could have wept when he felt it go slack.

The new arrival helped him to his feet and offered Floyd his hand.

"My name is John," he said in a British accent.

"Joshua Floyd, Captain, US Army. How did you...?"

"I advised them that executing a US soldier would have repercussions. I'm sorry, I only just learned of your capture, otherwise I would have been here sooner."

The elder said something to John.

"He says I must pledge my honor for you."

Floyd looked lost.

"It means they'll execute me in your place if it turns out you are a spy or a thief," John explained gravely. "Don't worry," he added, breaking into a smile, "he has no intention of killing me. He's just trying to save face."

John replied to the elder, and a murmur rippled through the crowd.

"Come on, let's get you out of here."

John steered Floyd toward the exit and led him out into the freezing night.

CHAPTER 20

FLOYD HAD NEVER been more pleased to feel himself shiver at the cut of an icy wind. The stars had never shone so brightly, nor the air tasted so sweet. Floyd's British guardian angel led him along a rough track that ran between two rows of terraced houses, and every step felt like a gift. The bleak threat of death had brought the little things of ordinary life into sharp relief for him.

"Harsh conditions can create harsh people," John said. "It probably won't seem like it now, but that's not true of the Kom people. They're usually very friendly and welcoming. It must have been the uniform. Americans haven't done much good here."

The track was illuminated by lights in the windows of the houses they passed. To Floyd's left, the roof of the nearest house formed a support for the one above, and beyond that stretched an unbroken run of five similar step structures built into the mountain until the next lateral track, which cut through the town. Narrow alleyways separated each run of houses from their neighbors, and enabled people to access the homes in the center of each "staircase." The same pattern of construction was visible to Floyd's right, going down the mountain.

"This place is something, isn't it?" John remarked.

Floyd nodded.

"I couldn't believe it, when I first saw it. That people managed to build like this in these mountains before modern technology. Or that they'd want to. But spend long enough here, and you understand why."

Floyd hadn't reached that revelatory moment yet. His lungs were acclimatizing to the thin ice-cold air, and he was still getting over having almost been murdered.

"Live at the limits of existence," John said, "and you understand what it means to be truly alive."

It sounded like a snowboard manufacturer's tagline.

"You been here long?" Floyd asked.

"Uh-huh," John replied. "Some years."

Floyd could appreciate the majesty of the place, but he couldn't think of anything better than being curled up on the sofa with his family, watching a movie and munching caramel pop-corn. He didn't need to be on the edge to appreciate life. He'd been close enough to the brink far too many times to forget the view. Tonight was just the latest and most painful trip.

"Up here," John said, and hurried left, along one of the lateral alleyways that ran directly up the mountain.

Floyd's heart starting pounding a little harder and his breathing grew labored. He envied John, who marched ahead as though the slope wasn't there. Kamdesh was located at an altitude of six thousand feet, well above the point at which most people noticed a reduction in oxygen. Floyd told himself it didn't mean the Englishman was any fitter than him, only that he hadn't just come around from a sharp blow to the head.

He was glad when John slowed by the third house. The Englishman walked past the stable level and went up some steps and through a door that led to the upper floor. He held it open for a puffing Floyd to follow.

"Took me months to acclimatize to the altitude," John said as Floyd shuffled inside.

He entered a small hall with two wicker benches and a run of wooden pegs along one wall. There were boots arranged on the benches and thick coats on the pegs, a combination of modern mountain gear and traditional Nuristani garb.

John removed his coat and boots, and Floyd took off his boots and rubbed his aching sides.

"Any idea who has my flight jacket?"

"We'll find it," John replied. "Now you're not dead, it's not a trophy. Taking it would be theft, and, as you've gathered, thieving is taken very seriously here."

Without his coat, John looked lean and muscular. He wore a traditional sweater adorned with an eight-pointed red star woven into blue wool. He opened an inner door, and Floyd was greeted by a blast of warm air and an umami, meaty aroma that lit up his taste buds. He started salivating almost immediately and his stomach growled.

They stepped into a large, open-plan living area. A rustic kitchen with a wood-fueled stove was located in the heart of the space, beneath a hanging stone chimney. There was a rough dining table, and around it rugs and throws that created a living area focused on the hearth. Toward the downslope, a set of curtains had been drawn back to reveal the rooftops of the houses below, and beyond them the dark shadows of the mountains on the other side of the valley. To the right of the window was a screened sleeping area with a large mattress on the floor.

A Western woman in a traditional Nuristani dress tended a pot on the stove. She glanced at Floyd. Her light brown hair fell straight around her shoulders. She had a tiny, almost button nose, and a wide mouth with thin lips. Her cheeks and nose were covered with delicate freckles. At first glance, she seemed fragile, but her eyes gave her away. They were beautiful wide ovals of amber brown, but there was a hardness to them that Floyd had only ever seen in the eyes of soldiers.

"So they didn't kill him?" she asked. Floyd immediately recognized a Californian accent. "I'm Christine. Chris to my friends."

She came over and offered Floyd her hand. He felt nothing but confidence when he shook it.

"Joshua Floyd. Captain, US Army. How did you two wind up out here?"

"Life is full of surprises, right?" John replied. "How about you? First time in Afghanistan?"

Floyd smiled at the evasion. "First time on the ground."

"You sightseeing?" Christine asked. "Or looking for something in particular?"

"Heading for the border. I lost some friends." Floyd's mood darkened at the thought of the pitched battle that had cost so many lives.

"Sorry to hear that," John replied. "We understand your loss."

The two of them shared a knowing look.

"I told the elders I would make sure you're not a threat to the village," John said.

"No threat. Just passing through."

John nodded thoughtfully.

"Is there a phone anywhere?" Floyd asked.

John shook his head. "No cell signal up here, and the landline went down yesterday. Happens pretty regularly. Usually a couple of weeks before it's fixed."

"Nearest phone outside of Kamdesh is about three hours' drive. Maybe four in these conditions," Christine said. "There are government checkpoints on the roads, which I'm guessing you want to avoid."

Floyd nodded. "I just want to get home to my family."

"We might be able to help you get to the border," she said.

"Can you ride?" John asked.

"Badly," Floyd replied.

"Good enough." John smiled. "We'll go tomorrow."

"In the meantime, you look like someone who's forgotten the taste of food," Christine said. "Let's eat. Pull up a chair. It's goat stew and rice."

"Smells delicious," Floyd replied, smiling at the prospect of sating the worst hunger he had ever experienced.

CHAPTER 21

MOST OF THE people around me wore the same strained expression. Worry pulled their features tight, conversations were quiet, smiles false and fixed. I was in the emergency room in the Mid-Hudson Hospital in Arlington. I'd ridden in the ambulance with Jessie, who'd been knocked unconscious in the collision. Ted Eisner had been brought along in a separate vehicle. The tough old veteran had insisted Jessie go first, so I'd been in the waiting area when he was wheeled in, sitting upright on the gurney, complaining to the paramedics that they were being overcautious and that he was, in his own words, "As spry as a prime steer."

There were a dozen people in the waiting area. A couple had been there longer than me, but most had come in after I'd arrived, a little over an hour earlier. The waiting area was made up of six rows of ten green plastic chairs. I was sitting opposite the vending machines on the same side of the room as the reception desk, watching the double doors that led to the ER ward.

I sensed movement to my left and saw Rafael Lucas, Private's go-to New York attorney. Rafael was a Spaniard who worked for one of the world's largest law firms. He was an elegant, handsome man from an old aristocratic Cantabrian family, and there was a hint of the 1930s in the way he dressed. He was wearing a black herringbone top coat, tailored suit, and vest with shirt and tie. He looked out of place in this provincial hospital.

"You OK?" he asked as he took the seat next to mine.

I nodded.

"And Jessie?"

"She was pretty beat up when I pulled her out," I replied. "They're checking her now."

"I guess I owe you," a voice said behind me, and I turned to see Ted Eisner scowling and not looking the least bit grateful. "I told the damned quacks there was nothing wrong with me. Now I've got to deal with all the goddamned insurance paperwork."

"Do you know who those men were?" I asked.

"No. And I don't know you either," he snapped.

"I told you, Mr. Eisner, my name is Jack Morgan and I run Private, a detective agency. This is Rafael Lucas, my legal counsel. I'm looking for Elizabeth Singer, and I need to find her before the men who assaulted you do."

Ted fixed me with a hard stare. I could sense him taking the measure of me.

"What do you reckon they want with her?" he asked.

"I don't know, but it's clear they're prepared to kill to get it."

"And what do you want from her?" Ted asked.

"Someone who loves her has hired me and my organization to bring her back safely," I replied. "I want to help her."

A medic in blue scrubs came through the double doors and scanned the room. His eyes settled on me and he headed over.

"Mr. Morgan?" he asked.

I nodded.

"Your colleague is asking for you."

"How is she?"

"She has a fractured rib and some minor contusions, but she seems OK otherwise. We'd like to keep her in overnight to rule out any neurological damage, but at this stage I don't expect any complications. She should make a full recovery."

"Give me a second, please," I said, and the medic nodded and went to wait by the doors to the ER. "Please, Mr. Eisner, we just want to help Beth. If you know anything…" I left my remark hanging.

He shook his head and looked down at his feet, which kicked aimlessly at the linoleum.

Giving up on Ted, I turned to Rafael. "Coming?" I asked, and he nodded.

We headed for the emergency room, and that was when Ted Eisner finally spoke.

"I have a tracker on my car. Put it on a couple years ago when they offered me a discount on my premium. I gave Beth my car."

"Thank you for trusting me, Mr. Eisner. I appreciate it. Can you find out the details?" I asked Rafael. "Give them to Maureen Roth. See if she can get a fix."

Rafael nodded and hung back to talk to Ted.

I followed the medic through the double doors and along a corridor into the emergency room. Bays were separated by screens and drapes, but I still managed to see some of the human misery concealed within: a man with a bloodied stomach who looked as though he'd been stabbed; a kid with a broken arm; an emaciated woman who was totally out of it, being questioned by a doctor who was asking about her opiate intake.

The medic led me to the sixth bay, and behind the curtain I found Jessie sitting up in bed. She was wearing a hospital gown, and pulled up a thin blanket when I entered.

"I'll leave you to talk," the medic said, before withdrawing.

"Sorry, boss," she said.

"What for?" I asked.

"Not being quick enough. Letting myself get taken out."

"Don't even start," I said. "They were pros. They would have made rough work of anyone."

"Well, I feel bad about it." She moved and immediately grimaced.

"How do you feel?"

"Like someone dropped an elephant on my chest. They want to keep me overnight."

"That's OK. I'm going to follow up a lead," I said. "Ted Eisner's car is fitted with a tracker. He lent it to Elizabeth Singer."

Rafael entered, his phone to his ear.

"Mo-bot has been able to get a location," he said after he hung up. "The vehicle is parked outside a motel in Bloomsburg."

"You bring a car?" I asked, and he nodded. "I want you to stay with Jessie a while. Make sure she's OK…"

"I don't need a babysitter," she cut in, but I ignored her.

"Take care of any insurance and bills, and make sure she rests," I told Rafael. "You know how stubborn she is."

Jessie scoffed and immediately gasped in pain.

"The silver Mercedes M-Class parked out front," Rafael said, handing me his car key.

"Thanks," I replied. "I'm going to drive out to Bloomsburg and see if I can find Beth Singer and the kids."

"Be careful, Jack," Jessie said.

"Always," I replied.

CHAPTER 22

FLOYD WOKE TO a mouthwatering sweet smell. He took a moment to orient himself, and remembered he was on the floor in Christine and John's mountain home in Kamdesh. They'd given him horsehair cushions and a set of colorful blankets, and told him to bed down in an area in the far corner of the open-plan living space, away from the window and partition that marked out their sleeping quarters. Floyd had slept in some unusual places, but there was something odd about sharing a couple's home while they slept a few yards away, separated by nothing more than a woven drape and some screens. Christine—or

Chris as she preferred to be called—had explained over dinner that the Kom people had a communal approach to life and many generations of the same family would share a space like this. Floyd didn't consider himself a prude, but the idea of sharing such an intimate space with others didn't appeal to him. He had thought about insisting on sleeping in the stable on the ground level.

When he sat up, Floyd was very glad he hadn't. The stable didn't have any windows, and sleeping there would have deprived him of one of the most breathtaking views of his life. The snow-covered rooftops of Kamdesh were laid out before him like powdered steps, and beyond were wispy clouds of mist, an expansive valley, and the cedar-packed slope of a high mountain peak. It was a truly beautiful scene and Floyd understood why John and Chris had positioned their sleeping area near the window, even though it couldn't have been the warmest place in the house.

"Morning," John said.

He was standing over the stove in a pair of boxer shorts and a T-shirt, stirring something in a small cast-iron pot.

"Hungry?" he asked.

"Uh-huh," Floyd replied.

"We're going to be stuck here a while." John nodded toward the window. "That mist is the edge of a storm front that's rolling in."

Floyd was itching to get started. He needed to reach a phone or an internet connection. "Can't we beat it?"

John shook his head. "Radio forecast says two but I reckon we've only got an hour before it hits. It will be a complete white-out."

Floyd sighed.

"Forecast says it should be OK by the end of tomorrow," John said, by way of consolation.

"It will be gone by nightfall," Chris said, appearing from behind the drape that demarcated the sleeping area. She was dressed in a pair of black leggings and a black sleeveless top.

John shrugged. "I've learned never to bet against her ability to read the sky."

"We can spend today preparing supplies and packing. Aim to leave first thing in the morning," she said.

John took the pan off the stove and put it on a black warming plate that hung over the open fire. He spooned white meal into three earthen-ware bowls and carried them to the table.

"Get it while it's hot."

Floyd got to his feet and joined the couple.

"What is it?" he asked, taking a seat at the table and lowering his head to breathe in the scent of the steam coming off his bowl.

"*Juvór*," Chris replied, as she sat down opposite him. "It's a maize porridge."

"I like it with cinnamon and honey," John added.

"Too much honey," Chris remarked.

"How did an American and a Brit end up here?" Floyd asked.

He took his first mouthful. It was heavier than oat porridge and required more chewing, but he could tell it was good mountain fuel.

"Sometimes life takes strange turns," John said. "I found this place five years ago while on assignment. I was a journalist covering the war."

"And you fell in love with the place?" Floyd asked.

"Sort of. I realized it was a good spot to get lost," John replied. "Off the beaten track. World doesn't change much up here."

"Doesn't change much at all," Chris agreed. "Makes you realize what's important."

She took John's hand and squeezed it.

Floyd ate his breakfast and resisted the obvious question. If these two wanted him to know why they needed to disappear, they would have already told him. He didn't want to alienate the people who'd saved his life and offered to guide him home, simply to satisfy his own curiosity.

"This is good," he said instead.

"Don't compliment his cooking," Chris cautioned. "It goes straight to his head."

"Ignore her. Compliment away! And when you're finished we'll see about getting you some less conspicuous clothes. And supplies for the journey."

"Thanks," Floyd replied as he looked toward the window. The first flakes of snow were already falling.

CHAPTER 23

THE STORM MEANT I made slow progress through the night. Snowplows had cleared and salted the highway, but the flakes fell so thick and fast, new layers had settled and tested the car's traction control. The snow obscured my view, but every now and then I was dazzled by the blinding lights of an oncoming vehicle the other side of the highway. Thankfully, most sensible people had sheltered from the storm and other road users were few and far between.

The snow finally abated when the first fingers of sunlight were reaching for the clouds, tinting them a cotton-candy pink. I was passing through the outskirts of Bloomsburg when I saw the Relax Inn, the motel where Mo-bot had traced Ted Eisner's car. I moved into the outside lane of the highway to take the next exit. The car drifted a little as I changed direction, but I steered into the skid and started down the ramp. I took a left and passed beneath the highway, and then followed the road south for half a mile through a run of industrial units until I came to the single-story, cream-colored motel.

As I pulled into the parking lot, the front door of one of the first-floor rooms burst open, and two masked men emerged, dragging two children with them. I recognized them instantly as Daniel and Marianne Singer. While I continued moving across the parking lot, as yet unnoticed, a third masked man pushed Elizabeth Singer through the open door. Elizabeth and her children were in their pajamas and all three of them were crying as they were shoved toward another black Escalade that waited in the slushy gray snow.

I realized the gang must have found out about the tracker on Ted Eisner's car, which was parked in the space next to the large SUV. Had they gotten the details from his insurance company? Was that the call the tall gunman had received at Eisner's house? Was that why he'd suddenly become expendable?

Marianne and Daniel were bawling as they were forced into the back of the Escalade, and Beth struggled furiously, but her resistance melted when one of the men produced a pistol and held it to Danny's head.

I made a split-second calculation. My chances of following them in this weather were slim, and there was no way I could wait for the police to arrive. There was only one option.

I gunned the engine as Beth was pushed into the back seat next to her children, aiming the Mercedes directly at the man who'd been holding her. He quickly turned and momentarily froze with surprise on seeing the large M-Class racing toward him. He tried to leap out of the way but I swerved in his direction, sending the car into an uncontrollable skid.

Time seemed to slow as the line of motel rooms spun dizzily before me. I looked out the driver's window and saw the masked assailant raise his hands to his face. The car hit him hard, knocking him flying into Ted Eisner's Buick Enclave.

I might have imagined the crack of bone, but there was no mistaking the man's agonized scream.

The low thud of suppressed gunfire and snap of breaking glass told me I was under fire. I scrambled onto the passenger seat and tumbled out of the car. Peering around the open door, I saw the other two men had gotten into the Escalade. While the passenger fired back in my direction, the driver started the engine.

If I was going to stop them, I would have to leave the safety of my position behind the car door and expose myself to fire. It was a suicide mission, but if I didn't act fast Elizabeth and the children would be lost.

CHAPTER 24

I JUMPED TO my feet and ran toward the passenger side of the Escalade. As I did so I saw Elizabeth Singer lean forward and punch the gunman in the back of his skull as he was taking aim at me. His shot went wild, and he was so angry, he forgot about me and turned to hit her. The children screamed, but his fist flew though empty air as Elizabeth ducked the blow. The car was moving now, but I managed to reach the passenger door and yanked it open as I jumped on the running board. The gunman made the mistake of trying to kick me away, so I slammed the door on his outstretched leg. He howled, and I did it again.

The driver reached into his jacket, but Elizabeth was on him before he could produce his gun.

She clawed his face, and he instinctively stepped on the gas. The car accelerated and I couldn't hold on as it gathered speed. I was thrown off the running board, winding myself as I tumbled onto the slush-covered asphalt. Beth kept fighting. The Escalade veered into a line of parked cars. Metal ground against metal and windows shattered as the big SUV crashed into an old Plymouth parked across two spaces in front of the motel office.

I sprinted toward the vehicle and pulled open the rear driver's side door. Elizabeth and her two children were dazed, and the two masked assailants were equally stunned.

"Come on," I said, pulling Elizabeth's arm.

She allowed me to drag her from the car. As I yanked the children clear, the driver came to his senses.

"Get back!" he yelled, reaching for his gun.

I urged Elizabeth and the children on. "Move!"

As we ran, I heard the crack of gunfire. I turned to see the driver climb unsteadily out of the Escalade while trying to target me.

I pushed Elizabeth and the children over to the Mercedes and bundled them in the back.

The driver started running toward us as I jumped through the passenger door and slid into the driver's seat. I started the engine, which growled to life, threw the car into reverse, and stepped on the accelerator.

I reversed toward the exit as bullets made holes in the windshield. I flipped the gearshift, stepped on the brake, and spun the wheel, forcing the car into a violent turn. We spun out of the parking lot, bounced over the sidewalk, and were facing forward when we hit the road.

CHAPTER 25

AARON VANCE WATCHED with horror as the Mercedes SUV screeched out of the motel parking lot. He surveyed the line of wrecked cars.

This can't really be happening, Aaron thought with a growing feeling of shock. It was the stuff of movies, but the small part of his brain that wasn't numb with disbelief told him it was real and that he needed to do something.

He'd managed the Relax Inn Motel for three years. The owner, Esther Tucker, was a mean-spirited, greedy old woman who liked to pay low and charge high. She was probably crooked, but never revealed enough about the business for Aaron to be sure. He had standing instructions never to call the police and to always phone her first if anything happened. But this wasn't a forged check or a wallet snatched from a room. This was carnage, and at least one of those men out there was seriously injured.

Aaron lifted the phone and dialed.

"Nine one one, please state your emergency," a voice said.

The first gunshot knocked Aaron back, and he looked down to see blood oozing though his gray shirt. It spread like an ink blot around his shoulder and soaked into the Relax Inn badge that was sewn above his breast pocket. He looked past the hole in the window and saw a masked man moving toward the office, smoking pistol in hand.

"Hello?" the operator said. "Hello?"

Aaron made a rasping sound before he found the strength for words. "I've been shot. He shot me."

He dropped the receiver and shuffled around the reception counter toward the door. He had to lock it and buy a few moments to get the revolver he kept in the safe at the back of the office. He became aware of a burning pain in his shoulder as the reality of the gunshot wound finally hit him. He almost doubled over as the fire of agony spread throughout his upper body, but he resisted the urge and forced himself on. Tears sprang to his eyes but he pressed forward and was a yard away from the door when the masked man crashed through it. The edge of the door hit Aaron's forehead and there was a blinding flash of light.

When the whiteness faded, Aaron found himself flat on his back. His eyes focused just in time to see the man standing over him and the muzzle flash. He didn't feel the bullet enter his gut, but the crack of his head against the floor jarred his spine.

I'm hurt, he thought as he watched the masked man walk to the discarded phone.

The gunman kept a disinterested eye on Aaron as he picked up the receiver.

"Yes, hello," he said. "Yes, that's right...Yes, gunshots. The manager has been shot. He got into an argument with a man calling himself Morgan. Jack Morgan. The guy shot the manager before abducting a woman and her two kids."

Aaron's mind struggled to process the deception. Everything was fading and he sensed time running thin, like the last grains of sand tumbling through an hourglass.

"No, I'm afraid not," the masked man said into the phone. "The manager is dead."

Aaron was surprised not to feel sick at those words, and bewildered by how remote the world seemed. Finally, it dawned on him. Time had run out for him.

CHAPTER 26

I SLOWED DOWN once we reached the highway. I turned onto the ramp and joined the interstate heading for New York.

Stunned by what had happened at the motel, neither Beth nor I said anything. Our soundtrack was the gentle, intermittent thud of the car rolling over highway section dividers, the spray of tires pressing through slush, and the muted sobs coming from the children in the back. Beth tried her best to soothe them, but they'd been badly shaken by what had happened. Finally, they settled into stunned silence.

"Who are you?" Beth asked me at last.

"Jack Morgan," I replied. "I'm a private detective. Your father hired me to find you."

I sensed her shift in her seat and glanced over to see her eying me with suspicion.

"You're Elizabeth Singer, right? And these are Daniel and Marianne?"

"Beth, Danny, and Maria," she corrected me. "I'd like to see some ID."

I reached into my pocket and handed her my wallet. She checked my identification and placed the wallet on the central console.

"Why were those men after you?" I asked.

"Can you pull over?" she said. "I think I'm going to be sick."

She looked pale and was gulping for air, so I slowed and steered the car to a halt on the shoulder.

"Are you OK, Mom?" Maria asked.

"I'll be fine. Just wait here," Beth replied hurriedly, before jumping out.

She left the door open, and the cold wind blew snow into the car. She ran over to the barrier, and I watched her buckle against the metal and heave. I turned to the kids, who were watching their mother fearfully.

"It's OK," I assured them. "Probably just nerves."

"Mr. Morgan," Beth yelled, still leaning over the barrier. "I need you. I need your help."

"You'll be OK, kids," I said, releasing my seat belt and stepping out.

I hurried over to Beth. "What is it?"

The blow came out of nowhere. She spun around with a rock in her hand and clocked me on the temple. I went down immediately and my vision blurred. I couldn't pass out. Not here. Not now.

I dug my nails into my palms and the pull of oblivion receded. I came to my senses and saw Beth jump into the driver's seat of the Mercedes.

"Hey!" I yelled. My mouth was full of saliva and I felt nauseous. "Stop!"

Beth glanced at me, put the car in gear, and stepped on the gas as I staggered to my feet. I stumbled forward as the wheels spun in the slush. They caught the road surface and the sudden friction sent the car lurching forward at speed. Beth had misjudged terribly. Almost immediately the car went into a fishtail skid. It veered toward a passing truck and Beth overcompensated, turning the wheel so hard, the M-Class swung around, sped across the shoulder and hit the barrier. The collision brought the car to a grinding halt, and I forced myself toward it. My legs felt weak and unsteady, but I had to get to them.

I opened the back door to find Maria and Danny crying. The car stank of fuel and silicate dust.

"Are you OK?" I slurred. "You hurt anywhere?"

Maria shook her head.

"Mom!" Danny cried.

The children had been wearing seat belts but Beth hadn't put hers on. The airbags had deployed but somehow her head had hit the driver's window. There was a bloody crack in the glass.

I opened the door and leaned in.

"Are you OK?" I asked.

She was groggy and bleeding from a wound on her forehead.

"Get away from me," she said, her words barely decipherable.

"Why? Why are you trying to escape from me?"

"My father," she groaned. "My father..."

She took a deep breath, clearly struggling to speak.

"My father is dead," she said before passing out.

CHAPTER 27

THE OSPREY WAS lit up by flames dancing within the fuselage. Floyd was drawn toward a figure standing in front of the wreckage. He knew who it was before he reached her. He wanted to call out, to warn her to step away from the inferno, but he had no power over his body and drifted like an automaton. As his wife turned toward him, Floyd saw tears in her eyes and her face was riven by distress.

"The children..." she cried, but Floyd heard no more.

He was woken from the nightmare. It took

him a moment to bridge the gap between dream and reality.

John crouched beside him, the concern on his face clear even by moonlight.

"We need to go now," he said. "There are men moving through the town. Mercenaries. I think they're looking for you."

Floyd got to his feet and hurried across the large living room to the window that overlooked the valley. He could see flashlight beams swinging to and fro in the shadows of the men wielding them as they moved from house to house further down the mountain. Outraged cries and aggressive commands filled the air.

"Get dressed," John said, handing Floyd some clothes. "Chris is downstairs getting the horses ready."

Floyd pulled a pair of woolen trousers over his shorts, and slipped a cotton tunic over his head, before putting on a heavy Soviet coat badged with the hammer and sickle. John was similarly dressed. He handed Floyd a pair of Nuristani riding boots and pulled on a pair himself.

Floyd heard more cries in Kamviri in the distance, and demands made in Russian.

"We don't have long," John said.

He pulled back the corner of a rug to reveal a trap door. He opened it and led Floyd down a run of wooden steps to the stables. Chris was checking the saddle on a large horse.

"They're ready," she said. "Supplies and gear." She pointed at three backpacks at the bottom of the stairs. "Yours is the blue one."

Floyd picked it up and shrugged it on.

Chris grabbed a coat from a peg near the door and put it on. She and Floyd slung packs on their shoulders, and she took the reins of a gray horse and led it to the stable door. The horse's hooves scuffed and clopped against the door.

"This one's yours," John said, giving Floyd the reins of a brown mare.

Floyd patted its muzzle and followed Chris. Floyd brought up the rear with a brown and white stallion.

Chris paused by the door. "We lead the horses out on foot east along the alley. When we reach the main road, we mount up and head south. Got it?"

Floyd nodded.

Chris switched off the stable light and opened

the door. The hinges creaked, the horses snorted excitedly, and John's stallion pawed the floor. Floyd had never been so conscious of noise and tried to will the world into silence. He hardly noticed the blast of ice-cold air that hit him as Chris moved into the alleyway.

She looked both ways, then signaled to Floyd and John to follow. Voices drifted up the mountainside. They were close, perhaps only a few houses away. Floyd's horse tried to move back into the stable, but he patted her flank.

"It's OK," he said, and led her along the alleyway, past the neighboring house.

John followed and the three of them walked without saying a word, aware of people waking in the surrounding buildings. Floyd's breath formed clouds in the chill, and steam rose from his horse's nostrils. He realized he had no idea what time it was, that his watch must have been taken along with his flight jacket when he was sentenced to execution. It must have been late because the people who came to their windows looked stunned by sleep and annoyed to have been woken by commotion in the town. A few looked at the trio leading their horses and nodded, but most had their eyes turned toward the other end of the alleyway, which seemed to be where the trouble was happening.

A voice yelled in Russian. Floyd glanced over his shoulder to see the silhouette of a man in the light of the flashlights. He was looking their way.

"Come on. They've seen us," Chris said, mounting her horse.

The man at the other end of the alleyway yelled as Floyd and John climbed into their saddles. Chris urged her horse forward and Floyd's followed its lead. He hadn't ridden for years and gripped the reins tightly. He looked back to see John following, behind him a cluster of flashlights and figures running toward them.

The horses' hooves pounded with greater urgency, and clouds of vapor swirled around their heads as they gathered speed.

Over the beating rhythm of the hoofbeats came a sudden, ugly crack. Then another. And another.

"They're shooting!" John yelled. A moment later there was another volley and he cried out in pain.

Floyd looked back to see the Englishman

slump forward. He reined in his horse, but John raised his head.

"Go!" he barked through gritted teeth. "Don't let this be for nothing."

Chris pulled up. "I can't leave him," she said as Floyd passed her. "Head south. There's a map of the passes in your bag."

Floyd urged his horse on. It galloped out of the alleyway onto the main road through Kamdesh. Floyd glanced back to see Chris tending to John as a gang of men closed in on them.

Adrenaline surging, heart thumping, Floyd flicked the reins and turned the horse south. His mount raced forward at top speed and didn't seem to need further encouragement, but if there was more speed to be had, Floyd wanted it.

"Yah!" he yelled.

He heard more shouts behind him, but didn't look back. Soon he and the horse were lost to the darkness.

CHAPTER 28

MY SECOND TIME in the hospital in less than twenty-four hours. Danny sat next to me, grim and still as stone. I wasn't sure whether my reassurances had calmed him or if he was simply numb. Maria was pacing the lobby of the Berwick Commonwealth Hospital, her skinny arms folded, her brow furrowed.

"You sure there's no one I should call?" I asked when she came near.

She shook her head.

"Your dad?" I tried.

Danny was about to reply, but Maria shot him a dirty look and he clammed up.

After the ambulance had picked us up and we'd gotten Beth seen to, I'd tried to ask the children about their family, but neither of them would say anything. I quizzed them about their mother's revelation that the man who'd introduced himself to me as Donald Singer wasn't her father, but they weren't willing to talk about it. I'd checked this guy's background, so either Beth was lying or I'd fallen victim to some very sophisticated invention.

While I was thinking this through, I noticed myself appear on the TV on the wall of the waiting room. There was no sound, but the footage being broadcast was of the mayhem outside the Relax Inn. A picture of me and my name were inset into the main image, which cut to one of the motel guests being interviewed about what had happened.

I took out my phone and called Justine.

"Hey," she said. "I was about to call you. I just spoke to Jessie. Are you OK?"

"Fine," I replied. "Can you ask Mo-bot to run a reverse search? See if anyone is looking for us..." I broke off when I saw Dr. Sohal, a slim middle-aged man with designer glasses and a Stars and Stripes tie pin, come through the emergency room doors.

"I've got to go," I said.

"Jack—" Justine said before I hung up.

The doctor approached with a smile on his face. He was leading the team treating Beth, and his expression was one of relief. "I think she's fine," he said.

Maria stopped pacing and ran over. "Can we see her?"

"Of course," Sohal replied. "Come with me."

Danny got to his feet and joined his sister. I rose and followed the two kids who trailed the doctor into the ER. The moment I stepped through the doors, I was greeted by a nurse I recognized from Beth's response team.

"Excuse me, sir," she said. "I need to ask you some questions. The patient claims not to be able to remember her home address or date of birth. It could just be shock, but we need to book an MRI scan to check there's no neurological damage. For that I'll need her insurance details. Or yours. If I could have your name and details that would also be helpful."

There was something about the way the nurse

had framed the question. Her delivery seemed to waver between passive aggression and sweet apple pie, and her expression kept alternating between a bright smile and anxious concern. Had she seen the news footage?

"Let me go and ask who her insurer is," I said, pressing on before the nurse had a chance to object.

I hurried through the otherwise empty emergency room to the bay where Beth was leaning out of bed and hugging Danny and Maria. She tensed the moment she saw me.

"When can she move?" I asked Dr. Sohal.

"I just want to do an MRI to see about the memory loss—" he began.

"But she's OK?" I cut in.

"Probably, but—"

I cut him off again. "The nurse mentioned she wanted to check something with you about the insurance paperwork."

He smiled uncertainly. "Really?"

I nodded.

"One moment, please," he said, stepping out of the bay.

"Have you really lost your memory?" I asked Beth.

She shook her head.

"Good," I replied. "The men who attacked you at the motel have set the authorities on me. We're all over the news. We need to go."

Beth pushed herself upright and wobbled for a moment.

"Mom?" Danny remarked, his voice frail with concern.

"I'm OK, hun."

Beth slid off the gurney and got to her feet. I took her arm and the children clustered around us as we left the bay.

"Excuse me!" Sohal called out when he saw us.

Behind him, I saw flashes of blue clothing through the glass doors. Two uniformed police officers entered the lobby and approached reception.

"This way," I said.

We ran in the other direction, through the ER, and took a left turn onto a corridor that led to the X-ray department. If they had my identity, they might be able to track my phone, so I took the difficult decision to jettison it. I slipped it onto the middle shelf of a supply trolley we passed.

I heard a door slam and the sound of distant footsteps running in our direction.

"Come on, kids," Beth said, hustling the children forward.

I ran ahead and burst through the fire door at the end of the corridor. As I spilled into the freezing air, an ear-piercing alarm sounded. The children covered their ears as Beth hurried them out. I glanced around, then ran toward the street, where a cab waited at the hospital entrance. Its exhaust puffed a steady cloud.

"Come on," I said.

We ran across a patch of snow, crossed the salted sidewalk, and reached the taxi. I whipped open the door, bundled Beth and the children inside, and followed them.

"Easy, buddy," the driver said.

"Two hundred bucks if you get us out of here now," I said.

"Okey-dokey," he replied eagerly.

He slipped the gearshift and we started moving. We were about thirty yards down the street when the first police officer burst through the fire exit.

Beth and the kids ducked but I kept my eyes on him.

"Man who'd pay two hundred for a ride, would probably pay three," the opportunistic cab driver noted.

I locked onto his eyes in the rearview mirror.

"Freedom ain't free," he added knowingly.

I nodded. It was worth the price. As the hospital receded behind us, I settled back and thought about our next move.

CHAPTER 29

THE CAB TOOK us to West Summit, a small town north of I-80. I asked the driver to drop us by the Kalahari Resort, a vast hotel, waterpark, convention center, and shopping mall that lay at the edge of town. I'd talked to Beth about catching a bus to Chicago. After I'd paid the driver a fare that amounted to ten dollars for every minute we were in the cab and he'd driven away, I started walking west.

"Come on," I said.

"Where?" Beth asked.

She gathered the children to her and eyed me with suspicion.

"A Marine buddy of mine used to have a fishing cabin up by Stillwater Lake. It's about a mile that way," I replied. "It's somewhere safe, and most importantly, no one knows about it."

Beth hesitated and looked at Danny and Maria, who watched her uncertainly.

"I'm here to help you," I assured her. "I didn't know your father was dead."

"He is," she said. "Died a long time ago. Either you're not a very good detective or someone was clever enough to outfox you. Either way, it doesn't fill me with confidence."

The remark wounded because it was true. I knew I wasn't a bad detective, but, in the man who'd posed as Donald Singer, I'd encountered someone who'd outsmarted me. The backstory he'd built on the internet and public records was too convincing to have been the work of an amateur, and I was concerned by the thought I could no longer see the edges of this investigation. What had started as a simple hunt for a mother and her two young children had grown into something else.

"I know. I messed up, but I promise you'll be safe with me," I said. "Even if it's just until you decide you want to go your own way."

Beth nodded. "OK. Come on, kids." She gave them a squeeze and nudged them toward me.

I crouched down to their level. "I'm here to help you. You can trust me. I promise."

West Summit was a small Pennsylvania town of a few hundred people that lay to the west of Pocono Summit. It was popular with hunters and anglers during summer, but in the depths of winter it seemed to be hibernating. We went through a tunnel that took us under I-380 and followed a trail into the snowy woods that surrounded the town. I could see the roofs of houses nestled in the trees, but we stayed clear of civilization and turned northwest, sticking to the woodland trail until we reached the tiny commercial district that passed for a town center. There was a mini-mart and the bright lights of a pizza restaurant shone in the gloomy light.

We passed the mini-mart, which was surrounded by high drifts of snow, plowed to keep the parking lot clear. The store was open, but there were no vehicles in the lot. A sickly-sweet smell of pretzels and donuts drifted through a steaming air vent. I looked at the downturned faces of the cold children.

"Wait here," I said, and jogged into the store.

I picked up a couple days' essential supplies and some hot treats, and paid the bored teenager behind the counter. I hurried outside and offered Beth and the children warm pretzels.

"Thanks," Beth said.

The children nodded. "Thank you, sir," Danny remarked.

We kept moving as they devoured the sweet pastry and made good progress along Stillwater Drive, the quiet residential road that led to the lake. None of us wanted to be outside any longer than necessary. We walked briskly in an effort to ward off the chill. Beth tried to keep the children's spirits up by pointing out some of the more beautiful ice formations in the trees, or icicles hanging from the homes we passed.

"Not much farther," I said as I took them over a graying drift of icy snow that had been plowed over the mouth of a trail leading off the main road.

The track leading up to Leo Wylie's cabin was buried beneath deep snow, and we all had soaking wet shoes and pants by the time we'd finished walking the final quarter of a mile.

The cabin stood in the middle of a tiny clearing, and nature had most definitely encroached since the last time I'd seen it. Overhanging branches brushed against the walls and touched the top of the roof. Snow had drifted up to the first-floor windows on either side of the building. At first sight, it certainly appeared no one was home.

A porch ran the whole length of the front of the cabin, keeping the entrance free of snow, and large piles of seasoned logs stood either side of the door. At least we'd be warm inside.

I found a spare key hidden in a nook behind the mailbox that was fixed to the wall between the front door and one of the log piles, and we hurried inside.

A couple hours later, after a quick meal of mac and cheese, Beth put the children to sleep in one of the four bedrooms. They wanted to share, although neither would admit it was because they were scared. After a couple of failed attempts at getting them to settle, Beth joined me in the living room, where I'd managed to get a blazing fire going in the large stone hearth. I'd also found a bottle of Leo's wine and poured us two glasses.

The smooth red brought the twin comforts of warmth and calm. For a moment we sat saying nothing, listening to the crack of the burning logs, savoring the peace after the day's mayhem.

Beth's eyes were on the fire. She opened her mouth a couple times and I sensed she was building up to something.

"Can I trust you?" she asked earnestly.

I nodded.

"It's my husband," she responded, and tears welled in her eyes. "At least I'm pretty sure it is. I think he's the reason we're here. I believe he's in danger, and those men...those assholes who tried to take our children..." Her voice trailed off and she gulped in a calming breath. "I think those men are trying to use us to get to him."

"Why?" I asked.

She shook her head. "I don't know. My husband is a Special Forces pilot. I never know anything about his missions. He flies Ospreys for Third Special Forces Group. His name is Joshua Floyd."

CHAPTER 30

BETH TOOK A sip of wine and followed it with a deep breath.

"I know the Third," I said. "I flew a Sea Knight in Afghanistan."

"You look like you've seen combat," she replied. "Not that you're scarred or anything. It's in the eyes. Hard to describe. You've seen trauma, and it's left its imprint."

I nodded slowly. I knew exactly what she was talking about. The horror of battle, the deaths of friends, these were things that would never leave me.

"I was an Osprey pilot," Beth said. "That's how

Floyd and I met. I always said I'd never marry another soldier, but love makes liars of us all."

She had another drink.

"I took my discharge when Maria came along. We married soon afterward, but the nature of Josh's work means we kept the wedding secret. The Army classified his file. No one is supposed to know we're together, and we go to great lengths to keep it that way. He doesn't really go out when he's on leave, and the kids have been taught never to talk about him."

She put her glass on a side table, leaned forward, and peered at the flames.

"We have an arrangement. If he is ever captured, I'm supposed to take the kids to a cabin we have in the woods and hunker down with them until the danger passes."

"Makes sense," I observed. "Bad guys can't use you and the children as leverage to get him to talk."

She nodded.

"Three days ago, two guys posing as cops pulled me over when I was bringing the kids home from school. I escaped, but they used a drone to follow us to the cabin—I spotted it just in time before they showed up with others. We had to make it out on foot."

"And when you did, the guy posing as your father hired me to track you down," I remarked. "I checked him out thoroughly. His cover was impeccable. Whoever these people are, they're well-resourced and professional."

Beth nodded somberly, and I watched her wrestling with concern for her children and husband. I felt anger rising that the man calling himself Donald Singer had used me to put them in harm's way.

"I'm going to find out who's behind this," I assured Beth. "And I'm going to make sure you and your family—including Joshua—are safe."

Beth replied with a faint smile. Studying her face in the flickering light of the fire, I got the distinct impression she didn't believe me.

CHAPTER 31

A CHILL RAN down the back of Floyd's neck. He woke suddenly and sat up. He rubbed his chin and found it was wet. He looked up to see an icicle glistening in the morning sun. There was already another drop hanging at the very tip, ready to fall. He looked out of the mouth of the tiny cave that had sheltered him and his horse, and saw the deep valley was bathed in sunlight. The snow-covered slopes of the mountains opposite dazzled him, and the green flourishes of trees or the gray of rock could only be seen here and there. The snow was far too thick to be defeated, even by the most severe outcrops in the landscape.

Floyd had named his horse "Mule" in honor of what would politely be called its independent mind. He turned to see the creature pawing the cave floor impatiently. Floyd had wrapped himself in most of the clothes he'd found in the pack Chris and John had given him, and had covered Mule in the rough woolen blanket he'd also found inside. But the blanket had fallen off and the horse was stamping it into the frozen ground.

"Easy," Floyd whispered, getting to his feet.

The animal must have been freezing, and Floyd knew the kindest thing to do would be to get moving, but he was worried about the men who'd come looking for him.

"Shush," he said, reaching down for the blanket.

He placed it over the horse's back and patted the animal on the flank. Mule snorted again, and clouds of steam burst from her nostrils.

"Just wait here," Floyd said, but the animal didn't have much choice; it was still bridled and its reins were tied around a rock.

Floyd jogged out of the cave and went up

the narrow snow-covered path that led to the ridge overlooking Kamdesh. He slowed as he approached the end of the path, crouching as he picked his way between ice-crusted rocks. He reached the apex of the ridge and looked down at the town. He could see tiny figures dotted on the mountainside, gathered in groups of three or four, all in gray and white combat fatigues, very obviously searching for him.

Why would someone go to all this trouble for a Green Beret pilot? Floyd had never considered himself a high-value target, but someone was throwing a great deal of manpower at him.

He held his breath when he heard voices and slowly turned to his left to see three men moving through the trees, two hundred yards below him. They were checking every mound and bump, searching in the roots of trees.

Overnight snow had covered Mule's tracks out of town, but the sky was now clear, so as he withdrew, Floyd did his best to brush away the marks he'd left in the snow. When he was well below the ridge line, he turned and ran down the path to the cave. He couldn't stay there. It was only a matter of time before he'd be discovered.

He hurriedly packed his clothes and gear, and checked the map John had given him. He slung the backpack onto his shoulders, saddled Mule, and once the billet strap was secure, he untied the reins and led the horse from the cave. He moved slowly and cautiously, and patted Mule in an attempt to convey the need for silence.

They headed down the path into the valley—Floyd's plan was to cross it and climb the mountains to the south. The border was only eighty miles away as the crow flies, but in this terrain, it might as well have been eight hundred.

You'll do what it takes, soldier, he told himself, thinking of Beth, Maria, and Danny. When he was a safe distance from the men hunting him, he mounted Mule and set off down the slope at a trot.

CHAPTER 32

I WOKE EARLY the next morning and crept out of the cabin without waking Beth or the children. I walked over crackling snow and followed the trail back to the road, and from there, I headed into town. A few vehicles passed me, but it was quiet. The morning rush hour hadn't started.

Dawn's tendrils reached over the treetops as I neared town, casting everything in a weak light. The brooding clouds suggested day would come slowly, and when it did arrive there was likely to be snow.

I returned to the mini-mart we'd passed, and

offered the same bored teenager twenty dollars to use his cell phone.

"Forty," he said.

I nodded and handed the bills over in exchange for his cracked old iPhone. He unlocked it, and I moved to the back of the store to talk in private.

"Hello?" Jessie said. She sounded groggy.

"Sorry for calling so early," I responded.

"Jack!" She suddenly came to life. "I've been so worried about you. We all have. The thing at the motel—"

"A set-up," I assured her. "Designed to get the cops looking for me. They want me found. More importantly, they want Beth Singer."

"Rafael has been on damage limitation," Jessie replied. "Turns out there was an emergency call naming you as a suspect, but motel guests who witnessed the incident give a conflicting story. You're not a suspect anymore, but the cops want to talk to you to clear up a few questions."

"I can't do that until we know Beth and her children are safe from the people after them."

"Who are they?" Jessie asked.

"We don't know yet, but Donald Singer isn't who he says he is," I replied. "How are you?"

"Aching, but otherwise OK."

"Glad to hear it," I said. "I'm going to need a ride and somewhere safe to lie low."

"No problem," Jessie replied.

"Where do you want to meet?"

"Swiftwater, PA," I replied. "There's a bus depot just off the highway."

"I'll find it," Jessie said. "When?"

"Two hours," I replied.

"See you there."

"Also, I need you to fill in Justine—especially about Singer. But this guy has serious resources, so we need to be vigilant and careful in our communications."

"No problem, boss."

"Thanks, Jessie," I said finally, before hanging up.

I returned to the front of the store and handed the clerk his phone with a grateful thanks. He shrugged and started swiping it as I left the mini-mart.

I started across the parking lot, but changed direction when I noticed a couple of cops eying me from a cruiser that slowed to a halt on the other side of the street. They might have been genuine police or they could have been part of the crew who'd tried to abduct Beth and the kids. Either way, I couldn't risk being caught. I headed back toward the convenience store, and nodded at the teenage clerk.

"It's brutal out there," I said.

"Well, you can't live in here," he scoffed.

"You got a bathroom?" I asked.

"Ten bucks," he replied.

I shook my head at his greedy opportunism and laid a bill on the counter.

"In the back," he said, gesturing toward the floor-to-ceiling fridges that lined the rear wall.

As I hurried in their direction, I glanced over my shoulder to see the uniformed cops crossing the parking lot, heading straight for the store. I jogged along an aisle and saw a corridor that cut between the fridges. I went straight down it, ignored the bathroom, and headed for the fire exit. An alarm sounded when I opened the door. I sprinted around the side of the building, ran across the parking lot and over to the other side of the street to where the cruiser was parked. I took out a small pocketknife and dug it into the nearside tire.

"Hey!" a voice yelled as air rushed out.

I looked up to see the two cops racing from the store.

"Stop!" the closest yelled.

I ignored him and sprinted into the front yard of the nearest house. I vaulted a locked side gate, dodged a barking German Shepherd, and ran alongside the house until I reached a large garden. There was a chain-link fence at the end, beyond it the woods that surrounded town. I flew across the lawn, jumped onto the roof of a doghouse near the fence, and used a fence post to push myself up and over.

"Stop or I will shoot!" one of the cops yelled.

I didn't even bother looking around, instead starting to run the moment my feet hit the ground. I threw myself into the snow-laden firs and within moments was lost in their cold embrace.

CHAPTER 33

"WE HAVE TO leave," I said, shaking Beth awake.

She'd fallen asleep with Danny and Maria, the three of them cocooned under heavy blankets and breathing deeply when I made my announcement.

Beth sat up suddenly and stared at me in bewilderment, until she recalled who I was and where we were.

"I got spotted by a couple of cops—or people dressed as cops," I explained. "I went to make a phone call."

Beth eyed me with disapproval.

"I was calling someone who can help us."

"Come on, kids," she said, rousing the children.

They had all slept in their clothes, so getting ready simply involved wrapping up for the cold weather and grabbing provisions to take with us.

We were soon starting our journey through the woods. I decided against the trail and road to avoid unnecessary exposure, so we were going to make this journey cross-country.

"Where are we going?" Beth asked.

"Swiftwater," I replied. "One of my colleagues is meeting us there."

Beth nodded uncertainly and we continued through dense woodland. Swiftwater was about an hour's walk by road, but this terrain would take much longer to cover.

I heard a bird call and looked up to see the familiar shape of a golden eagle riding the morning updrafts high above us.

"Hey," I said. "You kids ever seen a golden eagle?"

Danny nodded and Maria rolled her eyes.

"We live in Garrison," she said. "There's a ton of eagles in the mountains."

"Maria," Beth chided.

"It's OK. I still remember when I was young enough to believe it was cool to be jaded about everything," I said. "If you're interested, there's one right over us."

Danny looked up immediately, and was captivated by the bird. Maria pretended not to look, but I saw her sneak a couple of glances. Beth smiled at me, and we walked on.

Ninety minutes later, we emerged from the woods onto a quiet road just south of Swiftwater. We hurried directly across Route 611, onto an inclined driveway that led up to the bus depot. We didn't have to walk far before I saw a black Nissan Rogue parked in a turnout opposite the depot. Jessie got out as we approached.

"Beth, this is Jessie Fleming. She runs our New York office," I said. "Jessie, this is Beth, Maria, and Danny."

"You guys look frozen," Jessie said. "Let's get you inside. I've got the heater on scalding."

Beth and the children climbed in the back of the Nissan, and I took the passenger seat beside Jessie, who hopped behind the wheel. The car was warm and stuffy, and after the chill of the long walk, I loved it.

"I brought you a phone," she said, handing me an iPhone. "And cash, and there are some clothes in the trunk. I've arranged a place for us to stay. Rye—just outside the city. Secluded and safe."

"Thanks," I said.

"Thank you," Beth added.

I checked the phone and saw many of my important numbers had already been added. I dialed one I knew by heart.

"Hello?"

"It's me," I replied.

"Jack!" Justine exclaimed breathlessly. "It's good to hear your voice."

"I'm sorry I couldn't call sooner," I replied.

"Jessie explained. Sci and Mo-bot have started very carefully digging into Singer's background to find out who he really is and how he produced such a convincing legend."

"Get in touch with Singer," I suggested as an idea formed.

I noticed Beth suddenly tense, but I signaled her to stay calm.

"Tell him I want to meet somewhere in the city this afternoon. Text me the location."

"Will do," Justine replied. "But be careful, Jack. I want you back in one piece. I saw what happened at the motel."

"I'll do my best," I assured her, before hanging up.

"You want to meet him?" Beth asked.

I nodded. "I don't like being played. It's time to turn the tables."

Jessie put the car in gear.

"New York?" she asked.

"New York," I replied. She swung the car around and joined 611 heading south.

CHAPTER 34

THE JOURNEY ACROSS the valley had taken most of the day. Floyd had followed the trail marked on the map, but thick snow had made the going difficult. He'd veered off course a number of times and had to retrace his steps.

The sun had gone down by the time the horse started to climb the mountain on the other side of the valley. Mule was clearly exhausted, and Floyd knew they wouldn't be able to go on much longer, so he began to look for somewhere to spend the night. The lower slopes were covered by big trees, which made it hard to spot any shelter from the trail. If they could get above the treeline, it would be easier to see a crevasse or cave.

Floyd urged Mule up the steep incline. As they trudged slowly on, he wondered whether Beth and the children had gone to the cabin. Would the Department of Defense have notified her he was missing in action? Would they even know? Or would they mistakenly count him among the fallen? He couldn't bear the thought of Beth worrying about him, much less the children, so he pushed such questions from his mind. Get to the border. Get to a phone. His task was simple, even if the execution of it was not.

Mule was breathing heavily, and ridges of white, foamy sweat had formed on her neck, but she kept going, and they were in sight of the rocky terrain that marked the end of the forest. The trees were thinning out, unable to thrive much higher. Floyd looked at the shadows up ahead and tried to see if he could spot shelter, but he was still too far away.

He was surprised to hear the low thrum of an engine, and recognized the frequency—too low for a car or a plane, the rhythm belonged to a chopper. He urged Mule off the trail, into the last of the trees, and the horse pushed through snow that came to its knees until Floyd pulled up by the trunk of a cedar. Mule settled and Floyd watched the sky. The tops of the trees swayed gently against the bright stars, but there was no sight of the aircraft. The sound of its engine grew louder, and Mule pawed the ground nervously.

Floyd's heart pounded as he began to make out the occultation of the rotors, which meant the aircraft must be close. Then it appeared, the distinctive silhouette of a Russian-made Mil Mi-24 Hind, commonly known as the flying tank: a fast, heavily armed chopper with trademark down-swept wings. The bird had no running lights and was a solid black against the gray and white of the mountains opposite. It flew toward Floyd and, as it banked in his direction, he saw something that sent panic rushing through him: the familiar green glow of an infrared night-vision system. Against the cold mountainside, he and the horse would light up in bright oranges and yellow.

Floyd looked around, desperately searching for somewhere to hide, but there was nothing other than trees and deep drifts of snow. As the chopper came straight toward him, he could see the pilot, co-pilot, and someone else who stood in the center of the cockpit. All three were staring directly at him. They couldn't land, but if the bird was properly equipped, they wouldn't need to. A team could drop-line down to him.

Floyd knew he only had moments to get out of there, but he had no idea how he could outrun a chopper. They would follow him through the mountains. His heart sank at the thought he might never see Beth and the kids again. Then inspiration struck. He dismounted Mule and smacked her rump.

"Get out of here!" Floyd said. "Go! Yah!"

The horse, which had grown increasingly nervous at the sound of the helicopter, didn't need much encouragement and bolted forward. As Mule ran off, Floyd jumped into a deep drift at the foot of the tree, burying himself in.

As he quickly scooped the last of the freezing snow over his face, Floyd saw the chopper turn toward the horse. With the trees and branches flickering in front of Mule, it would be impossible to tell whether there was a rider clinging to her back.

Floyd held his breath and prayed his gambit would work. Finally, he heard the noise of the chopper's engine fading away.

Floyd hauled himself out of the drift, dusted off the worst of the damp, clumping snow, and made his way back to the trail. He'd managed to escape capture, but his freedom had come at a high cost. He was now about to cross the Hindu Kush mountains on foot.

CHAPTER 35

JESSIE HAD ARRANGED for us to stay in an empty house outside Rye, Westchester County. The house belonged to the cousin of Dinah Palmer, one of Private New York's detectives, who was on vacation in the Caribbean for the winter.

I left Beth and the children there with Jessie, and took the Nissan into the city to see the man who called himself Donald Singer. Justine had arranged for us to meet at Le Loup, an upmarket restaurant on the corner of Lafayette and Howard in Manhattan. I parked in a garage on Lispenard Street, four blocks away, and walked the frozen streets to the meeting. A north wind whipped down the manmade canyons. I hurried on, eager to get inside.

Le Loup was situated on the first floor of a twelve-story Art Deco building. It was one of the city's top eateries, which made it a safe and public environment in which to meet someone potentially untrustworthy and dangerous. I stepped inside and was greeted by a blast of warm air infused with the smell of butter, onions, garlic, and wine. Le Loup was known for its traditional French cuisine but the décor was very much Manhattan. The walls had been stripped back to the brick, which had been painted clinical white. The tables and chairs were constructed of recycled metal and distressed wood, and low-watt filament bulbs glowed like fireflies.

"*Bienvenue chez Le Loup,*" the hostess said. "Do you have a reservation?"

"I'm meeting Donald Singer," I replied.

"This way, please, sir."

I followed her through a crowded bar into the main dining room. The man posing as Singer was sitting at a table in the middle. If he knew I was wise to the deception, he gave no hint of it.

"Mr. Morgan," he said.

As I took my seat, I checked out the people at the surrounding tables. None of them gave me a second glance, but there was a guy at the bar, linebacker in size, whose narrow eyes lingered on me a little too long. Singer's muscle, perhaps?

"I was glad when your colleague phoned," Singer said. "I'm very interested to hear what you've found so far. What would you like?"

"Water, please," I told the hostess, who nodded and withdrew.

I studied Singer more closely than I had when we first met. There was a faint mark on his chin—a faded scar. Or could it be a careless blemish left by a plastic surgeon? His eyes had the false warmth of a politician's and his smile seemed stuck on. Even his accent didn't have the ring of authenticity that I recalled.

"I found Beth," I said.

"That's great news!" Singer replied, with hollow enthusiasm.

"Unfortunately, she ran off. Someone set the cops on my tail and it spooked her. We were at a hospital. She was injured escaping from people who were trying to abduct her. It was shortly after we left there that she took off."

"Oh," Singer remarked, deflated.

"She's OK, by the way," I added. "Your grandchildren too."

"Good," he replied. "That's good."

"I'm sorry, Mr. Singer. You raised a very intelligent and resourceful woman."

"That I did," he said, nodding his head slowly. "Did you get much chance to speak to her? Did she give any indication why she was on the run?"

He wasn't sure his cover had been blown.

"No," I replied. "We didn't get much chance to talk." I paused for effect. "But one of my detectives did make an interesting discovery. Did you know Beth is married?"

The man pretending to be Donald Singer leaned forward conspiratorially.

"We're not supposed to talk about it. That's why I didn't tell you. It's classified."

"Joshua?" I asked.

He nodded. "How did you find out about my son-in-law?"

"My team are very good at uncovering information," I replied. Now was the time to lay my bait. "We also learned he's missing in action. The

Pentagon are searching for him. According to my sources, they have a fix on his locator beacon."

"That might explain why Beth vanished," Singer suggested. "Something to do with whatever trouble Joshua finds himself in."

"I think it does," I agreed. "The people pursuing her are professional and highly dangerous. She is doing whatever it takes to get away from them."

The hostess returned with my water, but I got to my feet as she put the glass on the table.

"Thank you," I said.

She smiled.

"And thank you, Mr. Singer. I'm sorry to have let you down, but I can assure you it won't happen again. Stay strong and I'll be in touch as soon as I have any news."

"If there's anything I can do..." His voice trailed off.

"I'll be sure to let you know," I said, before heading for the exit.

I walked through the busy bar, wondering whether he would take the bait.

CHAPTER 36

AS I WALKED out of Le Loup onto the street, I noticed the linebacker who had been sitting at the bar followed me out. I knew if this was any kind of serious operation, he wouldn't be working alone. I made my way south along Lafayette, squeezing past pedestrians who were swaddled against the chill, listening to the slush and spray of passing vehicles. Suddenly someone barged into me—a young blonde woman in a short coat. She looked up at me, nodded, and smiled politely.

The moment she'd walked on, I checked my coat and found a disc about the size of a quarter had been dropped into my left pocket. I recognized the close-range tracker immediately.

I glanced over my shoulder to see the linebacker about twenty paces behind me, and then about ten paces behind him was a red-haired woman I recognized from outside Le Loup. They were doing such a bad job at staying hidden, I wondered if it was a ruse. I picked up my pace and hurried along the salt-covered sidewalk through the shadow of the tall buildings around me.

The Broadway lights were in my favor. I crossed with the crowd and ran down the steps into the Canal Street subway station. When I got to the bottom, I ducked around the corner and dropped the tracker that had been planted on me. I turned back the way I came and raced up the stairs as the linebacker came into view.

His eyes widened, startled, when he spotted me rushing toward him. Before he could produce whatever he was reaching for inside his coat, I drove my shoulder up into his gut, grabbed the back of his legs, and flipped him over my back. He tumbled down the stairs with a cry, and the people around us gasped and moved swiftly away. The redhead caught my eye and turned to run, but I was too fast. I caught her on the top step and grabbed her arm.

"I don't know who you're working for," I said—there was no point letting the man posing as Singer know he'd been made—"but if you come near me again..." I looked down at her colleague who was flat out on the hard tiled floor at the foot of the stairs.

I released her and walked on. When I glanced over my shoulder, I saw her running down the subway steps. I walked the neighborhood for another twenty minutes, doubling back on myself to reveal any other tails, but found none. I used the time to check my clothes for further tracking devices, in case I'd missed a plant. Once I was convinced I was safe, I headed for the parking garage on Lispenard Street.

CHAPTER 37

IT WAS MIDAFTERNOON by the time I reached the safe house Jessie had arranged. Located in suburban Rye, Westchester County, the house was situated on a tiny peninsula called Pine Island, which jutted into Long Island Sound like an upside-down "T." Lying northeast of Manhattan, Rye was popular with financiers and Wall Street types, and this was reflected in the houses, which grew bigger the closer I got to the waterfront. The safe house was on the water's edge, at the heart of an acre lot, and was approached through electric gates and a private drive. The snow was pristine and sparkled in the low sun as

I pulled to a halt outside the house in the expansive driveway. Looking south, I could see Manhattan through the bare branches of the mature trees that surrounded the grand two-story home.

I rang the doorbell and moments later Jessie let me in. I was grateful to step out of the bitter cold into the warmth of what was a beautiful family home. We entered a large hallway with a sweeping double-sided horseshoe staircase.

"Quite a place," I observed.

"Yeah, it's not bad," Jessie replied. "We're through here."

She led me under one flight of stairs and through a doorway that took us into a huge open-plan living space. It was a family room, dining room, and kitchen rolled into one, and glass doors ran the length of the exterior wall, offering a magnificent view of Long Island Sound and the Manhattan skyline.

Beth, Maria, and Danny were seated on a couch, watching TV. The kids didn't notice me come in, but Beth waved and I nodded in reply.

"Well, it seems to have worked," Jessie said, leading me to an open laptop on one of the kitchen counters.

"Is that you, Jack Morgan?"

There was no mistaking Mo-bot's voice.

Jessie pulled the laptop around so I could see the screen. Mo-bot was in the Private Los Angeles computer lab with Justine and Sci.

"Hey, Jack," Justine said.

"Boss," Sci added.

"What have you got?" I asked.

"I ran surveillance on the line Justine used to arrange your meeting," Mo-bot replied. "The moment you left him, the guy posing as Singer made a call."

"So he believed my story. You hear what he said?" I asked.

"I'm not a magician," Mo-bot replied. "But I was able to trace the other number. Or at least the cell tower it connected to."

She paused. This wasn't going to be good.

"The phone he called was inside the Pentagon, Jack. Singer called someone in the Department of Defense."

I'd suspected an intelligence component the moment I discovered Beth's husband was Special Forces, but I never imagined it would lead to the Pentagon.

"Can you find out who he was talking to?" I asked.

"I can try," Mo-bot replied. "The Pentagon has all kinds of countersurveillance to prevent identification and tracking, even of cell phones, but I can dig around, see what I can find."

"Thanks," I said. "Any leads on who this guy really is?"

"Not yet," Sci replied. "We're working on it."

"OK," I said. "This makes life a little more complicated. If this guy is connected to the Pentagon, we have no idea who we can trust."

CHAPTER 38

"IT GETS WORSE," Sci said.

I sensed movement and glanced around to see Beth Singer heading over. The children were still engrossed in their movie.

Sci paused when he saw Beth approaching.

"Go on," I said.

"I was able to call in a favor from a pal in the State Department," Sci said. "It seems Joshua Floyd was on a mission in Afghanistan and his aircraft was shot down."

Beth's head drooped. Jessie moved around to comfort her.

"The State Department is making representations to the Afghan government to let an investigative team visit the scene," Sci revealed. "But the Afghans are saying…" He hesitated.

"Tell me," Beth pleaded. Tears were forming in her eyes.

"The Afghans are saying there were no survivors," Sci revealed.

Beth shut her eyes and inhaled deeply. Tears traced their way down her face, but she wiped them away and turned to me.

"He's alive," she said. "And I'm not saying that as his doting wife. I'm saying that as one former pilot to another. If Josh was dead, they wouldn't need me and the children as leverage."

I didn't disagree. There was a slim chance the two incidents were unrelated, but the timing of the events and the nature of the people involved suggested orchestration. I nodded and turned back to the laptop.

"Sci, see if you can find out where the bird went down and whether there's been any activity in that area."

"Will do, Jack."

"We'll check in soon," Justine said, before ending the call.

I could see Beth struggling with her emotions.

"We'll find him," I assured her.

She replied with an uncertain nod. I'd been shot down in Afghanistan, so I knew the horror of the situation all too well, but I'd been lucky—which was more than I could say for most of the men who'd been in the bird with me.

"We'll keep you and your kids safe," I told Beth Singer. "And we'll find your husband in Afghanistan. We'll find him and we'll bring him home."

She responded with a faint smile.

"Moscow is our nearest office," I said to Jessie. "Get in touch with Dinara Orlova. Bring her up to speed."

"Will do," Jessie replied.

I backed away from the counter and took my phone from my pocket.

"Where are you going?" Jessie asked.

"To call in a favor," I replied, heading for the door.

CHAPTER 39

I STEPPED OUTSIDE and followed a path around the house. It was more a channel of shallow snow, in between the deeper drifts that covered the lawn and flowerbeds. I walked to the back garden and saw the gentle waves of the Sound lapping the beach not a hundred yards from where I stood. New York City loomed in the distance. I scrolled through my replacement phone looking for a number I was only supposed to call in an emergency.

I dialed, and as I waited for my call to connect, I watched the lights of cars zipping through Queens.

"Hello?" a voice said.

"I'm looking for Secretary Carver," I replied.

"And you are?"

"Jack Morgan, he gave me this number—"

"Hold, please," the voice said, and the line fell silent.

Secretary of Defense Eli Carver had given me the number after I'd saved his life from the Russian assassin Veles, at Air Station Fallon.

"Jack Morgan," Eli Carver said when he came on the line. "I'm glad you called. Not a day passes when I don't think about what I owe you."

"I did what I had to, Mr. Secretary," I replied.

"I'm pretty sure I told you to call me Eli," he responded with a friendly laugh. "But I'm guessing you didn't call to reminisce. What can I do for you?"

"Last week, a Special Forces bird went down in Afghanistan," I said, and felt his mood change.

"And you know about that how?" he asked somberly. "Never mind, I forgot who I was talking to. Go on."

"A man claiming to be the father-in-law of one of the men on that aircraft hired me to track down his daughter. It turns out he's an imposter who might be trying to use her as leverage."

"Local intelligence says there were no survivors, Jack." Carver's tone could not have been more serious. "It was a massacre."

"I'm very sorry to hear that, Mr. Secretary, but I believe there was at least one survivor. These men wouldn't be trying to abduct my client and her children if her husband was dead."

I barely registered the ease with which Beth Singer had become my client. She hadn't asked me, she wasn't paying me, but I felt ashamed of how easily I'd been misled and I needed to put it right. This wasn't just about getting off the bench and putting myself on the front line anymore. This was about protecting an innocent woman and her children.

"Why don't you come in?" Carver asked. "Show us what you've got. We can protect your client, take down the bad guys."

"That's where things get complicated, Mr. Secretary," I replied. "One of those bad guys might be in your department. The man who hired me appears to have a Pentagon connection, which makes me think that someone at the Department of Defense might have given up the mission in Afghanistan. Someone who is now working with hostiles to capture a US service-man and his family."

Carver whistled. "That's a heck of an allegation, Jack."

"I know, Mr. Secretary. That's why I called you and you alone."

"I appreciate it, Jack. But now I'm not sure who's doing who the favor."

"I'd suggest going through everyone who was cleared for the Afghanistan mission. Run vetting, full background, and comms checks," I said.

"Why don't you help us work this from the inside?" Carver suggested. "A Department of Defense contractor."

"I trust my team," I said. "I hope you won't take this the wrong way, Mr. Secretary, but I don't trust yours. It looks very much like you have at least one traitor at the Pentagon, and until we know if that's true and who it is, I'd rather not take any chances."

"Not even with me?"

"Not even with you, Mr. Secretary. With all due respect."

"You're a careful man, Jack," Carver said, and I could tell from his tone that he was smiling.

"Wisdom earned from hard lessons," I replied.

"Can I reach you on this number?"

"Yes, sir."

"Well, let's keep in touch," Carver said. "I'll let you know if I find anything."

"Likewise, Mr. Secretary."

"You be careful. And, Jack?"

"Yes, Mr. Secretary."

"What do I have to do to get you to call me Eli? You saved my life, remember?"

"I remember, sir," I said. It was my turn to smile. "Maybe if we ever share a beer it'll feel more natural to call you by your first name, but until then I can't seem to shake the habit, sir."

Carver scoffed. "Good luck, Jack."

"Thanks. And you, sir," I replied, before hanging up.

CHAPTER 40

I WAS ALONE in the living room, watching the blazing lights of the city in the distance. It was during these rare quiet moments that I sometimes questioned the life I'd chosen. I could have picked any apartment, any office, any bar, and found people who knew what each day would bring, whose lives were comfortable, certain. I wondered whether having lived a life on the edge, never settling, had changed me beyond redemption. Could I be happy with a comfortable, certain existence? Was my time in LA away from all this a sign I wanted out? But I hadn't been entirely content there. I'd felt a gap in my life that had been filled ever since I'd taken this case. As I looked at the city and pictured the lives being lived there, I struggled to imagine Justine and myself ever slotting into anything so normal. Were we doomed to live life on the edge? Would she be happy with such an existence?

While I was getting philosophical, Jessie had withdrawn to the study to attend to some essential work. The New York office was one of Private's busiest, and she was balancing her other duties with her work with me on the Singer case.

Rather than worrying about my distant future, I needed to focus on my next move. Sci, Justine, and Mo-bot would dig up something on the man posing as Singer, but he wasn't my prime concern. My main worry was Joshua Floyd. Beth and her children would never be completely safe as long as Floyd was at risk.

My new phone rang and Justine's name came up on the screen.

"Hey," I said.

"How are you?" she asked.

"OK. Safe."

"And Beth and the children?"

"They're fine," I replied.

"You've got a call. Dinara Orlova from Moscow."

I checked my watch. It would be after midnight there. "Put her through."

The line went dead for a moment before the call was connected.

"Dinara?"

"Jack Morgan. It sounds as though you've been getting into trouble," she said. Dinara had transformed Private Moscow from a deadbeat operation into a roaring success and it had done wonders for her spirit and confidence.

"Nothing new there," I replied.

"We looked into the situation down south," she said. I was glad she was being cryptic in case we had any unwanted listeners. "And there have been reports of a lot of unusual activity."

"What kind of activity?"

"The loud and dangerous kind," she replied. "The sort of heavy response I'd expect from someone who'd lost something."

"Can you pinpoint it?" I asked.

"Yes. Some of my old friends have been very helpful."

Dinara was a former FSB internal security

agent with excellent connections within Russia's intelligence community.

"Do you think you could have a team meet me there?"

"I can do that," Dinara said without skipping a beat.

"Good. I'll send you my travel plans once I have them."

"OK," she said. "You know, you're crazy, Jack. I say that with the greatest respect."

I laughed. "I'll be in touch."

She hung up and I waited for the inevitable.

"She's right," Justine said after a moment's pause. "You are crazy. You told me you were going to New York for a run-of-the-mill case to ease yourself back into the field. Now you're going to Afghanistan. Really, Jack?"

I thought Justine might stay on the call, but hadn't wanted her to find out my plans this way.

"I have a young family with me whose lives will be in danger until this man is brought home safely."

"But why do *you* have to bring him home, Jack? What is the point of having teams set up across the globe if you always go in yourself?"

"It's too big a risk and I can't ask other people to take risks that I'm not willing to take."

"This isn't about other people, Jack. This is about you. No matter what you achieve, no matter what you have, it's never enough. You're acting as if you have something to prove. What do you have left to prove?"

"I don't know." I said the words so quietly they felt more like an admission to myself. "Maybe it's just who I am."

"Is it, Jack? And what about me? What about us? One day your luck will run out. Time catches up with everyone eventually. The people who live a long life don't try to outrun it. They outsmart it."

"What other option do I have? There's reason to believe the Pentagon is compromised. The DOD can't even get a team into the country to investigate. I've served in Afghanistan. I know the country. I have the resources and the capability."

"But it's too dangerous," she said, getting down to basics.

"I'll have a team with me. We're on a rescue mission, not going into battle. I won't do anything that will get me, or anyone else, killed. I promise you, I'll come home."

Justine was silent and I knew what that meant. She didn't approve, but she wasn't going to disagree.

"You wouldn't love me if I wasn't the man I am."

"You're so stubborn. If you let anything happen to yourself, I swear I'll find you in the afterlife and make you suffer."

"I'm not going anywhere," I assured her.

"Just to Afghanistan," she said bitterly.

"Yes, just to Afghanistan."

CHAPTER 41

"YOU DON'T HAVE to do this," Beth Singer told me.

She'd left the children watching a movie in the family room and had joined Jessie and me in the living room.

"I know," I replied, and turned to Jessie. "Hadn't we better get going?"

She checked the time and nodded. "Alvarez and Taft should be here any moment."

A buzzer sounded. Jessie went to the video intercom and lifted the receiver. On the screen, I saw the faces of two operatives I recognized: Roni Alvarez, a tough, snarky former Bronx cop, and Jim Taft, a huge, bull-necked ex–Secret Service agent. They were here to guard Beth and the children.

Jessie buzzed them through the gate and turned to me. "Let's go."

"Please be careful," Beth said. She took my hands and squeezed them tenderly. "Thank you."

"I'll be in touch through Jessie," I replied.

I checked I had my phone, passport, and wallet, and followed Jessie outside, where we met Roni and Taft.

"Traveling light?" Roni asked.

"Yeah," I replied.

"We'll keep them safe until you get back," Roni said.

"Stay frosty," Taft added.

"Thanks," I scoffed.

They went into the house and shut the door, and Jessie and I got in the black Nissan and started out for LaGuardia.

Brooding clouds hung low over the quiet highway. Jessie drove cautiously through the slush and salt. She'd chartered a private jet, so there was no danger of the aircraft leaving without me.

"Do you want me to come with you?" she

asked as we rolled along I-95. "Roni and Jim will be okay with Beth and the children."

"She trusts you," I replied. "She might need a friendly face with her."

There was no need to explain why. We all believed Joshua Floyd was still alive, but the report there were no survivors might be true.

"Dinara is sending a team to Kabul," I added. "I'll be fine."

I'd used Private's secure messaging system to send Dinara Orlova my travel plans, and she'd replied to let me know a member of the Private Moscow team would be in Kabul to meet my plane when it arrived.

"You need to learn to trust people, Jack," Jessie said.

"I do," I replied. "Otherwise I wouldn't be leaving Beth and the children with you."

"It's not my place to analyze you," Jessie said, "but most people running a company of Private's size don't get involved in frontline operations. You've got nothing to prove."

"I'm not trying to prove anything," I replied, but somewhere inside I knew that wasn't entirely true.

"You don't have to save the world single-handed." Jess smiled.

"I know. I've got you to help me. We all want to be heroes. That's why we're in this business."

She shook her head and grinned broadly. "You've always got an answer, Jack Morgan."

We spent the rest of the journey discussing operational issues at the New York office, and after fifty minutes, Jessie delivered me to the executive jet terminal at LaGuardia.

I saw my Gulfstream G650 waiting on the tarmac, and, after thanking Jessie for the ride, passed through border control without issue, grateful Rafael Lucas had cleared the person-of-interest alert off my record following the motel incident. A few minutes later, I was airborne.

CHAPTER 42

LOSING THE HORSE had cost Floyd dearly. He was trying to reach the Pakistan border on foot, crossing some of the harshest terrain and most dangerous mountain passes in the world.

Floyd was nearing the summit of a mountain that, according to the map John and Chris had given him, would take him to a pass leading into the neighboring valley. There was supposed to be a trail, but it had been covered by deep snow and Floyd was having to use a stick to feel for the edge of the mountain. He was on its shoulder and a wrong step would send him to his death, eight or nine thousand feet below. There were no trees up here, and nothing to protect him from the brutal wind, which seemed to find its way through the layers of clothing, scarves, and gloves he was wearing. The jagged shards of cold bit through his skin and flesh and gnawed at his very bones. This was a brutal environment, and the darkness robbed the world of any color. The only things he had to give him warmth were the images of Beth, Maria, and Danny he held in his mind and the burning love for them that filled his heart. After everything he'd been through, he would not allow himself to die in this strange and inhospitable place.

Other than the relentless cold, he felt fine physically. John and Chris had given him clothes and food, and he estimated he had rations for two days, which wasn't going to be enough. He was burning a lot more energy than he would have been if he were completing the journey on horseback as planned, and it was going to take him four times as long. Floyd had a knife and a gun, and when he made it into the next valley he would try to find a wild goat or deer to replenish his supplies.

The men hunting Floyd weren't as careful as he

was. Every so often, he would see the telltale green glow of night-vision goggles in the valley below, and he heard the distant thrum of choppers. He had been lucky so far. They hadn't searched the route up to the pass. Maybe they lacked the local knowledge. Or perhaps they didn't think anyone would be foolish enough to attempt the journey at the height of winter. Floyd wasn't foolish, just desperate. He would get home no matter what.

He looked to the east and saw the sky turning gray. It would soon be dawn and he would need to find shelter from his relentless pursuers. Breathless, cold, and exhausted, he conjured images of Beth, Maria, and Danny and held them in his mind.

Guide my steps, he asked of them, and his family gave him renewed strength to press on.

CHAPTER 43

EVERYTHING WAS ON fire and I could hear my buddies screaming. I was standing by the wreckage of my Sea Knight, watching it burn, reeling from the horror of the situation, desperate to run in and save more of the men whose lives I was responsible for.

Then the horror was gone and I was being shaken awake by the co-pilot of the Gulfstream.

"Mr. Morgan, we're coming in to land, sir."

"Thank you," I said, my heart rate beginning to calm.

He went back to the cockpit and I took advantage of the copious space to stretch my arms and legs. I hadn't been troubled by that particular nightmare for some time. It used to be a regular specter, and for years I felt as though I was living two lives. One in the present, the other trapped in the nightmares of my past. Like many veterans, I carried the trauma of battle in my unseen wounds, but time had healed the worst of them so I was surprised to be reliving the old horror again, but maybe I shouldn't have been. This was where my military career had ended: Afghanistan. Maybe that's why I'd been eager to return. Perhaps there was something I needed to lay to rest here.

I looked out of the window and saw the chaotic city of Kabul spread out in the sunshine. Ancient buildings mixed with new. The roads were crowded with livestock, bicycles, motorbikes, trucks, buses, a cavalcade of vehicles of all ages, shapes, and sizes, playing a city-wide game of Dodgem. This was a country that had spent over one hundred years locked in war with an ever-changing roster of enemies, but from the air there were few signs of the scars the country bore.

We landed without incident and taxied to a spot away from the main terminal. I thanked the pilots and walked down the airstairs, where I was met by an Afghan immigration official. He eyed two figures who stood nearby. His wary demeanor suggested he'd had a run-in with them. While he watched them nervously, I grinned at the pair. I should have known they would come. Looking back at me with mischievous grins on their faces were Dinara Orlova and Feodor Arapov, the huge bear of a man who'd been of considerable help during the investigation into Karl Parker's murder and everything that followed. Dinara's cascade of long brown hair was today bunched beneath a woolen hat, and her athletic figure was concealed by a thick long coat. Feodor had bushy brown hair and a thick, matching beard, natural insulation against the cold. He wasn't wearing a coat but relied on a heavy-duty pullover to protect him from the elements.

The immigration official stamped my passport and welcomed me into the country before retreating to an airport cart and taking off for the terminal. I walked over to Dinara and Feo.

"What did you say to that guy?" I asked.

"I told him I would crush him if he gave you any trouble," Feo replied.

I smiled and shook my head. "I thought you were going to send a team."

"And miss the opportunity to return to this beautiful country?" Dinara replied.

I couldn't tell whether she was being sarcastic, but got the feeling it was a genuine remark. I knew she'd spent time in Afghanistan when she'd worked for the FSB.

I hugged her warmly and immediately found myself taken back to the night I'd almost confused my personal and professional feelings for her. I smiled awkwardly as we parted, and thought I could see her blush slightly.

"I'm glad you're here," I told her.

"And what about me, American?" Feo asked. "Are you glad I'm here?"

"Of course, Feodor Arapov. Who wouldn't be glad to see you?"

"I'll tell you who," he said, leaning forward conspiratorially. "Bad guys. That's who."

He pulled me into a bear hug. "But you are not a bad guy," he said as he squeezed the breath out of me.

I stepped back and looked at them expectantly.

"Do we have a car?" I asked.

"A car?" Feo boomed. "What use is a car in the Hindu Kush in winter?"

"That's our ride," Dinara said, pointing at a Bell 429 GlobalRanger a few stands away. "We chartered it for the week. I assume that's OK."

I nodded. "That's more than OK."

"Good," Feo said. "Then let's go. I hear you are a pilot."

"I haven't flown for a while," I replied.

"Oh, no," Feo countered. "You are not flying. I just wanted to know whether you would have the expertise to appreciate real artistry in the sky."

"Feo was once a police pilot," Dinara explained.

"I was *the* police pilot," he added.

He patted me on the back and set off for the aircraft.

I looked at Dinara and grinned. "He's not short of confidence."

"He's Russian to his bones," she replied, as though that explained everything. "We've got clothes and supplies on board."

I nodded and followed her to the Global-Ranger. Within minutes Feo had cleared us with the tower and we were airborne, heading for the Osprey crash site, deep in Nuristan.

CHAPTER 44

THE STEADY HUM of the engines remained constant as we traveled away from Kabul. Feo was an excellent pilot and kept us at five thousand feet as we flew over the desert that stretched between Surobi and Mihtarlam. There were rocky snow-capped peaks in almost every direction, but beneath us the folds of earth were arid desert—long sloping inclines of sand and rock that offered little shade or shelter. I wasn't warm even in the Russian winter coat Dinara had given me, which fended off the worst of the chill. The three of us wore radio headsets that facilitated easy conversation, and I had brought them up to speed on the investigation.

"So we believe Joshua Floyd is still alive?" Dinara asked.

"Yes," I replied, "and, if he hasn't been captured, he's likely to try to head for friendly territory."

"Pakistan," Feo observed from the cockpit.

Dinara and I were in the main cabin, sitting on benches that faced each other.

"That's where I'd go," I agreed.

"What would anyone want with a pilot?" Feo asked.

It was a good question and one I'd pondered myself.

"Maybe he's a foreign intelligence operative who's turned," Dinara suggested. "Maybe they want to bring him back under control?"

I hoped not for the sake of Beth and the children. I knew from bitter experience what it was like to discover someone you cared about was a traitor.

"I thought it might be something to do with a past mission," I said. "Maybe someone is out for revenge?"

"That's a big grudge," Feo remarked.

"Special Forces go up against people with the resources and funds to be able to hold big grudges," I countered.

"Maybe they want something from him—intelligence from a past mission?" Dinara suggested.

"What are your comms like?" I asked. My phone had lost signal three miles outside Kabul.

"Satellite phone and full data," she replied.

"Can you send a message to Mo-bot?" I asked. "See if she can get access to Floyd's operations file and find out what he's been doing."

Dinara nodded. "Sure."

"You better buckle up," Feo said. "We might get some chop in the mountains."

I stood up and leaned through the gap between the cabin and the cockpit. Ahead of us were the foothills of a vast mountain range. The peaks were rich in snow, and I could see clouds of the stuff being blown off the steep summits by harsh winds. Snow-dusted forests rose to about six thousand feet, above which there was just ice and jagged outcrops of rock. It looked a deeply inhospitable place, and it pained me to think Joshua Floyd might be braving it alone.

"Where are we heading?" I asked, as Feo took us up.

"Kamdesh," he replied. "Local intelligence says there was some trouble there a few nights ago."

I nodded and returned to my seat in the back.

The chopper started to dance in the updrafts and I pulled on my seat belt. I knew Afghanistan well. This was going to be a bumpy ride.

CHAPTER 45

IT WAS BITTERLY cold. Justine shivered as she and Sci walked along West 81st Street. They'd arrived in New York that morning, having caught the red-eye with Mo-bot. Jessie Fleming had met them at JFK and driven them to Private's office at Forty-One Madison, a thirty-six-story black glass and steel skyscraper that stood on the corner of Madison Avenue and East 26th Street, overlooking Madison Park. Private New York was headquartered on the thirty-fifth and thirty-sixth floors, and they'd been given a meeting room that was to act as the base of operations for their investigation into the man posing as Beth Singer's father.

"You've been pretty quiet," Sci observed as they weaved around another couple heading along the icy sidewalk.

"Just thinking," Justine replied.

"Pining?" Sci remarked with a knowing smile.

"No." She elbowed him playfully.

In truth, she was worried about Jack. The thought of what he could be facing in Afghanistan was almost too much for her to bear, particularly after what had happened in Moscow. She'd insisted they come to New York, not just to be closer to the guy they were investigating, but because she wanted to be there the moment Jack stepped off the plane on his return.

She had tried not to worry and had focused on getting the local investigation up and running. She didn't have Sci's forensic skills or Mo-bot's knowledge of computers, but as one of the country's leading criminal profilers, Justine knew people.

"You don't have to worry," Sci said. "Jack knows how to take care of himself."

"I'm not worried," Justine replied, but that was less than the truth.

She wasn't just worried about whether or not Jack would come home. Each of these major investigations took an emotional toll on him, and while it might remain hidden from others who only saw the confidence and bravado of a hero, she saw beneath the façade. The Moscow investigation had been particularly grueling, and even Jack acknowledged how much it had affected him. It wasn't often that Jack Morgan benched himself. Justine knew Afghanistan already held traumatic memories for him. She prayed that he would not pay too high a psychological price for whatever was to come.

"If you say so," Sci responded. "Although I'm a little offended that after all these years working together, you don't think I'm smart enough to read you like a book."

Justine elbowed him again.

"Cut it out," he said. "Try to be professional. We're almost there."

Mo-bot had traced the cell phone Justine had called to contact Donald Singer to an apartment building on West 81st Street, one block from

Central Park. Justine and Sci had volunteered to see if they could pin the phone to a specific apartment. It hadn't moved since it had been taken into the building.

38 West 81st Street was a grand old building with a green awning that traversed the sidewalk. It was the kind of prime real estate foreign investors would pay a premium for. It was a short walk from the park, and apartments on the upper levels had balconies that overlooked the small playground in the broad West 81st Street median. It was a beautiful part of New York City, and ownership of an apartment in the building would have been a status symbol for a certain class of jetsetter.

A liveried doorman opened the brass-bound door for them and smiled as they entered a huge vaulted lobby. There was marble everywhere and lush potted plants abounded, as did expensive abstract artwork. Justine didn't need to be an expert to know these were all costly originals.

She and Sci crossed to a long marble reception desk.

"Can I help?" the suited receptionist asked.

"I hope so," she replied. "My colleague and I

work in Fisher's, a jeweler on Fifth. One of your residents was in the store yesterday and he left his billfold. We have his address for delivery of a bespoke piece he ordered, but we'd like to make sure he gets his money back sooner rather than later."

Sci produced the billfold containing three thousand dollars in hundreds.

"My colleague accompanied me for security," Justine said.

The receptionist's smile was condescending. "Quite. Well, if you'd like to leave it with me?"

"We'd rather not," Justine replied. "It's quite a lot of money."

The receptionist's teeth remained on show even though Justine could tell he was offended.

"We don't have any dishonesty in this building," he said coldly.

Justine fought the urge to scoff.

"Could you give me the resident's name?" he asked.

"Donald Singer," Sci replied.

The receptionist frowned. "We don't have anyone here by that name."

Sci produced his phone and showed him a photograph of the man posing as Donald Singer.

It had been lifted from the false Singer Investments property company website.

"Ah, Mr. Andreyev," the receptionist said. "A very private man."

"Naturally," Justine responded. "Many of our clients use pseudonyms for reasons of discretion."

Sci handed the receptionist the billfold. "Can you make sure he gets this?"

"And could you also ask him to phone Fisher's and confirm receipt?" Justine asked. "Just to put my boss's mind at rest."

"I can certainly ask," the receptionist said. "I will run this upstairs immediately."

Sci and Justine thanked him and headed for the exit. The doorman smiled as he let them out. When they were a short distance from the building, Justine spoke into the microphone concealed within the cuff of her sleeve.

"You got it?"

"Yes," Mo-bot replied into Justine's earpiece. "I'm following it through the building now."

The billfold contained a tracking device that would enable Mo-bot, sitting in the warm comfort of their operations room at Private New York, to pinpoint Andreyev's exact location.

"And I've started running the name," she added.

"We're on our way back," Justine said, satisfied with their work.

In a few minutes they would know exactly where their target was based, and soon they'd know who he really was.

CHAPTER 46

KAMDESH WAS A small town located high in the Hindu Kush mountains. I'd flown these ranges before, but still found their majesty breathtaking. We approached from the south, flying up the valley, and I looked out of the chopper in wonder as huge peaks loomed to our north, their snowcaps dazzling in the morning sun. The lower flanks were a kaleidoscope of purples, grays, and blues in the bright light, and further down there were deep greens of cedar and fir. I couldn't help but feel insignificant in the presence of something so vast, and these were only a handful of the mountains stretching to the north and west as far as the eye could see.

My body ached and the bones in my feet felt as though they'd shrunk away from my soles. My eyes were heavy with jetlag and I could feel the ominous signs of a headache forming, but all these nagging discomforts melted away as I took in the awesome landscape.

We flew into Kamdesh a little after five. The town was a feat of engineering, built into the mountainside in terraces so that one home was constructed almost on top of another. Steep roads and alleyways carved through the clusters of buildings.

I joined Feo in the cockpit as he circled, searching for a place to land. Beneath us, people emerged from their homes and looked up at the aircraft. Some of the men carried rifles, others were armed with machine guns. A few were shouting instructions and pointing up at us.

"They don't look friendly," I observed.

"A thousand friends are few, one enemy is too many," Feo replied. "It's a Russian proverb that teaches people to be cautious. Like them, I hope."

I hoped they were just being cautious too.

"Down there," I suggested, spotting a shoulder of land that protruded to the north of the village near a track that led out of town.

Feo nodded and said something in Russian. I looked back to see Dinara smiling.

"He said he hates backseat pilots," she revealed.

"She's lying," Feo objected with a broad grin. "I would never say such a thing about my boss."

I buckled myself in as he swung us around and began his descent. A crosswind coming up the valley buffeted the chopper, but Feo compensated expertly and we were soon on a snow-covered patch of ground.

Outside, a group of armed men were coming along the track.

The yelling started the moment Dinara opened the cabin door. She swung it back and was greeted by a barrage of anger delivered in Kamviri. I unclipped myself and hurried back to join her. She jumped down and replied in Pashto. It wasn't the local dialect, but most of the men there understood her.

They moved forward, close now, their guns pointed at us, their voices still loud and angry.

Dinara spoke again and Feo climbed out of the chopper. He held an SR-2 Veresk submachine gun and had an MP-443 Grach pistol in a holster slung under his arm. The size of the man, coupled with the hardware he was toting, only served to fuel the crowd's hostility.

Dinara carried on talking. Slowly the angry shouts morphed into low grumbles.

"Their village was attacked three nights ago," she revealed. "A unit of Russian mercenaries. They killed three people and wounded another twelve. They think we're part of the same unit."

She turned and spoke some more. A young man who couldn't have been more than twenty yelled at the others and, a few moments later, they dispersed and headed back toward town.

"I told them we're friends of the pilot, the man the Russians were looking for," Dinara explained.

The young Nuristani man stepped forward and slung his AK-47 over his shoulder.

"Hello," he said. "You speak English?"

"Yes," I replied.

"My name is Vosuruk," the young man said. "After my grandfather. He was an important man here."

"Nice to meet you, Vosuruk. You can call me Jack."

"Welcome, Jack. Come with me, please. There is someone who can help you."

CHAPTER 47

I KNEW FROM experience that when you weren't facing them across a battlefield, the Afghan people were warm and welcoming, and Vosuruk was no exception.

"Did you come from America?" he asked as he led us along the track that ran into the village.

I nodded.

"We came from Russia," Dinara replied.

"The Russians killed my uncle," he remarked. "But that was long ago."

"I'm sorry," Dinara said.

"What for? We fight with honor. We die

with honor. And my uncle killed many Russians before he died. So maybe I also should say sorry."

Feo laughed. "Smart kid."

Vosuruk smiled in reply. He was about a foot shorter than me and wiry, but I could sense strength in the way he moved. The mountains punished weakness, so the people who lived here had to be tough.

"I want to go to Moscow one day. And America. I want to see cities where there are more people than there are stars in the sky."

He turned right onto a narrower track that lay between two rows of houses. "This way," he beckoned.

We followed and I admired the simple but resilient architecture and construction methods used to build homes in such a difficult environment. Square, functional, built with a mix of brick and concrete, much of which had been clad and whitewashed, there were still enough distinctive flourishes to distinguish one house from another. A blue ceramic plaque of Quranic text hung beside one door. Another had red-painted window frames. A third featured a wall that was covered in an abstract artwork formed of brightly colored cubes. No matter the conditions, wherever I've been in the world, people always seek beautiful ways to express their individuality.

"Have you seen a Ford F-350?" Vosuruk asked. "It is a pickup truck."

"It's a good truck," I replied.

"It is another dream. One day I buy one from America and bring it home. I see it in a magazine and I feel in love."

"Where did you learn English?" Feo asked. He towered over the slight Afghan.

"From my teacher. We're going to see him now," Vosuruk replied. "He's English. Proper English. Not American or Russian. Original English teacher."

I wondered what could have led an English person to this remote mountain village. There were worse places to live, but it wasn't somewhere I'd imagine was rich in opportunity for the foreign settler.

Vosuruk took us to the house on the corner at the far end of the alleyway. I looked south down a narrow road toward the bottom of the village and saw evidence of recent battle. There were blast craters and bullet holes in the thick walls of nearby houses, scorch marks on the white paint.

"The men who came here did that," Vosuruk explained.

He knocked on the door of the house on the corner and a moment later a woman's voice responded in Kamviri.

"She says to come in," Vosuruk said. He opened the heavy, weatherworn door.

We stepped inside a small room that was full of shoes, boots, and coats in two sizes. Vosuruk took us through an interior door into a large open-plan space that consisted of a living area decorated with richly colored cushions and throws. A kitchen was built around a large hearth and a stone chimney hung above it and stretched up to the steep ceiling. A couple of screens partitioned a sleeping area by the large window overlooking the valley.

A slim, brown-haired woman stood near the screen.

"These people say they're here to help the American pilot," our guide said.

"Thank you, Vosuruk," the woman replied, and the young man nodded and withdrew.

"Who are you?" the woman asked. She sounded Californian.

"Jack Morgan," I replied. "I run Private. It's a detective agency. These are my colleagues, Dinara Orlova and Feodor Arapov."

The woman studied us but said nothing.

"What do you want with him?" a voice asked from behind the screen. The man spoke with an English accent.

I heard a soft groan and someone shuffling around, then a tall, athletic man appeared from behind the screen, placing his hand on the woman's shoulder. He wore a vest, and there was a bandage over his right shoulder. He looked pale, and I guessed from the nature of the dressing and the flecks of blood seeping through the bandage that he'd been shot.

"We're here to take him home," I replied. "We're working for his family. Vosuruk said you'd be able to help us."

"The paramilitaries who came here and shot the place up were well equipped and sophisticated," the man said. "The kind of people who might come back to try a softer approach. How do we know you're not working with them?"

His accent suggested he was British.

"We're nothing to do with them," I assured him. "I don't know who they are or what they want with Joshua, but you're right to say they're sophisticated. They've been operating in the US at the same time, to try and capture his family."

The man and woman judged us silently. Feo kissed his teeth and exhaled in frustration, but now wasn't the time for confrontation.

"If you know where he is, please tell us so we can take him home. His family is in danger, and getting Joshua to safety is the only way to protect them."

The man and woman exchanged a skeptical look before she fixed me with a piercing stare. "Convince us."

"Convince us you're telling the truth," the man added. "And then we'll see if we can help."

CHAPTER 48

FLOYD WOKE SUDDENLY. He hadn't been dreaming; he was too exhausted. He came around from a black void that felt like death, and immediately wished he could go back to that blessed oblivion. Every muscle ached and his eyes burned with fatigue. He felt feverish, as though there were hot coals somewhere deep inside him, but when he touched his skin his temperature seemed normal. He suspected he was starting to experience the combined effects of altitude sickness and exhaustion.

He could see bright sunshine through the tiny crawlspace that allowed access to the cave where he'd planned to spend the day. He saw a shadow cross the light, and the hairs on his neck bristled. His stomach filled with acid as he realized something must have woken him. Was it a creature of some kind? A branch blown by the wind? He held his breath and listened closely, but heard nothing except the breeze through the trees.

He rolled onto his stomach, grabbed the coat he'd been using as an extra blanket, and slid it over his shoulders. He crawled to the cave mouth, which was only a little broader than his shoulders and taller than the width of his torso. He'd found the tiny entrance at dawn, after having spent much of the early hours looking for a place to bed down. He was at the foot of the last mountain before the range that would take him to the border. One final push up and over the next set of peaks would take him into the adjacent valley, on to a pass that led to the border with Pakistan.

To ears that had become attuned to silence, the scratching of loose rock sounded like the applause of a crowd of thousands. Floyd tried to move more quietly, but it was hard to do when crawling. He approached the end of the tunnel and used his forearms to inch forward and pull himself to the lip. He poked his head out and saw nothing but snow and the trunks of cedar trees. He hauled himself out carefully and slowly.

"Don't move," a voice said in a thick Russian accent.

Floyd glanced around to see a man in blue, gray, and white snow camouflage and a gray ski mask standing on a rocky outcrop above the cave mouth. He had a Vityaz-SN submachine gun aimed at Floyd's chest.

"Get on the ground," the gunman ordered, before saying something in Russian into a hand-held radio.

Floyd knew other men would soon join them, and his odds would diminish with every new arrival. He also knew that if they wanted him dead, he would have been shot already. He was alive for a reason, and he was determined to play that to maximum advantage.

The gunman jumped off the rocks and landed in the snow a few feet away from Floyd.

"I said get on the ground!"

Floyd rushed him, aiming his shoulder at the man's midriff. People with guns are accustomed to being obeyed, and Floyd knew he would have the element of surprise. The gunman raised the submachine gun as if to strike, but Floyd reached him before he could do so. He felt a satisfying compression as his shoulder hit the man's abdomen. The Russian groaned as he was thrust back into the rocks around the cave mouth. Floyd stood tall, grabbed the man's head, and forced it back. There was a loud crack as it hit the rock and the man's eyes rolled back in his head. His body went limp and Floyd allowed him to fall to the ground. He searched the man and took the Vityaz, along with three spare magazines of ammunition and the radio.

"Hey!" a voice yelled, and Floyd turned to see other men moving through the trees toward him.

He flipped the safety off and fired a short burst from the Vityaz, which he swung in an undirected arc. The gunfire had the desired effect, the men scattering for cover. Floyd seized the moment he'd bought himself and ran west, heading into the thickest part of the forest.

Snow-covered branches whipped at him and huge clumps of powder pelted him as he pressed through the trees. There was an eruption of gunfire above and around him, and the air filled with woodchips and the smell of cedar. He knew they were aiming high and wide in an attempt to frighten him into stopping, but he wasn't that dumb.

Memories of Beth, Maria, and Danny gave his exhausted spirit a much-needed boost, flooding his battered body with an infusion of energy. Floyd knew that if he stopped and allowed these men to take him, as soon as they had whatever they wanted from him, he'd be completely expendable. He couldn't let that happen. He had to escape.

CHAPTER 49

I TOLD THEM a condensed version of my story: how a supposed relative of the downed airman had hired me to find people close to him and how I'd discovered my client was a liar, using me to gain leverage over Floyd. I kept things vague so I didn't compromise Beth and the children.

"You're being sketchy on the details," the Englishman said. "Is that because you don't trust us?"

I smiled. "Just being cautious."

"But I'm still not convinced," he replied. "Any one of the men who attacked us could have told that story."

I studied him and the American woman

carefully. They were outsiders. Not just in this village. Whatever had driven them to these mountains had made outcasts of them, by choice or necessity. I didn't think they were living at the edge of the world because they were on the run from the law. They were too open and empathetic. I believed they were good people, and hoped I was right.

"I used to fly Sea Knights in the US Marine Corps," I said. "I flew them in Afghanistan. Over these mountains. I was shot down here, so I know exactly how Floyd feels. I know the grief he's carrying for his comrades, for his brothers. I was lucky enough to be rescued but he is alone out there, hunted by men who will stop at nothing to capture him. Men who are also hunting his family.

"When I left the military, I took over my deadbeat father's detective agency—Private—and I've devoted my life to building it into the most successful detective agency in the world. I sacrificed everything for it. Why did I do that? Because I want to help people. *Semper fidelis*. It's the motto of the US Marine Corps. It means 'Always faithful.' That spirit doesn't leave a person just because they take off the uniform."

I paused.

"You want me to convince you with physical proof? I can't do that. I can show you my ID, you can check out my backstory, but I can't show you proof of my motivation for finding Joshua. All I can do is lay it all out and hope you recognize the sound of the truth when you hear it. I need to find this man because I made a promise to his wife that I would bring him home safely."

"Everything he says is true," Dinara said. "Use Google. Check him out."

"No internet," the Englishman said. "Not till the phone line comes back, at least."

It was the American woman who came to my rescue. "I've heard of Private," she said. "From my days in the Bureau."

She studied me closely and I held her gaze. She was sizing me up, and I was wondering how an FBI agent wound up in the Hindu Kush mountains.

"I believe him, John."

"I do too," John said, looking at the woman and nodding. "Give him the route, Chris."

The woman walked over to a set of drawers and took out a map of the region that she handed to me. It was marked with a route through the winter passes, which could get a person to Pakistan.

"This is the route Joshua is taking to the border," she said.

"Thank you," I said.

"And if you run into the men who did this"— Chris indicated John's bandaged shoulder—"send them our regards."

I nodded. "I'll be sure to do that."

We hurried out of the house and ran back the way Vosuruk had led us.

"That was well done," Feo said. "The way you told your truth."

I nodded my appreciation. I didn't often open up, particularly about my father. My family have been a huge source of pain and betrayal in my life, and I try to think about them as little as possible.

We made it back to the chopper and were airborne a few minutes later. I navigated, guiding Feo along the route plotted out on the map given to me by Chris and John.

Our flight path took us over some rough terrain. We flew over a forest, then above the treeline and through a pass between two high peaks, across a valley, and up into another pass. This was a long journey on horseback, but in the chopper we were clocking 150 knots, or about 170 miles per hour over ground, so we covered what might have taken Floyd days in a matter of minutes.

"I've got something," Dinara said through the comms system. She was using a radio scanner to monitor the airwaves. "Encrypted chatter. A lot of it. Multiple signals, rapid communications, and quick responses."

"Down there, two o'clock," Feo said as we came out of the pass into another valley.

I saw what he was pointing at immediately: the flash and flare of machine gunfire. Even at a distance, it was clear multiple gunmen were converging on a single shooter, who was trying to fight them off. They were moving in on him quickly, and judging from their relative positions, we didn't have long before the single shooter, who we assumed was Floyd, would be overwhelmed.

"Take us down," I said to Feo. "Fast!"

CHAPTER 50

FEO PLUNGED THE chopper into a swift and steep dive. I unclipped my seat belt and hauled myself into the main cabin, where Dinara was sorting through a gear bag, checking weapons. She handed me an SR-2 Veresk submachine gun and a couple magazines. I strapped myself in beside her as the aircraft rode the bumpy drafts down.

"I'm going out," I said. "I want you in the chopper covering me."

"I should—" she began.

"In the chopper, covering me," I said emphatically. "If it gets too hot, you bug out and we'll rendezvous at the Pakistan border. Got it?"

She nodded.

"Floyd is moving away from us," Feo said.

The chopper banked and I saw the solitary shooter running through the trees.

"He thinks we're hostile," I remarked. "Get us as close as you can."

There was the sound of a hailstorm beneath us and I felt the rattle of bullets hitting the fuselage. I looked down to see masked, camouflaged shooters firing at us.

"Get ready," Feo said. "He'll be at your twelve when we touch down."

Feo banked hard and the bird dropped like a stone. The trees loomed close to the window and the ground raced upward worryingly quickly. Then there was a sudden roar from the engines, a surge, and a moment of inertia. We were down.

"Go now!" Feo yelled.

Dinara opened the door and I unclipped and jumped out. I could see Joshua Floyd directly ahead, racing through the trees. We'd pulled ahead of him and he was shocked to see the helicopter, and changed direction, running north.

"Captain Floyd!" I yelled, but my voice was lost beneath the rotors.

"Jack," Dinara said, touching me on the shoulder.

She pointed skyward and I registered what she'd seen: two heavily armed Mil Mi-24 Hind helicopters, their distinctive silhouettes black against the blue sky. We had two minutes at most.

I started chasing Floyd. Bullets peppered the trees around me, filling the air with splinters.

"Floyd!" I yelled. "Captain Floyd!"

He glanced back. Maybe it was the use of his name or my accent that caused him to hesitate.

"Beth sent me," I shouted. "She sent me to get you out."

That stopped him dead. I raced to catch up as bullets zinged around us.

"Who are you?" Floyd asked.

"My name is Jack Morgan. I run a detective agency and I'm here to help."

The shooters were closing on us in an arc, their gunfire designed to keep us pinned down. The camouflaged men were less than a hundred yards away. In the sky, the heavily armed Hinds were getting closer.

"Come on," I said, grabbing Floyd and pulling him east.

We were close to the base of a huge mountain. As we ran, I could almost have reached out and touched the cliff face that supported the vast peak. My plan was to circle around the GlobalRanger and approach it from the south. Floyd fired short bursts in the direction of the men closing on us. I stayed close to him, to avoid being picked off. There was little chance any of the attackers would risk killing their target, but they wouldn't hesitate to shoot me if they were given the opportunity.

I ran hard, my lungs burning. I saw the GlobalRanger chopper rotors whirring through the trees as we raced forward. I caught a glimpse of Feo in the cockpit, distracted and yelling at Dinara. She was leaning out of the door on the other side of the chopper and had her back to us. Her head was darting one way and then another, and I could tell she was looking for us. I saw her turn to Feo and bark a reply. He grimaced and shook his head before looking to the north.

I followed his eye line and saw the two Hinds bearing down on the GlobalRanger.

"Get out of here!" I yelled, but we were too far

away for them to hear me over the noise of the rotors.

The Hind was equipped with two launchers, each of which was capable of delivering thirty-two high-explosive rockets. I watched in horror as first one rocket, then a couple of seconds later another, flew from the lead Hind. The projectiles tore forward, leaving trails of fire and smoke.

"Feo!" I yelled uselessly.

He had seen them and taken immediate action. The GlobalRanger leaped off the ground and got into the air just moments before the rockets passed beneath it.

Then realization dawned that both rockets were now heading straight for us.

I felt Floyd pull me back.

"Come on!" he yelled.

I started to move, but outrunning the rockets was simply impossible. In a few seconds they would hit and there was nothing we could do about it.

CHAPTER 51

DINARA MOVED ACROSS the cabin as the rockets passed underneath them. The relief she felt as she watched the explosives roar away from them, quickly turned to horror as she saw what was in their path. She watched helplessly as, some three hundred yards away, Jack Morgan and Joshua Floyd went sprinting through the trees, trying to get away from the missiles bearing down on them.

"Jack!" she screamed.

The first rocket struck the mountainside. A thunderous explosion and shockwave buffeted the rising aircraft. Dinara cried as a fireball obscured her view of Jack and Floyd. She prayed it was sufficiently to their east not to have harmed them, but if they had survived, they were lost to flames and smoke. Any hopes she had that they might survive were obliterated when the second rocket hit the mountain instants later, striking the cliff directly ahead of where the two men had been. The explosion shook the GlobalRanger and created a huge fireball that consumed the forest for fifty yards around. Nothing in its path could have survived, and Jack and Floyd had been less than a couple of yards from its epicenter when she'd last seen them.

She watched the angry flames burn white hot, tears running down her face.

"Feo!" she cried in anguish. "Jack!"

"I know," he replied grimly. "Strap in, we need to get out of here."

She staggered to the co-pilot's seat in a raw state of shock and slumped down. She absently reached for the four-point harness and clipped in. She couldn't shake the horrific images of Jack's death from her mind.

Feo pulled the chopper into a steep climb, and accelerated away from the chaotic scene. Dinara glanced down as they banked. She saw the flames recede, leaving nothing but charred devastation and clouds of smoke in their wake. All around the blast zone, camouflaged attackers who hadn't been killed in the explosion staggered as though badly injured. Everything caught in the blast radius had been incinerated.

Fresh tears came as Dinara realized Jack had truly gone. They had failed in the worst possible way.

Feo took them up toward the blue sky as the two Mil Mi-24 flying tanks set down and camouflaged men jumped out to attend to their injured comrades.

Dinara watched them with rising anger. She burned with hatred for them and longed for revenge.

Feo touched her arm reassuringly. A moment later they banked around the shoulder of the mountain and left the horror far behind.

CHAPTER 52

"VICTOR ANDREYEV IS a Russian venture capitalist with interests in shipping, energy, chemicals, and armaments," Mo-bot said. "He served five years in the Russian Army and rose to the rank of colonel."

"Intelligence asset?" Sci asked.

"That would be my guess," Mo-bot replied.

Justine pinched the bridge of her nose and inhaled deeply. Private had almost been ruined going up against a rogue Russian intelligence plot in Moscow. This investigation was getting out of control, and she couldn't help but think of Jack facing these people out there in Afghanistan. She leaned over to get a better view of Mo-bot's laptop. They were seated around the board table in the main meeting room on the thirty-sixth floor of Private New York's headquarters. They were facing the windows and the blackout blinds were down, so there was no chance prying eyes could see the content Mo-bot was sharing.

"We traced the billfold to the penthouse apartment," she went on.

"Figures," Sci remarked. "Looking at his profile, he's definitely a penthouse kind of guy. Top of the heap."

"What do you want us to do?" Jessie asked.

In Jack's absence, they were looking to Justine for leadership.

"Put a tail on him," she replied. "Find out where he goes, who he talks to."

"What about counterintelligence?" Mo-bot asked.

Justine nodded. "We should notify the Bureau. Share what you've found. If there's an intelligence cell operating in New York, they need to know about it."

"Send an anonymous tip to Max Pimenta. Tell

him to look into it himself," Jessie said. "He's a good man."

The phone on the console that stood against the back wall rang. Jessie rose to answer it.

"Do you think you can map out his business interests?" Justine asked Mo-bot while Jessie took the call.

Mo-bot nodded. "I have some of it already. I can complete the picture."

"Yes... Yes, I'll just get her," Jessie said, and Justine registered the change in her tone immediately. "Justine, it's Dinara. She's on the satellite phone. I can't get any sense out of her. She says she wants to talk to you."

Justine rose slowly. Somewhere deep within, she felt a dark dread building.

She crossed the room and took the phone. "Hello?"

"Justine. It's me—Dinara."

Justine didn't need to hear any more. She knew from Dinara's cracking, tearful tone, the croak in her voice.

"No," Justine said quietly.

"I'm sorry," Dinara replied. Justine heard

shuddering sobs. "There was nothing we could do. Nothing. I'm so sorry."

Justine felt a hand on her arm.

"What's happened?" she heard a voice ask, without registering whose it was.

The room shrank away to nothing, as though the foulest darkness had oozed from the receiver and consumed her world. There was no shape, no form, no meaning.

"No!" Justine cried. "Bring him back! Bring him back to me!"

"I can't," Dinara replied. "There was an explosion. Jack and Joshua…"

"No," Justine said. "No. This isn't real."

It didn't feel real. She was alone. Utterly alone in a void. Holding a phone that connected her to somewhere she despised. A source of misery.

Justine dropped the receiver and heard it clatter against something. Tears flowed, and she heard herself gasping for air, sobbing, but it was all so distant, as though it was happening to someone else. She was aware of ghosts clustering around her, trying to soothe away the pain, but they were shades, existing on a different plane.

They couldn't touch her grief, nor do anything to make it better.

She was aware she kept repeating the same phrase over and over.

"He's gone. He's gone. He's dead. Jack's dead."

CHAPTER 53

"THEY HAVE MY name," Victor Andreyev said. "They seem competent."

He was standing on the rooftop of the gray stone building on the northwest corner of Madison and East 26th Street, diagonally across the broad intersection from Private New York's headquarters, using an Optika Blu, a Russian handheld version of Camero's XAVER LR 80 field imaging system, which enabled him to see what was happening inside the meeting room. Taras Gurin, the cunning psychopath headquarters had assigned to be his head of operations in America, held a directional microphone that had picked up almost all of the conversation that had taken place between Jack Morgan's team.

Taras had a reputation as a man without conscience. He was rumored to have undertaken some of the most difficult interrogations during the Ukrainian uprising. He had a narrow face that almost seemed too small for his muscular body, and his eyes were set close, which Andreyev had always thought signaled a lack of intelligence, but this man was sharp and possessed of a rough street cunning that made him very insightful and dangerous. As an enemy, Taras would be formidable, but he was fiercely loyal to Russia and served Andreyev with devotion.

Taras had discovered the signal transmitter concealed in the billfold the Americans had left at Andreyev's apartment building. It was an effective if unsophisticated ruse, although he was surprised they had been able to discover the location. It suggested they had advanced surveillance techniques he was not yet aware of. If his phones were compromised... he would ask Taras to conduct a full sweep to be sure.

Taras had traced the signal from the billfold to its receiver, turning Private's tricks against them. There was now no doubt these people knew Andreyev wasn't really Elizabeth Singer's father, which meant subterfuge and deception with them would no longer be useful. Hostilities were inevitable.

"Do not overestimate their competence," Taras replied with a smile. "The billfold tracker is available from any gadget store. A child could have used it."

"American law enforcement has never troubled us," Andreyev countered.

"True, but that is no measure of competence," Taras sneered. "What should we do about them?"

Andreyev had been alarmed to hear the woman babbling that Morgan and Floyd were dead. That was a major setback. He would have to verify the report with Kolokov, who was leading the Afghan mission, but he very much doubted Private would be giving false information. There was little to no chance they knew they were being watched. The death of Morgan was of no concern; Floyd's death, however, was more of a problem.

"We need to find the wife," Andreyev replied. Elizabeth Singer would know the location of the

Bull, and her children would be all the leverage needed to make her talk. "Put a team on these people," he said, nodding at the figures on the infrared display.

They were gathered around the grieving woman, and he felt sorry for her in the way one might pity a cat pining for a mate that had been hit by a car. Sad, but ultimately the fault of the animal for playing on the road. "One of them will lead us to the target," Andreyev said.

Taras nodded, and Andreyev stepped away from the edge of the roof, heading for the stairwell. A hot bath then perhaps a cognac before lunch would warm him up after exposure to the elements, he thought. He hurried inside, eager to get to his chauffeur-driven Bentley Mulsanne, which waited on the street a couple blocks away.

CHAPTER 54

NIKITA KOLOKOV WAS furious. He'd spent days tracking the American pilot across Nuristan. Despite the mistakes of others, he'd executed the mission to near perfection. The first error had been the trigger-happy operator who was supposed to disable the Osprey once it was on the ground and the American troops had deployed. Instead, he had opened fire on the aircraft as it had been coming in to land. Thankfully, Floyd had not been one of those to die on impact, but the rocket had made their job much harder. The Americans had been ready for a fight, rather than running into the ambush Kolokov had planned.

He had lost five men to the Americans, but they had been in a strategically inferior situation and their defeat had been inevitable. Kolokov could have engaged them far more effectively if he hadn't been under strict orders to capture Floyd alive. So five comrades died—six if he included the trigger-happy operator, who was quietly executed for his failure.

Now, after everything he'd done to successfully entrap Floyd, another trigger-happy maniac had blown up their target, along with half a mountain.

The loss of their target wasn't Kolokov's only problem. He now had eleven wounded soldiers and had lost another three to the explosion. He had no idea of the identity of the man killed with Floyd, or where the Bell GlobalRanger helicopter had gone, but he was certain he would find out. Some intelligence analyst would compile a comprehensive report. Kolokov would do his best to ensure the bony finger of blame stayed away from him.

He was walking through the smoldering forest amid the embers of the fire. Trees had been incinerated, leaving only blackened stumps here and there. The mountainside was a shattered mess of boulders and rocks, and the earth itself had been scorched by the powerful explosion. The scent of rocket fuel lingered in the air, mingling with the stench of ash, burned flesh, and metal. The three men he'd lost were simply gone. There were no bodies to bring home. Kolokov shook his head at the scene of devastation.

"Come on," he commanded. "Gather the wounded. We're moving out."

Nestor, his second-in-command, started barking orders. His men abandoned the search for survivors and started moving toward the two flying tanks, helping the wounded as they went.

Kolokov kicked aside a smoldering chunk of charcoal. Part of a tree? Or a person? He couldn't tell and didn't care. He wanted to get as far away from the scene of failure as possible. He hurried toward the Mil Mi-24 helicopters and tried to avoid making eye contact with the pilot of the aircraft on the left. If he spent too long looking at the sheepish man who'd fired the missiles that had killed their target he might feel impelled to execute him instantly, and that would not be wise considering the pilot was needed to get them out of this godforsaken place.

Kolokov chose to ride in the other aircraft and consoled himself with the knowledge that the man would be properly dealt with when they returned to Moscow.

CHAPTER 55

JUSTINE WAS ON her own, sitting on the couch in Jessie's office. She'd needed some time by herself. She couldn't even begin to imagine how she'd move on from this, but she had to find a way to function at the very least. She was no use to anyone in this state. She felt exhausted. Her eyes burned with the salt of so many tears, and her mind was numb.

She checked her watch—it was 11:05 a.m.—and got to her feet. She left the room, stepping into an open-plan office that was largely empty. The nearest desks were vacant, but a couple of investigators were working at the back of the room. Justine avoided meeting their eyes.

She hurried to the meeting room on the corner of the thirty-sixth floor, knocked, and entered to find it empty. She saw the phone receiver she had dropped on the floor had been replaced. She walked over to it, and shivered as she touched it. She looked around the room where her life had changed forever, suddenly struck by the intense desire not to be there. Not just in the room, but in the office, maybe not in Private at all. Without Jack there was nothing for her here, and the thought of spending each and every day working at an organization where she would constantly be reminded of him filled her with dread.

She left the room and almost walked into Jessie, who was coming along the corridor outside. She looked pale and her eyes were puffy with grief.

"Mo-bot is in the computer room, working. She's pretty cut up, but losing herself in the machines is her way of dealing with it."

Hearing Jessie talk about the grief of others made Justine choke up. Jack had meant so much to so many people, she felt selfish only to have thought of how his death had impacted her. Fresh tears ran down her cheeks. She wiped them away.

"I just don't know what to do," she said. "I can't believe he's gone."

Jessie put a consoling hand on Justine's arm. "Me neither."

The warmth of human touch caused Justine to break down again, and she shuddered as she sobbed.

"Come on," Jessie said. "We should get you out of here. I'm supposed to relieve Alvarez and Taft in a couple hours. Let's go now. Beth and the children will give us something to focus on. They need us."

Justine nodded and allowed herself to be steered through the office to the elevators. The receptionists looked at her with sadness and sympathy but said nothing as they stepped into the car that would take them down to the parking garage. Minutes later, they were on the road to the safe house in Rye.

The gray winter light robbed everything of color and much of the world was shrouded in thick snow, creating a canvas of grief onto which Justine projected memories of her time with Jack. She'd loved him from the moment they'd met.

Others knew him as a tough man of action, but she'd seen a different side. He'd had a generous spirit and felt deep compassion toward anyone who experienced suffering. And then there was his sense of humor. Not a day had passed when he hadn't managed to make her smile. As the drab landscape sped by, she wondered whether she would ever laugh again. They'd had their ups and downs, but after the Moscow investigation Justine had felt things might be getting serious. She winced at the thought of all the moments they would never have together. Wherever she looked, she saw images of an unlived future. A wedding. Children. A life together growing old. All gone. Taken by violence. She wept, but kept looking out of the window because these shades of what she'd lost were all she had left of Jack.

Jessie didn't say anything, and when Justine glanced at her she saw a grim-faced woman who was trying to weather her own storm of grief. They traveled without speaking, with nothing more than the rhythm of the wheels rolling over the highway to break the silence.

Sixty minutes after leaving the office, they

rolled into the driveway of the shorefront house on Pine Island. There was a blue Chevy Suburban parked near the front door.

"It's not easy, is it?" Jessie remarked.

Justine shook her head and wiped her eyes. Jessie reached over the armrest and embraced her, an act of kindness that prompted more tears. When they let go, the two women stepped into the bitter cold and headed for the house.

CHAPTER 56

JUSTINE HADN'T YET met Elizabeth Singer, but she recognized her from the photographs she'd seen. She had long dark hair and was about five feet six, with an athletic physique. She sat at the kitchen counter, eating lunch with her children. Roni Alvarez and Jim Taft sat on couches by the television. They were on their phones and had CNN on low. They stood the moment Jessie and Justine entered, and Taft, a gruff former Secret Service agent, spoke first.

"I'm sorry, boss," he said to Jessie. "We heard." He indicated his phone. Justine shouldn't have been surprised. Very little stayed secret in the days of instant communication.

"My condolences," Roni said. She was a former FBI agent, who had seen her fair share of action, but the tears welling in her eyes told Justine that Jack's death had affected her deeply.

"Thanks," Justine replied.

"Condolences?" Beth Singer asked. "What for? What's going on?"

Justine felt a wave of nausea. They hadn't told her what had happened. Maybe they hadn't known Floyd and Jack had been together.

"Roni, could you take Danny and Maria next door?" Jessie said. Beth's expression immediately hardened from puzzlement to concern.

"What's going on?" she asked fearfully.

Jessie didn't answer. Roni mustered the children and led them into a living room that lay off the main family room. They looked confused and frightened.

"Don't worry, kids," Roni assured them. "Ms. Fleming just wants to talk to your mom."

"It's OK, guys," Beth said.

Roni shut the door and Jessie and Justine

approached the breakfast bar. Justine felt immensely sorry for Beth because she knew the crushing blow that was coming her way.

Beth must have read the news in the other women's expressions because she clutched the countertop, saying: "No."

"I'm afraid we have reason to believe your husband was killed today," Jessie said.

Justine started crying herself when she saw tears spring to Beth's eyes. She'd never before met this woman, but she walked over and embraced her. They were bound by grief.

"No," Beth said. "It can't be true."

"Our operatives witnessed an explosion," Jessie said, and Justine felt Beth shake and shudder against her.

"What am I going to tell the children?" she said between sobs.

Justine didn't know what to say. No words would make the slightest difference to her pain because death was something that couldn't be soothed away. It was a permanent wrench, the destruction of a future and the forced imposition of a different path, one devoid of the company and companionship of the departed. Nothing could make it better, so Justine just hugged Beth tightly.

A loud digital alarm sounded. Taft went over to the TV stand and picked up the device that was making the noise. Roni emerged from the living room.

Justine saw Taft pick up an iPad and examine it carefully.

"We installed motion detectors in the grounds," he said. "Two of them were just triggered."

CHAPTER 57

FEAR CONQUERED JUSTINE'S grief. She stepped away from Beth and went over to Taft, who studied the iPad.

"Roni, can you bring the kids in here?" Jessie said.

She nodded and ducked into the living room. "Come on, guys. We need to go back," she said. A moment later she appeared at the door with Danny and Maria and ushered them into the family room.

"Where are they?" Justine asked, peering at the iPad.

"We've had two triggered at the back on the

outer perimeter, either side of the property. Looks like they came along the beach."

He pointed to an on-screen digital representation of the property. Two markers near the waterline were flashing red.

"Could it be someone walking a dog along the beach?"

"It's private," Taft replied. "Shouldn't be anyone out there. And…"

He stopped talking and gestured to the screen where a third marker, this one further into the garden, had been activated. "We've got another one."

"We need to get to the cars," Justine said.

Jessie nodded.

"What's happening, Mom?" Maria asked.

"We've got to leave," Jessie said, before Beth could answer.

Justine racked her mind, replaying the journey from Manhattan. Had she and Jessie been so wrapped in grief they'd slipped up and failed to notice they were being followed? Or had their location been compromised some other way? She had no doubt whoever was out there wanted Beth and the children.

"I'll take point," Taft said, producing a Glock 19.

Maria gasped and looked at her mom.

"It's OK, honey," Beth assured her.

Justine wasn't a fan of guns, but she was glad to see one at that moment.

"Alvarez, you watch our six," Taft said.

"We'll split for the vehicles," Jessie added. "Beth, you come with me and Jim. Justine, you take Maria and Danny in the Suburban with Roni."

"I'm not leaving my children," Beth said firmly.

"We need to separate the targets," Jessie replied. "It's too great a risk for you all to be in the same car."

"I am not leaving them!" Beth shouted.

Jessie shook her head. "OK. Beth, Maria, and Danny come with Jim and me. Let's move."

Justine nodded and fell in beside Maria, who looked up anxiously. Justine smiled at her but got no response.

They followed Taft to the front door. He checked the windows on either side, gave the thumbs-up, and opened the door. There was a crack and a whistling sound. Taft clutched his throat and fell to his knees: he'd been shot in the neck.

CHAPTER 58

MARIA SCREAMED AND Danny started wailing. Justine instinctively grabbed the girl and pulled her close, so she couldn't see the horror. Beth did the same with Danny.

"Jim!" Roni yelled.

Jessie tried to pull him inside, but a second bullet struck his skull and his head whiplashed with a sickening crack. Justine had to choke back bile. She swallowed the acrid liquid as Taft fell forward onto the icy porch. That was when Justine saw them: three masked men, all in black, holding machine pistols fitted with suppressors. Jessie tried to shut the front door, but Taft's body blocked the threshold.

The men were close now, running across the drive past the Nissan. Jessie grabbed Taft's gun and fired a couple of wild rounds. The men scattered, taking cover behind the vehicles.

Justine heard a noise behind her and turned to see three black-clad men at the glass doors overlooking the waterline. One was working the lock. Roni shot at the man. The bullet made a perfect hole in the glass, hitting him in the shoulder. One of his accomplices dragged him away from the door while the other returned fire, the glass splintering around them.

"Come on," Roni said. "Upstairs!"

Jessie loosed a couple more rounds to buy time, before pushing Beth and Danny toward the stairs.

Justine and Maria followed behind them as they crossed the marble hallway. Roni was laying covering fire as they ran to the right-hand flight of stairs and raced up them. Justine held Maria's hand and pulled the distressed girl up after her onto the curved balcony that joined the two staircases.

"He's setting a charge," Roni yelled, sprinting after them.

Jessie followed her. As Justine watched the two women race up the staircases, Roni on the left and Jessie on the right, she heard a small explosion and the sound of glass shattering.

"This way," Roni said. They ran into a corridor leading off to the right.

The children whimpered and cried as they all dashed past a number of bedrooms before reaching a master suite at the very end of the corridor. They bundled inside and Roni shut and locked the door.

Justine heard heavy footsteps on the stairs and the low indistinct sound of whispered instructions.

"They're coming," Roni said in a low voice. She ran to the front window. "I'm going to jump," she said, looking down. "You need to throw the children down to me and then jump after them."

Danny sniveled and Maria wept.

"We've got to do it, kids," Beth whispered fiercely. "I bet it's not even that high."

Justine heard a door being kicked open further along the corridor. They were checking all the bedrooms.

"Come on," she said, pulling Maria over to the window.

The girl resisted, but Justine was insistent. She knew they had no choice. If they didn't get out in the next few seconds, all would be lost.

Jessie moved into position by the door and covered it using Taft's Glock.

Roni holstered her pistol, opened the window, and climbed onto the sill. She looked down one last time and dropped. Justine heard a thud and a groan, but when she looked down, Roni was on her feet and had her arms held up to catch the children.

Justine helped Maria onto the sill. "Just don't look down," she said.

Maria whimpered and Justine said an inward prayer for forgiveness as she pushed the girl clear. Maria cried out as she fell, but Roni caught her.

Gunshots erupted behind Justine. She turned to see Jessie's gun smoking and two bullet holes in the door. Jessie signaled there were people on the other side. Justine could hear movement.

"Come on," she said, trying to control her rising panic.

Beth helped her lift Danny onto the sill.

"Don't be scared, Dan," Beth said. "Maria's done it."

He turned to face the opening, and Justine pushed him. He squealed as he fell, but hit Roni as intended and the two of them tumbled into the snow.

"Go," Justine told Beth. She clambered onto the sill and jumped without hesitation.

Jessie fired another couple shots through the door.

"Let's go, Jess," Justine said, urging her colleague over.

Justine heard a gunshot then a scream. She looked down to see Roni clutching her chest and staggering before she fell to the ground. Three masked men were dragging Beth, Danny, and Maria away.

Jessie ran over, but there wasn't a clear shot.

"We can't go out that window," she said. "We'll be picked off as we hit the ground."

She ran back to the door, stood to one side, flung it open, and peered around the frame.

"It's clear," she said.

She waved Justine forward and the two of them hurried through the house. They met no resistance. All the rooms were empty. They ran down the stairs, Justine feeling a renewed wave of nausea as they passed Taft's body. They got out-side just in time to see Beth being bundled into an unmarked white van at the end of the drive. Before the side door was closed, Justine caught a glimpse of Maria and Danny inside, both held by masked men. The door slid shut and the van sped away.

Justine ran to the Nissan.

"It's no good," Jessie said, indicating the wheels of the SUV and the adjacent Suburban.

All four tires on both cars had been slashed. They'd be next to useless in normal conditions, but completely out of action in the snow.

Justine fell to her knees. Jack was dead, and now Beth and the children had been taken. The crushing weight of defeat bore down on her and made her feel as though she couldn't breathe. Her whole body shuddered and shook. When she was finally able to draw breath, she started to weep and felt as though she might never stop.

CHAPTER 59

DRIFTING THROUGH DARKNESS, I wondered if this was death. But where at first there was nothing, I suddenly saw her face: Justine. I came around to pain. I felt as though I'd been to hell and back. My ears were ringing, my head throbbing with pulsating waves of pressure. Acrid fumes had burned my sinuses and my lungs had been stripped raw. All I could taste was high explosive and smoke. Every muscle in my body ached as though pummeled by giant meat tenderizers. Even my bones felt sore. I had no idea whether I'd been blinded or if it was genuinely as dark as the grave.

Then there was sound and light. I turned my head to see Joshua Floyd holding up a windproof lighter. The flame seared my eyes and I looked away, turning toward a mass of tumbled rocks. Then it all came rushing back. We'd caught the edge of the first blast and it had flung us against the rockface at the base of the mountain. The explosion had dazed me, but Floyd was alert to the fact it had thrown us almost exactly to the place he'd been running for. He'd grabbed me and pushed me into a narrow opening in the rock I would never have noticed on my own. Together we had scrambled further into this cave a split second before the second explosion hit. The rocket blast had shaken the mountain and caved in the entrance to the tunnel, but the rock-fall had at least protected us from the flames. We'd felt their heat all around us. For a time the cave had become like an oven. The fierce temperature had done something odd to the air and, feeling suffocated, I'd blacked out. My last thought had been of Justine, and she was the first thought that had greeted me on waking.

I turned back to Floyd and we grinned at each other like a couple of idiots.

"I owe you," I said.

"It was dumb luck," he replied. "If I hadn't found this place last night, we'd be a couple of briskets out there."

"Dumb luck or design, I still owe you."

"You OK?" he asked.

"I think so. You?"

"Probably about the same," he replied. "That was intense."

"Tell me about it."

"Did Beth really send you?" he asked, groaning as he rolled onto his knees.

"Sort of," I replied. "I was initially hired by a man claiming to be her father."

"Her dad died years ago."

"I didn't know that. Turns out the guy posing as him was part of the group hunting you. So this is me making good."

Floyd looked worried. "Are my family OK?"

"They're fine. My colleagues have them somewhere safe. If we can get out of here, I intend to take you to them as soon as possible."

Floyd nodded. "Thank you."

"Don't thank me yet," I said. "The rescue mission didn't start well."

"We're still alive, aren't we?"

"Let's keep it that way. Want to see if we can dig our way out?"

He nodded, put the lighter between two stones to keep it upright, and we crawled over to the tunnel mouth and started moving rocks.

"The intelligence reports suggested you were killed in the attack at the crash site," I said. "There were believed to be no survivors."

Floyd stopped digging and I saw him bow his head. Even though his face was lost in shadow, I could sense his pain.

"I lost a lot of friends. Brothers..." He trailed off.

"I'm sorry. I know that pain myself. Before I was a private investigator, I was in the Marines. I was a pilot too—I flew Sea Knights. I was shot down in Afghanistan. Most of the men I was carrying were killed."

He lifted his head to look at me. "I keep playing things back. Could I have done anything differently?"

"I know that one too." I had reached a heavy boulder. "Give me a hand, will you?"

Floyd shuffled over and the two of us strained to shift a piece of rock not much smaller than an oven. Our sinews stretched and our breathing grew labored as we dragged the obstacle clear of the tunnel and rolled it behind us onto the damp earth of the cave. We were rewarded with the appearance of a shaft of moonlight about the size of a human head.

"You did everything you could," I said to Floyd. "If there had been another way, you would have taken it."

"I guess," he replied. "But it doesn't ease the pain."

"Time dulls that. It heals like a scar. It's only on bad days that it feels like a fresh wound again."

He nodded thoughtfully.

"Let me check if I can see anything out there," I suggested.

I pressed my face into the gap as far as it would go.

"Just scorched earth," I said. "I can't hear any movement."

I withdrew and we carried on shifting stone.

"Hopefully they think we're dead," Floyd remarked.

I nodded in agreement. "Do you know why they want you?"

He shook his head. "I've been around. Done my fair share of things people might want revenge for, but since they didn't kill me, I'm guessing they're not going to all this trouble to settle an old score. They want something else, and it's been playing on my mind because I don't have the first idea what it is."

I knew he'd be bound by oaths of secrecy, but I sensed genuine puzzlement and got the impression he was telling the truth.

We worked for another hour before we finally cleared the entrance enough for us to wriggle out. It was cold and dark. Steam and smoke rose off the burned forest.

"You got a map?" I asked.

Floyd shook his head. "It was in my pack. I ditched it to get into the cave."

There was no point looking for it; the remnants would be among the ash and cinders that surrounded us. I cursed myself for leaving the map Chris and John had given me in the chopper.

"My feel is the pass is over there," I said, pointing at two peaks on the other side of the valley. "The border is just beyond it."

"That's my read, too," he replied. "Looks pretty simple. If two pilots can't plot a course there, I don't know who can."

I smiled, and we started walking.

CHAPTER 60

A SQUAD CAR had arrived at the house within minutes of Jessie calling the police. Now the place was a major crime scene with detectives and FBI trawling over every inch of the property, looking for evidence and examining everything they found. Justine sat in an FBI incident-response truck and watched Jessie through the window. The head of Private New York knew some of the agents on the scene and was talking to a couple of them who'd sat in on Justine's interview. The detective in charge, Charlie Nightwell, had led the interview and she crossed the driveway now to join Jessie's conversation with the special agents. Charlie Nightwell was the kind of tough New York cop who looked as though she'd stare into the face of evil without blinking. She exuded strength, and, in that moment, Justine longed to be like her. Justine used to think she was tough, but she certainly didn't feel that way now. She was far more vulnerable than she'd ever realized.

Beyond Jessie, Nightwell, and the two special agents, forensic investigators were working the scene alongside uniform cops and FBI agents. A photographer was taking pictures of Roni's body. Taft's was hidden by a screen, but Justine couldn't shake the memory of the gruesome head shot he took. These two brave people had been cut down before their time. They'd been murdered while trying to protect others. There had to be justice, or if not that, vengeance.

Justine had given her statements and was glad to be alone. Jack's death had created a gaping wound in her soul, and this professional failure only deepened it. She hadn't felt so low in years. Guilt gnawed at her, alongside the grief she felt for Jack. The deaths of those two agents were on her. If she hadn't been so caught up in her own loss, would she have noticed a tail? Would she have suggested they sweep the car for bugs before leaving the New York office? Justine would never know for certain if they had been followed or what she could have done differently, but she found it hard to shake the feeling that if she'd been at her sharpest, those two people would still be alive.

The trailer door opened and Justine steeled herself to put on the brave face she reserved for strangers. It faded away the moment she saw Mo-bot and Sci climb the steps.

"Oh, Jus," Mo-bot said, crossing the truck to embrace her. "I'm so sorry. Jessie told us what happened."

"We lost them," Justine responded tearfully. "They killed two of our own and they took Beth and the children."

"They'll pay for this," Sci said. "We'll make sure of it."

"Have you told the feds about Andreyev?" Mo-bot asked.

Justine nodded.

"That might explain why he's gone to ground," Mo-bot replied. "The billfold showed up on a flight to Moscow."

"You think he's left the country?" Justine asked.

Mo-bot shook her head. "I checked immigration photos of everyone on the flight. No record of him on the plane. My guess is he gave it to someone else to make it look like he'd flown. We sent a couple of operatives to his apartment. It's empty. He has what he wanted. He can burn his cover."

"What do we do now?" Justine asked, wishing Jack was there to guide them.

"We're going to find Beth and her children," Mo-bot replied. "Whatever it takes. We will find them and we will bring them back. And then Andreyev will pay for what he's done."

CHAPTER 61

THE COLD BURNED, scalding my extremities, causing tingling pain in my hands and feet. Floyd and I were dressed for the conditions, but even these clothes weren't designed for nights on a mountain. Any normal expedition would now be in a tent, tucked in sleeping bags, but we weren't a normal expedition; we were fighting for our lives.

We'd lost our gear and were trying to make it to the Pakistani border before we died of exposure. We were high up the mountain, maybe ten or twelve thousand feet, close to the pass that I remembered being marked on the map Chris and John had given me. I'd been climbing a few times in the past with buddies who were addicted to the adventure of scaling mountains. Here, high up in the peaks of the Hindu Kush, with the stars so close it felt as though I could reach out and touch them, with air so thin and cold each breath was an intoxication and the majesty of the Earth stretched out far below, I finally understood why the mountains caught and held my climbing friends in their addictive grip. I was on the very edge of survival. Maybe it was only by coming so close to death that I could fully appreciate the beauty of life.

We were following the winter trail up to the pass. From memory, I estimated it was a short distance from the pass to the border, located on the other side of this mountain, in the next valley. The summit loomed above us, glinting in the moonlight. Every crystalline sparkle reminded me how cold it was, but I couldn't look away because it was a wondrous sight. The sides were steep and snow clung to them in patches, on top of ice that was diamond blue. The peak itself rose into the sky like a jagged tooth, reaching for stars and galaxies that were rich in depth and color. There weren't many more beautiful places to die.

Floyd trudged beside me, but we didn't talk. Our boots crunched ice and snow, and our breathing was fast and labored, made worse by regular sections that required us to scramble up steep runs of sheer rock. All around us the world was still. No sane creatures would travel here, particularly at night.

Down there in the valley where air and energy were cheap, we'd chatted about our respective military experiences, discussed the merits of different aircraft we'd flown, traded war stories and anecdotes about those we'd served with. He'd told me about the men who'd been killed when the Osprey had been shot down, and I had shared my similar experience. It wasn't something I often discussed, but it was cathartic to share with someone who truly understood.

He had spoken about Beth and the children, and asked me questions about them, how they were and whether they were safe. I told him what we knew about the man posing as Beth's father, and assured him his family was safe with my team.

Then I spoke about Justine. I told Floyd how much she meant to me and spoke about her in terms that would have made a love-struck teenager ashamed, but there was no one to hear me except the mountains and Floyd, who was expressing similar emotions about those close to him. I didn't give voice to my darker worry. I had no doubt Feo and Dinara thought we were dead. If they'd managed to escape, I expected they would have informed Justine by now, and I couldn't stand the thought of her suffering. I didn't share that concern with Floyd because if Justine had been told we were dead, it was likely Beth had too.

The mountain had silenced our easy chatter halfway up. We saved our breath for the arduous climb. When I looked at Floyd now, I saw the familiar, grim struggle of a man determined to push his body beyond its natural limits. I probably wore the same bleak expression. It was hard going, and a small part of me just wanted to lie down in the snow and rest until all the pain was gone.

"Nearly there," I grunted, and Floyd nodded in reply.

We pushed on the last few steps and then saw the pass open up as we turned a bend that marked the shoulder of the mountain. There was a relatively flat gap between the peak of this mountain and its neighbor, and we could see clear sky and distant ranges.

I looked at Floyd and forced a smile, and he offered one in reply.

We pressed on, trudging through deep snow for another quarter of a mile until we earned the reward our exhaustion deserved. The pass ended abruptly, and beneath us was a sheer cliff that dropped a few hundred feet before going into a gentler slope. Far below, on the valley floor, beyond an expanse of forest that covered the bottom of the mountain, I could see lights and the faint outlines of small buildings. They stood beside a single-track road, which would have been lost to darkness had it not been for the headlights of a truck approaching the buildings. We had reached civilization, and the sight sent my spirits soaring.

I could see it had the same effect on Floyd because he grinned at me, relief in his expression.

"This way," I said, gesturing toward a trail that was almost lost to snow. It would take us east, leading, if I remembered the map correctly, to the border and to safety.

CHAPTER 62

THE VALLEY WAS a few blissful degrees warmer than the pass. It had taken us three hours to stagger and stumble our way down the mountain. We were breathless and exhausted by the time we reached the snow-covered forest that spread across the lower slopes. We picked our way between tall cedars and pines, and soon the ground started to level out. We were on the gentle slope that led to a group of buildings we assumed were the border station.

"Look," Floyd said, pointing through the trees.

I saw a light and we both picked up pace. My legs had been pummeled by the ascent but the descent had been worse, fighting gravity with every step, resisting the pull of the ground with muscles that had very little left to give.

I don't know whether it was my bleary eyes, general exhaustion, or fogged mind, but I didn't realize our mistake until it was too late.

The light we'd assumed was the border post was in fact a landing light fixed to the under-carriage of a Hind helicopter, which stood in a clearing not fifty paces from us.

I motioned to Floyd to stop, and we both dropped into a crouch.

My senses were suddenly alert. I heard every-thing: the creaking of branches moving in the wind, the distant hoot of an owl, the brush of pine needles against each other, and the low chatter of men talking in Russian. I saw a unit of twenty in snow camouflage standing around the helicop-ter. This was the group that had been hunting Floyd, I was sure of it. There was only one chop-per. Perhaps the other had left already. None of the men appeared to be injured, so I guessed the first had been used to transport the wounded who would have undoubtedly been caught in the rocket blast. The men were just standing around, smoking and talking. Then the reason for their presence here became clear. A pilot in conventional green fatigues emerged from beneath the aircraft clutching a wrench and spoke to a tall man in snow camouflage. He had the bearing of a commander. They must have been forced to land here and make repairs.

I signaled to Floyd to go back the way we'd come. The chopper stood between us and the border post. We'd have to give it a wide berth if we were going to avoid being spotted. We moved back slowly and silently, but we'd only gone a few yards when I saw something that stopped me in my tracks: the green glow of infra-red goggles pointed directly toward us.

CHAPTER 63

THE RUSSIAN BROUGHT the goggles down from his eyes and ran over to his commander. They exchanged some words and the commander took the IR goggles, pointing them in our direction.

"Don't move," I whispered.

I saw the commander looking directly at us. My heart sank when he lowered the goggles. His eyes shone with the hunger of a predator, and there was a faint smile of satisfaction on his face.

"Run!" I yelled, and we turned and sprinted east.

At the same moment, the commander barked

at his men, who instantly went from casual soldiers to disciplined hunters. The forest filled with shouts and the crashing of boots, and then came the gunfire. I stayed as close as I could to Floyd because I knew they wouldn't risk killing him. The gunfire was intended to confuse and intimidate, so I tuned out the fear and harnessed the adrenaline.

Floyd and I were making good progress. The dangerous part would be when we turned south for the border post. I could see men in camouflage gear tracking us, running through the trees, trying to cut us off to the south. They moved like shadows whipping through the forest. We had to outrun them. The border post was about two hundred yards beyond the chopper. Guards had come out of the building to look in the direction of the gunfire.

"Come on," I said to Floyd, and we pivoted south, sprinting through the trees.

I lifted my legs high to avoid fallen branches and roots, but still I stumbled. Floyd did too, but neither of us fell. Flames burst around us, spitting from muzzles, and bullets shredded the forest, but we pressed through the storm of gunfire, driven by thoughts of the people we loved.

A man stepped out from behind a tree and swung the butt of his machine gun at Floyd's face, but I bundled him to the ground and we tumbled at the man's feet. I jumped up as he swung again, blocked the blow with my left forearm, and drove the palm of my right hand into his chin. His head snapped back and he let out a pained groan. I seized the opportunity to punch his exposed throat. He instinctively raised his hands to the injury and I hit him in the solar plexus, before grabbing his gun and wrestling it off him. I saw two other men coming through the trees, quickly turned the machine gun on them and fired. They went down and Floyd ran over to them. I drove the machine gun's butt into the face of the man clutching his neck, knocking him out cold. I heard shouts behind me and turned and opened fire.

I saw shadows scatter as I ran to join Floyd. More gunfire and shouts followed, but Floyd and I weren't listening. We were running. We broke the treeline at a sprint, racing toward the border post and a group of jittery guards. They raised their rifles and barked commands, but there was no way we were stopping.

I looked back at the trees and saw the Russian commander run to the edge of the forest. I couldn't make out his face in the shadows, but I suspected he wasn't smiling anymore.

The Pakistani border guards were shouting furiously.

"Don't shoot!" I yelled in reply. "We're Americans. We pose no threat. We need your help."

CHAPTER 64

THE BORDER PATROL officers who staffed the station had taken our weapons. Their commanding officer, a Major Azar Khan, spoke excellent English and told us we were to be held until he had contacted his superiors. Floyd and I were taken to a holding room in the largest of the three buildings at the post. There was one structure on the Afghan side, but it was unmanned and looked abandoned.

The building we were in was constructed from whitewashed cinder blocks and contained six rooms: an office, a staff room, a bunk room, kitchen, toilet, and a holding room. Located at the back of the building, it wasn't a cell, but it wasn't far off. A trio of double bunks lined the windowless interior walls and a small electric heater struggled against the cold.

Floyd and I sat on bunks near the heater, trying to absorb as much of its pathetic warmth as possible. We'd attempted to persuade Major Khan to give us access to a phone, but the Pakistani commander refused. He was very aware of how easily two American strays hunted by Russian paramilitaries could quickly escalate into a huge diplomatic incident if everything wasn't done by the book.

"How long do you think we'll be stuck here?" Floyd asked.

I shrugged. I knew how slowly the wheels of bureaucracy could move. I was desperate to get to a phone so I could let Justine know I was still alive, and I had no doubt Floyd was itching to talk to Beth.

I heard raised voices beyond the locked door, and then footsteps. A key went into the lock and the door opened to reveal Major Khan. His gray-flecked mustache drooped with disappointment. There was an overwhelming air of apology about him.

"Are we done?" I asked.

"I'm sorry," he said. "There was—"

He was pushed aside by the familiar figure of the Russian commander. He had a blond crew cut and stood about six-three, looming over the Pakistani officer, who shrank against the wall of the holding room.

"My name is Nikita Kolokov," the Russian said. "You are now my prisoners. You will come with us."

Two of his subordinates moved into the corridor behind him and he barked a command at them in Russian. I didn't need to speak the language to understand the order: I was to be killed.

CHAPTER 65

"I AM VERY sorry," Major Khan offered. "There are too many of them for us."

"And we pay well," Kolokov added.

Major Khan flushed with shame and cast his eyes to the floor. I didn't care about the motives for his betrayal of us. My only concern was getting out of there alive.

"Come," Kolokov instructed, gesturing at Floyd. "Our chopper is ready to take you for processing."

Floyd didn't respond, so the commander stepped forward. I seized my chance. I grabbed Khan's pistol, popped it free of its holster restraint, drove my elbow into the shocked major's face, and opened fire on the two Russians in the corridor. My aim was true and both men dropped like stones. Floyd moved quickly as Kolokov raised his submachine gun at me. He grabbed the Russian commander by the neck and drove his head into the whitewashed wall, stunning him. I fired twice, hitting Kolokov in the chest. He clutched at the wounds, which had started to bleed into his gray and white uniform. He dropped to his knees and his eyes went blank before he fell face forward onto the floor.

"Get his gun," I said. Floyd took the Vityaz-SN submachine gun from the dead man.

I discarded the major's pistol and picked up a Vityaz and two magazines from one of the men I'd shot in the corridor. We moved toward an interior door that led to the open-plan office at the front of the building. The cheap pine door had no window, so we couldn't see what was happening beyond it, but I could hear movement and someone shouted a command.

The door opened and the Russian who appeared looked more surprised to see us than we were to see him. Floyd fired a burst that hit the man in the stomach. He staggered back, mortally wounded. Beyond him, I saw half a dozen Pakistani border officers gathered against the wall of the office. I couldn't see who was holding these men captive since they were concealed behind the door.

I heard shouts and signaled to Floyd to go low. He ran ahead of me in a crouch and I followed at head height. As we burst through the doorway, I saw three men in snow camouflage swinging their weapons toward us. Floyd picked off two and I shot the third before any of them had the chance to pull the trigger.

The Pakistani guards were relieved. One started talking hurriedly, but we didn't have time to listen. We rushed through the office toward the front door.

There was a rattle of gunfire. Glass shattered and a hail of bullets thudded into the desk next to me. I looked to my right and saw a man shooting through the window. I fired back and he ducked out of sight.

Floyd and I ran to the front door, splitting to stand flush against the wall either side of it. A volley of bullets burst through the wood. Floyd indicated the window to the right and crept toward it as I grabbed the door handle. He stood beside the window and signaled he was ready. I opened the door. Gunfire started immediately. As bullets peppered the far wall, the border officers ducked for cover behind their desks. I waited for the gunfire to stop before I stepped out. A man who stood some twenty yards away was reloading. I opened fire and he went down. I stepped forward and sensed movement to my right as another camouflaged Russian rounded the corner of the building with his gun trained on me.

CHAPTER 66

A SHOT RANG out and the man aiming at me was suddenly spun around and fell facedown into the snow. Floyd had shot him through the window, saving me from certain death. I heard yelling from the treeline. The rest of the Russian unit came running toward the building. I glanced to my right and saw some vehicles parked a short distance away. I ducked back inside.

"Who drives the truck?" I asked the border officers, miming turning a steering wheel.

The youngest of the group, a baby-faced guy in his early twenties, raised his hand.

"Let's go," I said, gesturing with the submachine gun.

He hesitated.

"Do you want to wait here until the Russians arrive?" I asked.

He shook his head and joined me by the door. Floyd led the way and we ran outside to be greeted by a hail of bullets. The Russians were aiming closer than they had been previously, perhaps because they were more desperate, or maybe because their commander wasn't there to rein them in. My heart was pumping adrenaline at a furious rate as we ran from the building toward a small parking area where a trio of vehicles were parked: an old Volkswagen, a Lada, and a Mercedes truck that had been converted into a personnel carrier. Bullets chewed the snow at our heels, but we made it to the truck and took cover behind it.

Our driver used a fob to open the cab and we all climbed in. He started the engine and we sped away as the Russian paramilitaries reached the border patrol station. The tailgate rattled as it was hit by bullets, and the rear window of the cab shattered, sending glass everywhere. But the engine roared and we were soon out of range of the shooters.

Floyd slumped in his seat and gave a sigh of relief.

"Pull over," I said to the driver, when I was sure a bend in the road concealed us from the paramilitaries.

"What the hell are you doing?" Floyd asked.

"We'll never outrun them in this," I replied. "We need to be smarter."

Our driver stopped and I jumped out, Floyd following my lead.

"Keep going," I told the frightened officer, who drove off down the road, eager to get away from men pointing guns at him.

I indicated to Floyd to move. He did so reluctantly. We ran into the forest, clutching our guns.

We tracked back, picking our way through the trees as fast as we dared. We were halfway to the border post when we saw the Volkswagen and the Lada speeding past along the road, almost certainly carrying the Russian paramilitaries who thought they were hot on our tails.

We ran on.

"You're not crazy enough to suggest what I

think you're going to suggest, are you?" Floyd asked.

"So you've thought of it too?" I replied. "We're a couple of pilots. Their commander said the bird was airworthy. Why drive when you can fly?"

Floyd scoffed.

We slowed as we neared the clearing. Our escape had thinned the personnel surrounding the chopper. There were now only three guards and the pilot, and all of them had their attention fixed on the border post expectantly. With the chopper now fixed, they were ready and waiting to take to the air whenever the rest of the unit returned.

I signaled Floyd to move to their rear and we crept between the trees. When we had the chopper between us and them, we broke cover and ran across the clearing. The side door of the Hind was open and I could see the pilot through the gap on the other side. He must have sensed movement because he turned and looked me square in the eye.

I raised my gun, but he shook his head fearfully. I recognized the look of an honest man who did not want to die.

He said something urgent in Russian and started running for the border post. The remaining paramilitaries followed, all four men racing away. I guess the pilot had told them they needed to help their comrades. If so, he wasn't lying.

Floyd and I jumped through the side door, scrambled into the cockpit, slid into the pilot and co-pilot's seats, and fired up the engines.

I looked to my right and saw the paramilitaries turning around, but it was too late. They managed a couple futile shouts and pointless shots before I took to the air. Thirty seconds later, after we had climbed past three thousand feet and were speeding north through the valley, Floyd turned to me and smiled. I responded with a wide grin.

We were heading home.

CHAPTER 67

THE MIL MI-24 Hind was fully fueled and packed with weapons and equipment. Floyd went through the gear bags while I flew north, tracking the contours of the valley. If the mountains had been beautiful when we'd been touching death near the summits, they were even more magnificent now viewed from the comfort of the chopper and in the knowledge that we had come through a situation where survival had seemed impossible. We were alive and on our way home, and that thought alone was all the warmth and rest I needed.

"I've found a satellite phone," Floyd said, joining me in the cockpit.

I recited one of the few numbers I knew by heart, and he dialed.

"Go ahead," he said, handing me the phone.

He took the controls. I removed my headset and held the phone to my ear. I heard a long and distant ringing tone.

"Hello?" Justine said. Her voice sounded weak and strained and I knew from that one word that she thought I was dead. "Hello? Who is this?"

"It's me, Jus," I replied.

There was nothing but silence and I didn't know if the line had cut out.

"Justine?"

"Jack?" she replied in disbelief. "Jack?"

"Yeah. It's me," I said, and felt a lump rise in my throat. "I guess Dinara and Feo thought we'd been—"

"They said you were dead," she interrupted tearfully. "I thought you were gone."

"I'm not," I responded. "We managed to escape."

"We? Is Joshua Floyd with you?"

"Yes," I said. "He's with me. We're coming home."

"Is Beth there?" Floyd yelled at me above the sound of the chopper.

"Did you hear that?" I asked.

Another pause, but this time I knew the line hadn't gone dead because I could hear Justine sobbing.

"Jus?"

"She's gone, Jack," she replied. "And the children too. They were taken."

"I see," I said flatly. "Can you connect us to Dinara?"

"Uh-huh," Justine said, before putting me on hold.

"Is she there?" Floyd asked.

I shook my head. "Justine isn't at the safe house."

His smile fell. Could he sense something was wrong? I felt terrible lying to him, but until I had the full details I wasn't going to share the bad news. It would only lead to worry, and there was nothing either of us could do about it from here.

"Jack?" Dinara sounded astonished.

"Dinara," I replied. "You bailed on us."

"I'm so sorry, Jack. We saw you..." Her voice trailed off.

"I'm kidding," I said. "You did the right thing. Where are you?"

"Kabul," she replied. "Getting ready to go back to Moscow at first light. Where are you?"

"Kom Valley, near Kamdesh," I said. "Heading your way. Wait there. We're a couple hours out. We'll meet you at the airport."

"OK," Dinara replied. "I'm so glad you're alive, Jack."

"Me too," I scoffed. "Justine, are you still on the line?"

"Yes," she replied.

"Can you arrange transportation home from Kabul?" I asked.

"With pleasure."

"And send Dinara a full report on what's happened in my absence, so I can get up to speed," I said carefully, so Floyd wouldn't become suspicious.

"Absolutely," Justine replied.

"I'll see you soon, Dinara," I said.

"We'll be waiting for the luckiest men in Afghanistan," Dinara responded before hanging up.

"Jack," Justine began. "I...When I thought you were...I realized how much you..." She was having trouble getting the words out.

"I know," I said, when it became clear she couldn't continue. "I love you too."

"Uh-huh" was all she could manage.

"I'll call when we get to Kabul," I said.

I hung up, handed the phone to Floyd, and put on my radio headset.

"Everything OK?" he asked, his voice tinny in the headset.

I nodded and gave him a thumbs-up. I hated being less than entirely honest, but I needed to find out exactly what had happened to Beth Singer and the children before I could figure out how to get them back.

CHAPTER 68

JUSTINE STARED AT her phone. She couldn't believe what had just happened. Had she imagined it? She went to her call list and found the most recent number. She checked the duration of the call. She definitely hadn't imagined it.

Jack was alive.

She jumped off the bed and punched the air. She'd never believed people did that in real life, but she was fizzing with energy and had to find some way to release it. A little over five minutes ago she'd been lying on her bed in the darkest of moods, mourning the loss of the most important person in her life, and now the world had burst into new and vibrant possibility with the news of his survival.

She went to the window. She wasn't sure if she ran or hopped or jumped. It didn't matter. She was buzzing. She'd never felt like this before. It was as though she had been reborn. She'd lived another life, a grim existence of loss and trauma, and it had been destroyed by a single phone call. She pulled back the drapes to reveal the Manhattan skyline illuminated against the dark winter's evening sky. She hit the glass with her palms, and pounded out a little celebratory rhythm. She was on the forty-second floor of the Langham Hotel. The people on Fifth Avenue beneath her looked tiny. She felt a moment of pity because whatever grief or heartbreak they'd suffered in life would be with them always and they'd never know what it was like to have those feelings lifted from them.

Then she suddenly thought of the families of Roni Alvarez and Jim Taft. She knew for a fact their loved ones would never have any respite from their grief. And then there were Beth, Danny, and Maria, lost to the evil men who'd murdered Roni and Taft. Those sad thoughts brought her back to earth and all her energy became newly focused—she needed to find Floyd's family.

She slipped on her shoes, grabbed her key card, and left the room. She took the stairs down to the thirty-seventh floor and walked the corridor until she found room 3708. She knocked, and Mo-bot's voice came from the other side of the door.

"Who is it?"

"Justine."

She heard movement. The door opened to reveal Mo-bot with a pair of half-moon glasses perched on top of her head. She looked beleaguered and depressed, but as she registered Justine's expression, her own changed.

"Well, I'll be damned," she said. "He's alive, isn't he?"

Justine cried with joy and stepped forward to hug Mo-bot. "Yes! He's alive. He just called me."

The older woman squeezed her tight. "Thank God," she said.

When Justine stepped back, she saw tears in Mo-bot's eyes.

"Come in," she said. "Tell me what happened."

Justine followed Mo-bot into a room much

like her own, a large suite with a corner view of the city. It had a living room, separate bedroom, and large bathroom. Mo-bot had set up her laptop on the desk in the living room and her workstation was covered in printouts and snack wrappers.

"Sorry the place is a mess," she said. "I comfort eat when I'm depressed. So, how did he do it?"

"I don't know," Justine replied. "I was so stunned to hear his voice, I can't even remember what he said really. It was all a blur."

"Knowing him, he probably swallowed the rocket," Mo-bot chuckled.

Justine was glad to see her laugh. A great weight had been lifted from both of them.

"He wants a report on what happened to Beth," Justine said. "Joshua Floyd is with him."

Mo-bot's smile fell. "Cops don't have anything. Nor do the feds. And we don't either. Whoever these guys are, they're pros. I think Russian intelligence. Sci is at Federal Plaza trying to get access to the ballistics reports, but my guess is it will be fresh steel—previously unused guns."

"Why don't we go through everything?" Justine

suggested. "It would be useful to do that anyway. We might see something we've overlooked."

Mo-bot shrugged. "OK. If Lazarus wants a report, Lazarus gets a report. People who come back from the dead can have whatever they want. It's the law."

Justine grinned, but she still couldn't quite believe it.

Jack Morgan.

Back from the dead.

CHAPTER 69

I HAD RARELY been happier to see the shimmering lights of a city. We'd used the chopper's course plotter to get us to Kabul, relying on pilot's instinct and grasp of general direction when the computer's Cyrillic threw up navigation waypoints we couldn't understand.

"OAKB, Kabul International, OAKB, Kabul International, this is Mi-4769," I said, giving the chopper's call sign.

"Go ahead, Mi-4769," the air traffic controller said.

"Mil Mi-24, requesting landing," I replied. "We're running low on fuel."

It wasn't a lie. These choppers weren't designed for long distances and we'd pushed the aircraft to the limit.

"Copy that, Mi-4769," the air traffic controller replied. "Proceed on heading two-nine. You'll see the helipad to the northwest of maintenance building Alpha Two."

"Copy that, OAKB control," I replied.

I banked right, changing to a heading almost thirty degrees off compass north. We flew low over the city, which was coming to life with the approach of dawn. The fluorescent lights of a few cafes shone here and there, and a line of trucks queued outside the city's famous bird market. Newsstands and bakeries were opening up and traffic was starting to build in the main thoroughfares.

Then I saw the outline of the control tower at Hamid Karzai International Airport, and the transit lights for helicopter approach to the airport. I swung us left a touch, adjusting to put us in the center of the path. There were no other aircraft in sight when we flew over the airport car park and some warehouses. I saw a large hangar with "A2" painted on its roof, and beyond it the helipad lit for our landing.

The GlobalRanger that had taken me from Kabul to Kamdesh was parked near the helipad. As we approached, I saw Feo and Dinara step out of the aircraft.

"Your people?" Floyd asked.

I nodded. "Good people."

I slipped the tail around and set the Hind down on the pad.

"Smoothly done," Floyd remarked as I powered down.

We climbed out of the cockpit and jumped onto solid ground. My friends hurried over. Dinara was crying, but her tears ran down her face into a beaming smile. She hugged me and kissed me on the cheeks over and over.

"Jack Morgan," she said. "Don't you ever do that again."

"You're a tough old bear," Feo said, pulling me away from Dinara and wrapping me in a suffocating embrace. "You make me proud. If I didn't know otherwise I would say you were Russian."

"I'm flattered," I said.

"You should be," he replied, as I stepped away. "How did you get a flying tank?" he asked, nodding toward the Mi-24 Hind.

"We asked politely," I replied with a smile. "This is Joshua Floyd. Joshua, this is Feodor Arapov and Dinara Orlova. Colleagues from our Moscow office."

"Good to meet you," Floyd said.

Feo shook his hand and pulled him into a crushing hug. "You cheated death, my friend. No need to pretend you are a stranger who is only worthy of a handshake. Did Jack save you?"

"Actually it was the other way around," I replied, as Floyd broke free of the man's embrace. "Joshua got us inside a cave just before the second rocket hit."

"Then we are all in your debt, Captain Floyd," Feo said.

"We've arranged your flight back to New York," Dinara said, leading us toward the GlobalRanger. "A G650 is ready to depart whenever you are."

She leaned into the cabin of the helicopter and produced a black flight case about the size of an oven.

"We've received a report from Justine, which is in here, along with some clothes and equipment you might need," she said.

"You ready to fly?" I asked Floyd.

"Are you kidding? I can't wait to see Beth and the kids," he replied.

Dinara shot me a knowing look, but neither of us said anything.

"We'll take you to the terminal," Feo said.

"That Hind is full of gear," I told him. "You might want to check it before you leave. See if there's anything you like."

"A little plunder?" he said with a deep laugh. "It's good for the soul."

I took the flight case from Dinara. "Thank you for everything."

"Anytime," she replied, before kissing me on the cheek.

"Let's go," Feo said. "Time for you lucky men to head home."

CHAPTER 70

BETH SINGER AWOKE from terrible dreams to find herself strapped to a pipe, her arms almost stretched to breaking point high above her head, her toes just touching the ground, so every movement was a strain and simply standing still caused untold suffering.

She had dreamed of a horrific cacophony assaulting her, death metal rock music alternating with the sounds of children screaming. Was it Maria and Danny? Where were her children? The nightmare had seemed to go on forever until in a moment of clarity she realized she was awake: the nightmare was real. It all came back to her then. How they'd grabbed her and the children. How she'd been knocked unconscious when she'd tried to fight the men off. And now she was here, alone.

Beth had completed an escape and interrogation course during her training at Fort Bragg and she guessed she was being prepared for questioning. The people who'd abducted her were trying to break her spirit. She'd been suspended in a stress position and the horrific sounds were a recording designed to grind her down psychologically. After countless hours, she came to recognize patterns in the traumatic loop.

"Please," she tried to scream, but she'd been gagged, so she couldn't tell them their efforts were unnecessary. She'd have gladly said or done anything they wanted in exchange for her children's safety. With Joshua gone, they were all she had left.

Beth had spent hours weeping for Danny and Maria, picturing their faces, imagining the worst, pleading with God, begging fate to intervene and for the universe to be kind to them. She'd cried with exhaustion. Wept with shame at her inability to protect her children. She cried with abject pity for herself, and finally, when she could cry no more, she hung there limp as a joint of meat, as numb as though she'd been anesthetized.

Beth lost all sense of time. The music no longer had any effect on her, nor did the screams. Drained of all hope, she felt nothing at all. Anger, fear, frustration—all these emotions were contingent on the idea that a situation could be improved, that an outcome could be avoided or escaped. But Beth had come to accept that she and her children were lost. Everything was lost. Jack Morgan and his people had failed them. And in the grip of that knowledge, she felt nothing. That was the true nature of despair. It was absolute. There was no emotion, because there was no hope.

It took a moment for her to realize the music had stopped, and she became aware of a crack of light at the bottom of her hood. Her ringing ears made out the sound of footsteps. Someone reached out and touched her belly. The thought of someone's fingers on her bare skin made her recoil. She'd been stripped to her underwear at some point, another ounce of her dignity she had been forced to surrender.

"Elizabeth," a man said. "Do you want to see your children again?"

They were alive, she thought, and the hope that she'd thought extinguished was rekindled. With it came longing, anger, and anxiety. Where were they? Had they been hurt? Would they live through this?

Beth felt hands reach under her hood and pull her gag down.

"Please." Her voice sounded thin and pathetic. She was ashamed to have allowed herself to get in such a vulnerable position. She—a trained warrior. "Please tell me what you want."

"The Bull, Elizabeth. We want the American Bull."

Beth started crying then because the flames of hope were once again dying. They'd asked for something she couldn't give them. Not because she refused to do so, but because she didn't have the first idea what they were talking about.

"The Bull, Elizabeth," he said. "Where is it?"

"Please," she begged. "Please let us go. I don't even know what that is. You've got the wrong person. I don't know what you're talking about. Please! Please let my children go. Please..."

She wept as the gag was forced back into her mouth. A heavy fist punched her naked stomach, but no matter how much it hurt, she couldn't double over, so she just hung there, taking the agony of further blows. Finally, when she felt as though something had ruptured, the punches stopped. More footsteps. Then the crack of light was replaced by total darkness. For a brief moment there was no sound other than her own muffled cries, then came the overwhelming noise of death metal and the screams of children.

She was back in hell.

CHAPTER 71

JOSHUA FLOYD SLEPT while I read the report Justine had sent. Beth Singer and her children had been abducted from the house on Pine Island, and so far we had no leads. I felt a deep sense of grief when I read Justine's account of the deaths of Jim Taft and Roni Alvarez. They had given their lives to protect others. I didn't need any further incentive to fight back but their deaths fired in me an intense need to bring Andreyev and all those responsible to justice.

The G650 hit turbulence and the sudden shudder shook Floyd awake. He yawned, stretched, and smiled.

"That felt good," he said.

We'd used the jet's bathroom to wash and change into the clothes Dinara had brought us. Floyd was in blue jeans and a green sweater, and I wore black trousers, a black sweater, and boots. Not my usual style, but at least they were clean.

"What have you got there?" Floyd asked, indicating the report.

"Can you think of any reason these people would be after you and your family?" I said, to avoid answering his question.

He shook his head. "Apart from revenge. But I'm just a pilot. If anyone had vengeance on their mind, I'd probably be pretty low on their list."

I grimaced. Having read the report, I didn't feel comfortable deceiving him any longer. He tilted his head toward me and his smile faded.

"I don't know how to break this to you," I began.

"No," he said.

"Beth, Maria, and Danny were taken. Two of my team were killed in an attack on the safe house."

"No!" He hit the table that separated us.

"We'll get them back," I assured him.

"I'm sorry." His tone softened. "I'm sorry about the people you lost."

I nodded. So was I. Alvarez and Taft were excellent operatives, and I could feel the horror of their deaths in Justine's words. "I appreciate that."

"Can I read the report?" Floyd asked.

"Of course." I handed it to him.

I'd been mulling over an idea since Justine told me about the abduction, and having read the report, it seemed like our only option.

"Captain Floyd," I said.

He looked up from the document, his distress evident.

"I think I know a way to get your wife and kids back, but you'll need to—"

He cut me off. "Anything. I'll do anything."

I nodded and picked up the satellite phone. I checked the list of useful numbers Dinara had included in the flight case and dialed the one I was looking for.

The call took a while to connect and, from the tones and clicks, it sounded as though it was being rerouted.

"*Na provode*," a voice said. I recognized the

Russian phrase people used when they answered the phone.

"Mr. Singer?" I responded. "I didn't catch that. Must be a bad line. This is Jack Morgan."

"Hello, Mr. Morgan." Andreyev's tone was hostile, and he wasn't making any effort to disguise his real Russian accent under the syrupy Southern one he'd invented for Donald Singer.

"I'm on my way back from Afghanistan. I've found Joshua Floyd," I revealed. "Can we meet when I get back?"

"Have you spoken to your team, Mr. Morgan?"

"Not yet," I lied.

There was a pause. I could hear Andreyev breathing.

"I don't believe you, Mr. Morgan. I think you've spoken to your team. I think you know who I am and what I've done."

"OK, Mr. Andreyev," I replied. "What's it going to take for you to release Beth and the children?"

"I don't want anything from you or Captain Floyd. I have everything I need. It's just a matter of time. If that changes, I will let you know."

Andreyev hung up.

Floyd looked at me expectantly.

"He doesn't want to negotiate. Which means Beth has whatever he wants."

Floyd clenched his fist. "What? There's nothing she has that could have provoked all this. And why go after me in Afghanistan? I don't believe she has anything."

"I hope you're right," I said. "It might help keep your family safe until we get them back. And we will get them back. I promise."

CHAPTER 72

I COULD SEE Justine standing beside a white Toyota Sequoia as we came in to land at Teterboro Airport, a small facility for executive jets located in New Jersey. Even at a distance, I sensed her anticipation, and shared it. I couldn't wait to hold her in my arms. In contrast, Joshua Floyd was impatient and irascible, which was completely understandable in the circumstances. I was coming home to someone I loved while his family were in the clutches of evil.

The pilot of the G650 brought the aircraft down and there was the slightest bump when the wheels kissed the runway. We taxied to the stand where Justine waited, and after a quick check by an Immigration and Customs Enforcement officer, we were allowed off the aircraft. I thanked the pilot and co-pilot, and hurried down the airstairs.

"Jack!" Justine ran over.

She looked exhausted, but she was beaming. My own wide smile made my cheeks ache. She rushed into my arms and I held her close. She whispered my name over and over and we kissed again and again.

Joshua Floyd came down the airstairs slowly, a frown on his face. He shivered as he looked around the desolate snow-covered airport. This wasn't much of a homecoming for a man who'd been through hell, and it was made worse by the absence of his family.

"Justine Smith, this is Joshua Floyd," I said. "Captain Floyd saved my life."

Justine shook his hand. "I don't know how I can thank you."

"Find my family," he replied flatly.

She looked at me awkwardly.

"We will," I assured him.

The back door of the Toyota opened and Mo-bot stepped out. She wore a thick ski jacket, hat, and gloves. In contrast to Justine's elegant trench coat, Mo-bot was dressed for substance over style. She barreled over and gave me a hug.

"It's good to see you alive, Jack," she said. "We're set up at the New York office."

"This is Joshua Floyd," I told her.

She and Floyd shook hands.

"We're going to get your family back, Mr. Floyd," Mo-bot said.

"Mr. Morgan," the pilot called.

I turned to see him holding out the flight case Dinara had given me, and ran back to take it.

"Thanks," I said.

I joined Mo-bot, Justine, and Floyd, who were heading for the SUV.

"What have you got there?" Mo-bot indicated the case.

"Clothes mostly, some notes, but most importantly a satellite phone," I replied. "I want you to take a look at it. It was on the aircraft that belonged to the men hunting Captain Floyd. There might be something useful on it."

"Hand it over," Mo-bot replied. "I've got my laptop and some of the gear in the car. I might as well get to work."

I put the case down by the back of the Toyota, opened it, and took out the satellite phone.

"Iridium 9575," Mo-bot remarked as I handed it over. "Good phone. Should have a lot of history, unless the last owner wiped it regularly. And even then there are ways to recover data. I'll get to work."

She hurried around the Toyota and got in the back seat. Floyd sat beside her.

Justine opened the trunk and I lifted the flight case inside. I closed the tailgate and, as I turned, she embraced me. Her eyes glistened.

"I never want to lose you again," she said. "Promise me?"

"I'll do my best," I replied.

She stared at me, but didn't say anything. After a moment, her expression softened.

"That will have to do," she said, before kissing me.

CHAPTER 73

BETH COULD HEAR someone whimpering and, after a few moments, realized she was the source of the pitiful sound. She'd been hanging from the straps around her wrists for what seemed an eternity. She could barely remember her life before the hell she was now experiencing, and when she caught flashes of what once had been, of the children running around laughing, of Josh taking her in his arms, those images caused nothing but pain.

She knew her life was gone. People like the men who'd abducted them didn't leave witnesses. They didn't believe in mercy, or in survivors.

They'd beaten her and she'd cursed them and sworn vengeance. Then she'd tried to bargain and negotiate, but they were relentless in their willingness to inflict pain and unyielding in their refusal to listen to her offers. They were only interested in one thing: the Bull.

Beth desperately racked her brains to try to figure out what they were talking about and why they thought she had anything to do with it, but she came up with nothing. She tried to make them understand, but they didn't believe her. She'd thought about lying and sending them to some made-up place, but knew they'd punish her more if they returned without the Bull. Even worse, they might punish the children.

The horrific screams and death metal stopped. Beth's ears throbbed in the silence that followed. A moment later, she heard footsteps and muffled crying. She recognized it immediately.

"Danny," she tried to say, but the gag muffled her voice.

Her hood was removed and her eyes burned in response to the sudden flood of light. She clenched them tightly shut while someone removed her gag.

"Please don't hurt him," Beth pleaded.

"Mom!" Maria screamed, before breaking into sobs.

Beth forced her eyes open. As they became accustomed to the light, she made out her children standing ten feet ahead in the center of what looked like a concrete-floored barn. Thirty feet behind them was a corrugated-steel door. Masked men stood either side of her children, each pressing a pistol to a child's head.

"Please let us go," Beth begged, her voice rasping and croaking, broken by all her crying. "I don't know anything about the Bull."

She sensed movement and heard steps behind her. She turned her tender head as far as she could to see a middle-aged man in a gray suit step into view.

"We are at the end of our patience," he said.

"You're the one behind this," Beth observed. She recognized his face from the files Jessie Fleming had been studying. "Victor Andreyev."

The man frowned and Beth immediately regretted revealing what she knew. She had increased the likelihood this man would kill them.

"Where is the Bull?" he asked.

"I don't know," Beth replied. She was on the verge of hysteria. "I swear I don't."

"Your husband took it from an associate of ours in Ukraine," Andreyev said. "We want it back."

"I don't know!" Beth cried.

"Mom!" Danny wept.

"It's OK, baby. It's OK," Beth tried to reassure him, but she didn't believe her own words.

"The price of your resistance will be a life," Andreyev said.

"No!" Beth screamed as he nodded at the men holding her children.

Danny and Maria struggled and cried, but the men held them firmly.

"You choose which one dies," Andreyev said. "Who is it to be? The boy or the girl?"

"I don't know about the Bull," Beth whimpered. "I don't know. I don't know. Please..."

"If you won't choose, then they will both die," he said, and nodded at the men.

Beth screamed and time slowed as she watched the masked men press pistols tight against her children's temples. Danny and Maria squirmed and cried, but they couldn't get free of their strong captors.

Beth mouthed "I love you" to her children as tears streamed down her face, but she didn't think either of them saw. She wept and cried like a wounded animal. She had failed her children. If they died, she was responsible.

"Wait! Wait!" Beth screamed. "I'll tell you where to find the Bull! I know where it is!"

"You're lying," Andreyev replied.

"I'm not! I'll tell you everything I know! Just let my children go!"

"Tell me then!" he yelled.

"It's in our house," Beth whimpered. "The Bull is in our house."

"Liar! We have searched it." Andreyev kept his eyes trained on her. "Kill them."

She watched in horror as two index fingers tightened around the triggers. She screamed as they were drawn back to firing points. Finally, she shut her eyes. She couldn't watch. She waiting for the inevitable.

Nothing happened.

She opened her eyes to see the shooters raise their pistols. The one holding Danny aimed his gun at Beth and pulled the trigger. There was a dull click. The gun wasn't loaded.

She screamed and the children broke into hysterical crying.

"She doesn't know anything," Andreyev said. "Cut her down. She's no use to us dead."

Andreyev stalked close to Beth as the man holding Danny handed the boy to his accomplice. Beth ignored Andreyev and kept her eyes on her children. She would never forgive these people for what they'd done.

"You might not have the answers we need, but you're still of use," Andreyev said. "Your husband survived."

Beth couldn't believe what she was hearing. Was this another game? Some kind of cruel torture?

"You are our leverage," Andreyev said. "You and your children."

The masked man who'd held Danny produced a hunting knife from behind his back and stood beside Beth to cut her bonds. She cried as she fell to the floor.

Finally released, Maria and Danny ran over and threw their arms around her.

Andreyev said something in Russian and the two masked men followed him out of the barn.

Beth's arms burned with pain. There was little strength in them, but she didn't care. She hugged her children to her as tightly as she possibly could, relishing every moment and praying this wasn't some kind of dream.

CHAPTER 74

WE WERE ON our way to Manhattan when the satellite phone rang. Mo-bot had it connected to her computer and was interrogating its registry.

She handed me the phone, but kept it plugged into her machine.

"Hello?" I said when I answered.

"Mr. Morgan?"

I recognized Andreyev's voice immediately.

"Yes."

"You said the pilot survived. Is he still with you?"

"Yeah, he's with me."

"Then we might be able to make a trade," Andreyev said. "The woman and children for the pilot."

"I'll have to check. Can I reach you on this number?"

I looked at Mo-bot and signaled to my watch. She nodded and indicated she'd had enough time to run a trace.

"Of course," Andreyev replied.

"I'll call you when I have an answer."

I hung up and turned to Floyd.

"He's offering Beth, Danny, and Maria in exchange for you."

"We do it," Floyd said immediately. "It's not even in question."

"I know this is going to be hard for you to hear," I replied. "But I think it's a bad idea. He'll take you and keep Beth and the children as leverage. Most likely kill you all when he has whatever it is he wants."

"We can stop that happening," Floyd countered. "Hold him to his deal. Or lure him out and take them."

I frowned. Both those suggestions were extremely high-risk.

"Mo?" I asked.

She shook her head. "He's routing the call through a number of networks. It's impossible to trace."

I looked at Justine, who was focused on the snow-flanked highway. She glanced over and shrugged.

"We make the trade," Floyd said firmly.

I didn't see what other options we had and was about to reply when I saw a familiar expression cross Mo-bot's face. The cat most definitely had gotten the cream.

"There is another way," she said. "I've found an old number on the phone. A couple incoming calls made two weeks ago from the same cell tower near the Pentagon we found when we tracked Andreyev's call. I think this number might belong to our mole in the Department of Defense."

CHAPTER 75

"GOODNIGHT, SIR," THE guard at the desk said, before pressing the button that opened the outer door to the Rotary Entrance.

A blast of cold air hit Rick Ferguson as he left the Pentagon and headed for the parking lot. He hurried along the raised walkway and down the stone steps that led to the premier tier of spaces, where the senior brass parked. He was a rung down the ladder, which meant he had to walk through the lot, braving the bitter night. He jogged across North Rotary Road, his breath rising in little clouds before dissipating into the clear sky. The stars shimmered brightly in the frozen air. Rick clapped his gloved hands and picked up his pace. This was not a night for tarrying. He passed a few more senior staff cars and finally made it to his spot beneath one of the streetlamps.

He opened the driver's door, grabbed his scraper, and removed an inch of crusted snow from the windshield of his late-model Range Rover Sport. He brushed loose snow off his gloves, replaced the scraper in the side pocket, and climbed into the driver's seat. He'd had the car a little over six months and it still gave him a buzz of pleasure to see it parked in the driveway in the morning. He'd told nosy Nancys and Normans at work that Ellie's mother had gifted them some money, but the truth was a little more complicated.

He settled back in his cream leather seat and reversed out of his space, then drove toward the gate. The guard in the gatehouse checked his license plate and ran an ID check on him before lowering the cheese-wedge barrier that was designed to keep out intruders. Rick gave a friendly nod and wave to the guard, before driving on. He turned left onto Washington Boulevard and headed for the Memorial Highway.

"Call home," he said.

"Calling home," his in-car assistant said, and a moment later Ellie came on the line.

"Hello?"

"Hey, hon, it's me."

"How was your day?" she asked.

The most banal of all questions, asked by billions of spouses every single day. Rick had complained once and regretted it.

"What are our lives worth to each other if we don't share them?" Ellie had asked, along with other emotive comments in that vein.

So he knew it was easier to just answer with his now habitual, "Oh, you know, same old, same old."

"I hear you," Ellie replied.

It was vacuous and a total waste of oxygen, but it gave her comfort for some reason.

"Tara gave me nothing but trouble today, and when I . . ." she began to drone.

"Honey, I'm about to hit the black spot," Rick said.

There was no black spot. It was a convenient invention that spared him from listening to the mundanities of her day.

"I just wanted to know if you wanted me to pick anything up?"

"No, we're good," she replied. "I made spaghetti and meatballs."

He endured Ellie's meatballs at least once a week and was getting tired of them. They were bland and dry, but if he ever told her that, they'd need to have another "chat," so it was easier to play nice.

"Yum," he lied. "And you can tell me all about what Tara did when I get home."

And I have a stiff drink in my hand, he thought.

"I will," she replied. "Drive safely. Love you."

"Love you, too," Rick said before hanging up.

He wasn't sure if he believed the words anymore. He had once, or at least he thought he had, but maybe he'd never felt love, just the thrill of chase and conquest. At least Ellie wasn't offensive. She came from a good family, and her father had excellent political connections. She was convenient. If he ever grew tired of her, she was too well bred to give him much trouble. He would have to budget a moderate amount for any divorce, but she'd never be able to get at the real money.

He switched on the stereo and flipped through his playlists to his favorite album of the moment, which was Alice Coltrane's *Journey in Satchidananda*, a trippy, soothing cascade of jazz. He shifted in his comfy seat and settled back for the opening bars.

Thirty minutes of classic harp, double bass, and piano later, he was heading up Birch Lane, a couple minutes from his beautiful home, passing all the other big houses set back from the road and nestled in their perfect wintry gardens. He was daydreaming about being on vacation in Catalina with someone more adventurous than Ellie, so he didn't notice the shadow to his right.

The collision came out of nowhere. A truck tore out of Spring Valley Drive and smashed into his beautiful Range Rover. The car was a sudden mess of airbags and silicate dust, but Rick still managed to hit his head on the side window. The world swam. As his mind floated, he saw an SUV pull up in front of the Range Rover and a group of masked figures jumped out.

This can't be happening, Rick thought, before he blacked out.

CHAPTER 76

ANTICIPATION IS KEY. Most interrogators don't give themselves anywhere to go. They start with the stuff of nightmares and the victim quickly retreats into a cushioned part of their mind, which helps insulate them and allows them to become accustomed to the pain.

I shook Rick Ferguson awake and let him take in his surroundings. He was in the burned-out shell of the Mill Wheel Tavern on Route 26, just outside of a tiny village called Chester, New Jersey.

Sci had found the place by running a crime-report search for bars that had been destroyed by arson. After taking Rick a couple blocks in a stolen truck, we'd flown him to New Jersey in a chopper I'd chartered.

The bar had been burned down five months back. It stood beside a quiet rural route that had very little traffic, which I guessed might be why the owner torched it—not enough passing trade to stay afloat. At this time of night, a little before eleven, there was no one on the road. The charred wreckage helped conjure the sense Rick had woken up in hell. The walls were black with tar, melted plastic was dotted here and there in misshapen pools, there were holes in the walls and roof that allowed snow and ice to take over large sections of the property. This was the kind of place where bad things happened, and I could see from the terrified look on Rick's face, he was smart enough to have figured that out.

Floyd and I wore black ski masks and leather gloves. I had laid a range of shop tools on the charred remains of a table. I wandered over to them and made sure Rick got a good look.

"Do you know who I am?" he asked. His voice trembled with the effort of his false bravado.

He wasn't as smart as I had hoped. Pentagon

personnel should know not to ask that question, and he really shouldn't be doing anything to reinforce a price value in the minds of kidnappers. Fortunately for him, we weren't kidnappers. We were the embodiment of justice, and this was his reckoning.

We had taken a gamble that the Pentagon mole hadn't been told about what had happened in Afghanistan when Mo-bot called the number she'd found in the satellite phone's registry. Her suspicions about it had been correct.

Floyd had claimed to be one of the Russian paramilitaries and did a pretty passable accent. Speaking in broken English, he kept the mole on the line with bogus intelligence reports and requests for clarification. That bought just enough time for Mo-bot to bypass Pentagon counter-surveillance measures and pinpoint his location. The lazy, arrogant fool hadn't even stepped out of his office to take the call. Rick Ferguson was program manager of the Advanced Field Technologies Group for DARPA, the Defense Advanced Research Projects Agency. That put him at the nexus of a great deal of high-level military intelligence on development and field deployment.

"This place will be swarming with cops within minutes," Rick informed us.

He was overcompensating, and beneath the bravado was a vast reservoir of fear. We would feed it.

I picked up a pair of pliers, saying nothing as I moved slowly through the ash and charred wreckage toward him. He was bound to a chair and fought against the restraints as I came near.

"Don't you touch me! Don't you come near me!"

The thin veneer of bravado cracked and flaked. It was time to burn it away entirely.

"I'm going to break a finger for each lie you tell," I said. "I'll start with the pinkie on your left hand and work across."

"No!" Rick yelled. "No! Help!"

"Help?" Floyd sneered mockingly. "Help!" He closed on Rick with a snarl. "No one can hear you."

He fought hard but his hand was bound too tightly. I placed the jaws of the pliers around his left pinkie finger. I squeezed it until I saw him grimace.

"Ahh! Ahhhhhh!"

He stopped struggling and settled into a grudging docility.

"Please, just tell me what you want."

"Who do you work for?" I asked.

"The Department of Defense," he replied hurriedly, glancing at his finger nervously.

"I'm not going to break it, because that isn't a lie. But there's another truth, which is the answer I'm looking for. Who else do you work for?"

I squeezed again and he winced.

"They'll kill me."

"They are not your most pressing problem," I replied. "You're in a new world now. One where you live minute by minute. Worry about what *we're* going to do."

I squeezed harder and he cried out. The desk jockey had never experienced anything like this.

"Please…"

"A name," I snapped.

"Victor Andreyev," he replied. "He's SVR. I report to him."

The SVR—Sluzhba Vneshney Razvedki— was Russia's foreign intelligence agency, headquartered in the Yasenevo district on the outskirts of Moscow. A building I knew well, having infiltrated it the last time I'd been in the city.

"Good," I said. "We know about Victor, so we know that's the truth."

Rick seemed surprised we already knew, but not as surprised as I was to hear confirmation he was an SVR operative. I'd suspected it because of the resources being thrown at this operation, but it brought back painful memories of the last time I'd been up against that institution. I'd lost a very good man.

"A team was sent to capture a pilot in Afghanistan," I said. "Tell me why."

"They were going to try to abduct him here, in the US, but it was too risky. A missing Special Forces operative would spark a full court press from law enforcement and the DOD, so I persuaded them we could set a trap somewhere lawless and out of the way. I made sure he was assigned to pilot the Afghan mission."

"And the pilot's wife and children," I added, "why have they been targeted?"

"They're just leverage," Rick admitted. "An insurance policy. To make sure he gives them what they want."

Floyd moved quickly—far too quickly for

me to stop him. He swung at Rick, and his big gloved fist connected with the man's jaw. There was a painful crack. Rick howled.

"My jaw!" he said, although it sounded like "Muh daw!"

I turned to Floyd and shook my head, even though part of me thought it might not hurt Rick to know there was someone in the room who really wanted to make him suffer.

"Where are they now?" I asked.

"Don't know," Rick replied.

I repositioned the pliers and squeezed.

"Ahhhhh!" he cried. "I swear I don't know! They wouldn't give me that kind of information. It's not something I need to know."

His words were distorted and pained, but I could still make them out.

"What do they want the pilot for?" I asked.

"I don't know," he cried.

I squeezed. Torture went against my personal beliefs, and breaking his finger was a line I wasn't prepared to cross, but I could get close.

"Ahhhhh! Please! I don't know what they want. I heard them talking about a bull. That's all I know."

Floyd stepped forward again and swung a one-two jab and cross that knocked Rick unconscious.

"What just happened?" I asked.

He removed his mask, and I did likewise.

"I think I know," he said. "I think I know what they want."

CHAPTER 77

FLOYD AND I dragged Rick outside to the Airbus H125 helicopter that stood in a clearing just behind the bar. Justine was waiting beside the aircraft. She didn't like wet work, but knew it was a necessary part of the job. In this particular case, when a mother and children's lives were at stake, I could tell she was prepared to overlook some excesses. There was no sympathy in her eyes as we dragged Rick into the aircraft.

"Where to now?" Justine asked.

"I need to go to the Catskills," Floyd said, and Justine and I exchanged surprised glances. "I think I might know what they're after. It has something to do with a mission I carried out in Belarus."

"What?" I asked.

He pursed his lips and shook his head. "I can't talk about it."

I sighed. I respected his commitment to the oath of secrecy he'd taken, but his family's lives were at stake. There was little I could do, though, short of taking him into the bar for interrogation.

"We need to make a stop first," I said. "Drop off the trash." I nodded at Rick.

I produced my phone and made a call that was answered within three rings.

"Hello?" a voice said.

"Secretary Carver, please," I replied.

"And you are?"

"Jack Morgan."

"Hold, please," the voice said, and the line fell silent.

"Jack Morgan," Eli Carver said a few moments later. "What earns me the privilege of two calls in a week?"

"I found your mole, Mr. Secretary," I said.

I couldn't see him, but I knew I now had the secretary of state's full attention.

"A DARPA program manager called Rick Ferguson," I revealed.

"I know that guy," Carver replied with a touch of irritation in his voice. "You got proof?"

"A taped confession. It won't hold up in court, but it will give him nowhere to go when your people get to work," I said. We'd had a Dictaphone recording the whole time.

"You going to bring him in?"

"No, Mr. Secretary," I replied. "Where there is one mole, there might be others."

"So what's your plan?"

"We're heading for Denville. Call the local police department and tell them we'll be dropping off a high-value suspect. We'll deliver Ferguson and the recording of his confession. They can hold him until your people are able to collect him."

"And you?"

"It's better you don't know, Mr. Secretary," I replied. "I can tell you we recovered Joshua Floyd. When the time comes, he'll have some interesting testimony."

"Are you planning trouble, Jack?" Carver asked.

I hesitated. "Like I say, it's better you don't know, Mr. Secretary."

"Is this going to be one of those conversations I need to deny ever having had?"

I stayed silent.

"Well, thank you anyway, Jack," he said.

"We'll speak soon, Mr. Secretary," I responded before hanging up.

"Denville?" Justine asked.

"It's a small police department. I don't think Carver will ask them to try to hold us, but just in case he does, I picked somewhere the odds would be in our favor."

"And I thought I was paranoid," Floyd observed.

"The word you're looking for is careful," I replied with a smile.

We climbed into the chopper and within minutes the ground was falling away as I took us skyward.

CHAPTER 78

BETH HAD MANAGED to calm the children and get them to sleep. There were three cots arranged against the back wall of the barn, away from the space where she'd been tortured. She dragged two of the army surplus beds close together and positioned them so the children could sleep beside each other. While they lay there, whimpering and crying, she'd ignored her burning arms and stroked their hair, soothing them to sleep. The children gave her focus and purpose and stopped her from dwelling on the trauma she'd experienced.

When the children were deep asleep, Beth

used a bucket of water and a small towel to clean herself up, and changed into some old jeans and a gray sweater that just about fit her. The sweater was moth-eaten and ragged, but it kept the chill at bay.

She explored the barn, which was about the size of two tennis courts. Above her head, struts ran between the walls and supported the A-frame steel roof. She checked the walls: corrugated steel that ran beneath the concrete floor line. The only door was a huge solid steel double gate that was designed for vehicle access. She tried the catch and found it was locked.

"Don't waste your time," a voice yelled from the other side.

She and the children were being guarded, which meant an escape through the front door would be unlikely to succeed. Beth looked around and her eyes settled on the pipe she'd been suspended from. About three inches in diameter, it came down from the roof about ten feet away from the door and ran the length of the barn, before disappearing through the back wall. Smaller pipes ran off it at regular intervals and were capped by sprinklers. A fire system perhaps?

Or a way of feeding animals? Either way, the central pipe was sufficiently thick to make a good weapon.

Beth hurried to the other end of the barn. Ignoring the pain in her arms, she lifted her cot as quietly as possible. The children stirred, but didn't wake.

She carried the cot to a point where the pipe connected to one of the sprinklers, and set it down directly beneath the roughly welded joint. She fought her aching body, stepped onto the cot, reached up for the pipe, and got to work.

CHAPTER 79

WE HADN'T NEEDED to worry about the cops in Denville. I set the chopper down on the baseball field next to the police department and three officers emerged from the building. I powered down the engine and Justine, Floyd, and I climbed out to meet the officers. The leader of the trio, a gruff middle-aged sergeant, said they'd been waiting for us after receiving a call from the Pentagon. They'd been instructed to hold a man who was about to be delivered to them.

"We've been trying to guess what kind of perp gets the royal treatment," the sergeant asked. "You got bin Laden's brother in there or something?"

"We've got a traitor," I replied. "A man who sold out this country. Make sure you lock him up tight."

The sergeant's eyes narrowed and his mood soured. "Ain't nothing lower than treason."

The officers dragged Rick Ferguson from the chopper and watched as we took to the sky.

I flew north for thirty minutes, heading deep into the Catskill Mountains. Below us, the bumps in the snow-covered terrain became large distinct folds, and the mountains soared as we flew deeper into the remote wilderness. Narrow roads and tracks criss-crossed the landscape. Floyd knew every landmark and directed me farther and farther into the mountains. Finally, a few miles north of Rondout Reservoir and Sundown Forest, he pointed to a clearing that I could just about make out in the faint moonlight.

"Set us down there," he said.

I circled around and began my descent.

"What's down there?" I asked.

Floyd had been cagey about our destination so far.

"Beth and I had a go-to place in case she and the kids ever needed to lie low," he replied.

"Somewhere they'd be safe if I was ever captured. At least, it was supposed to be."

"But you have another one?" I guessed.

And when I looked down, to the north of the clearing I saw hints of a structure through the snow-covered trees.

Floyd nodded. "Like you said, it isn't paranoia. It's about being careful."

The clearing wasn't much bigger than a baseball diamond. I took us down slowly. When we were on the ground, I powered down the H125 and we stepped out into the brutal chill of a Catskill winter's night.

"I bought this place using a dummy corporation a few years back," Floyd said as we trudged through the snow. "Land here is cheap. Picked up most of this side of the mountain and the cabin. It's somewhere we can come if things ever go real bad."

He took us through a gap in the trees and we followed a trail north of the clearing. I saw a small cabin ahead, tucked almost out of sight. It was the kind of place someone could disappear.

"What do you think they're after?" Justine asked.

"Three months ago, I flew a team into Belarus. We were tasked with stealing data and documents from the home of Konstantin Roslov, a Russian SVR operative who was believed to be coordinating operations across Europe."

"And?" I asked, the word hanging before me in a cloud as I exhaled.

"I went in with the team, probably shouldn't have," Floyd replied. "But Roslov wasn't there and the place was empty, so it was a safe target. We were under orders to make it look like a random burglary. So I took something."

"Spoils of war," I remarked.

Floyd nodded. "It's in this cabin," he said, pointing toward the tiny building.

Trees towered over it, with trunks like the legs of giants tightly packed as far as the eye could see. Shutters covered the cabin windows. Floyd pulled back a panel by the front door to reveal a key safe. He rolled the tumblers, opened the safe, and pulled out two keys. He used them to unlock the front door and let us in.

He picked up a battery-operated lamp and switched it on. We walked through a small hallway into a rustic living room. A couple of couches covered in blankets faced a large fireplace, and historical military paintings hung on the wood-paneled walls. Floyd went to a sideboard that was covered in trophies and mementos and picked up a brass statue, a small bronze replica of the Charging Bull that graces Wall Street. About ten inches long and six high, the figure was a perfect scale copy of the famous original, which symbolizes a strong financial market on the rise. The original figure, by Arturo Di Modica, is known the world over.

"This was on Roslov's desk," Floyd said. "I thought he was having a pop at American capitalism, so I liked the idea of taking it away from him."

He handed it to me, and I turned it over and examined it closely. "You take anything else?"

Floyd shook his head. "The other guys did, but not me. I didn't have a gear bag. I was just the pilot. There must have been hidden cameras in the place. They must have filmed us to know that it was me who took the Bull."

There was nothing unusual about the bronze figure. Not as far as I could see. "What about the documents and data?"

"I think they got something," Floyd said. "But I don't get told that kind of information."

"We need to get this into the lab," I said to Justine. "Find out why people are prepared to murder for it."

CHAPTER 80

BETH HADN'T BEEN able to break the main pipe—it was too strong—but she had snapped off a two-foot section of the thinner sprinkler feed. A little more than an inch wide, the pipe wouldn't be much use as a weapon, but it had potential as a tool. Beth had set to work using the jagged broken end to gouge away the concrete by the back wall. She'd been at it for over an hour and had created a hole beneath the corrugated-steel wall that was sufficiently large to put her hand in. She felt cold earth on the other side and her heart leaped.

Given the time, she knew she could dig her way out.

Every fiber of her being wanted sleep, and her muscles ached with fatigue, but she kept digging. Whenever she felt as though she couldn't keep going, she looked at her babies, who were still asleep despite the glare of the strip lights that hung high above them.

Maria and Danny were all the incentive Beth needed to force herself on. She would die for her kids, so pain and torturous labor were nothing in comparison. She kept working and forced the opening wider, a millimeter at a time. She groaned as she stood up to take a short break and stretch, but her rest was short-lived.

She heard an exterior bolt being drawn back and hurried over to her cot, dragging it to conceal the hole. She jumped into bed, tucked the length of pipe beneath her, and pulled a thin blanket up to her neck. She closed her eyes and pretended to be asleep as the door swung open.

She heard footsteps approach. A hand shook her. She turned over to see Andreyev standing close by her. He held a cell phone that was connected to some kind of digital relay about the size of a pack of cigarettes.

"We offered your husband a deal some time

ago," Andreyev said. "He did not take it. We believe he needs more convincing. You will talk to him and tell him to come to us. Or we will kill one of your children. We do not need you all."

Andreyev indicated the two masked men who stood over Danny and Maria. Both were aiming pistols at her sleeping children.

"No blanks this time," Andreyev assured her. "When I give the word, one of them dies."

CHAPTER 81

WE WERE THIRTY minutes from Manhattan Heliport when the satellite phone rang. Floyd passed it to me. I removed my headset before I answered.

"Mr. Morgan," Andreyev said. "I hoped I would have heard back from you by now. Maybe Captain Floyd needs some encouragement to reach a decision. Please put him on the line."

I could tell from Andreyev's tone what was coming next. The man was angry and he would take that anger out on Beth and the children. I had to try to buy some more time.

"He escaped," I replied. "I gave him your

offer and I think he must have gotten suspicious that we were still working together. He took off around Denville. Just made a run for it. We tried to chase him down, but he shook us off. We're out searching for him right now."

Floyd looked at me quizzically from the co-pilot's seat. Justine tapped me on the shoulder. When I turned, she shrugged as if to say: What's going on?

I signaled them both to be quiet and waited for Andreyev to respond. I could tell I'd taken the wind out of his sails. I just had to pray he hadn't heard about Rick Ferguson going missing yet.

"Do you have any way of contacting him?" he asked.

"No. He has no phone, no money. I don't know where he's going. We had a reported sighting outside a convenience store in Livingston. That's where we're going now."

"If I find out you're playing games—"

I cut him off. "What games? You think this is a game to me? I've already lost two agents in this. No more innocent people need to die. I made a promise to Beth to protect her and the kids. I want to take your deal and get them to safety. And I thought Floyd did too, but maybe he's more of a coward than I gave him credit for."

I shook my head apologetically at Floyd.

"You have twelve hours, Mr. Morgan," Andreyev responded. "Find him and call me. Or I will be forced to punish the people I have at hand."

He hung up and I made sure the call had disconnected.

"What the hell was that?" Floyd asked.

"I just bought your wife and kids more time," I replied. "We've got twelve hours to save them."

CHAPTER 82

I SET US down at Manhattan Heliport, which was located at the southernmost tip of the island. By the time I'd settled the charter, Jessie had arrived to collect us. As Justine, Floyd, and I made our way through the parking lot to the Toyota, I thought back to my last time here—chasing the assassin who'd killed my friend. Far too many people had died as part of the twisted games of state played by enemies set on destroying everything we stood for. I was determined that Beth Singer and her children wouldn't be added to the list of victims.

Jessie caught sight of the Bull replica as I

climbed into the front seat of the Toyota and she slid in beside me.

"Souvenir?" she asked.

"We think this is what they're after," I replied. "We need to get it into the lab."

She nodded, started the engine, and pulled out of the heliport, before heading north on FDR Drive.

"Everyone OK?" she asked.

I nodded, and Justine and Floyd did likewise. None of us said anything, though. I think we were all too aware of the ticking clock.

It was approaching 3 a.m. and everywhere was eerily quiet. There were hardly any other vehicles on the road, and as we turned off FDR Drive and made our way through the city, there were hardly any people around either. It was as though New York had inhaled and was holding its breath for a moment, pausing before breathing life into a new day. The bright lights of electronic billboards shone over frozen sidewalks and the LED advertisements stuck to the handful of yellow cabs that navigated the deserted streets danced across the lanes like fireflies.

Jessie drove us north to Madison and East

26th, where we parked in the subterranean garage before taking the elevator to Private's offices. Sci and Mo-bot were waiting for us.

"It's good to see you, Jack," Sci said warmly when we stepped out of the elevator. He clasped my hand and pulled me in for a hug.

"This is Joshua Floyd," I said. "Seymour Kloppenberg."

"Good to meet you. Congratulations on getting out of Afghanistan," Sci said, shaking Floyd's hand. "Call me Sci."

"Thanks, Sci," Floyd replied.

They all looked at me expectantly.

"Sorry to keep you all up," I told them. "But we think this is what they're after." I brandished the Wall Street Bull. "Taken off the desk of a Russian asset called Konstantin Roslov. We need a full analysis."

"We'll find out what we can about Roslov," Jessie said, and Mo-bot nodded.

"And I'll have a look at this thing," Sci remarked, taking the Bull from me. "It's heavy."

"I'll go with you," I said, but Justine shook her head and pulled me to one side.

"You're going to rest, Jack. You and Captain

Floyd must be running on fumes, and you're no good to us exhausted."

I looked at Sci, who smiled knowingly as he headed for the lab. Mo-bot and Jessie had already gone.

"You either trust your people to do right or you don't," Floyd observed. "Personally I could do with some shut-eye."

"We'll get you set up somewhere," Justine told him. "And the same goes for you, Jack Morgan."

CHAPTER 83

I WAS BACK in the mountains of Afghanistan, struggling for breath as I followed Joshua Floyd through the trees. He was running too fast for me to keep up, and seemed not to be bothered by the thin air. I was going to get left behind. I heard a furious sound behind me, the roar of some ancient, fearsome creature, and glanced over my shoulder to see two rockets tearing through the sky, propelled by hellfire. When I turned to look ahead, Floyd had gone, but how would I escape without him? I didn't know where the cave was. I made it to the cliff face and pawed frantically at the rock, searching for the entrance, but I wasn't going to make it. The rockets detonated and I was caught in the blast. I was tossed into the air and felt myself being consumed by the flames...

"Jack." Justine's voice cut through the nightmare. "Jack!"

I woke to find myself lying on her lap in the meeting room. I remembered she'd put me on the couch. She'd set my head in her lap and stroked my hair until I fell asleep.

"How long have I been out?" I asked.

"Little over two hours," she replied.

"How are your legs?" I said, sitting up.

"They've been better." She stood and stretched them out. "What's a little lost circulation? You've got a visitor."

I glanced around to see Mo-bot at the door.

"We've got something you should see."

I stood up and walked off the stiffness in my muscles. I could have done with another twenty-four hours' sleep, but that was a luxury I wasn't going to have for a while.

Justine and I followed Mo-bot through the quiet office. The lights were on energy save and most of the place was lost to shadows, which was just as well because my eyes were raw and struggled to adjust to the light.

We went through a security door into the corridor that led to the computer room. Another door and then we joined Jessie in a climate-controlled room full of servers and terminals.

"Feeling better?" she asked.

"I probably needed the rest," I replied. "I do feel a little better for it."

Mo-bot slid into the seat beside Jessie. Justine and I stood at her shoulder.

She opened an image file to reveal a photograph of a pale man with the puffy face of an alcoholic crowned by a mop of thick black hair. If he'd ever had a soul, it wasn't evident in this photo. His eyes were windows to a cruel void.

"Konstantin Roslov," Mo-bot said. "Colonel in the Russian Army before an honorable discharge. He went into commodities. Similar profile to Andreyev. Made a fortune buying up mining businesses that specialized in precious and heavy metals."

Mo-bot opened a file window to show the website of the Roslov Fund, a venture capital firm.

"He used money from his industrial empire to start a venture fund that invested in businesses all over the world. Same as Andreyev. It's a pattern. I think they figured out the way to beat capitalism is to get inside it. According to the CIA, the Roslov Fund is a front used to launder money to Russian-backed interests all over the world."

"Where is he now?" I asked. "Still in Belarus?"

Mo-bot shook her head. "He's dead, Jack."

She opened a Russian newspaper article and ran it through Google Translate. It featured a long-distance photograph of a corpse under a sheet, surrounded by police officers. It looked as though they were in a scrap yard.

"His body was found in a recycling facility outside Minsk," Mo-bot revealed. "The day after the raid on his house."

"Punishment for carelessness?" I suggested.

"Whoever killed him removed his limbs. The Belarusian police believe they were amputated while he was alive," Jessie said. "So it was either a punishment or a warning."

"Or maybe both," I remarked.

CHAPTER 84

"HAS SCI FOUND anything?" I asked.

Mo-bot shook her head. "Not last time I checked."

"Someone killed an entire unit of Green Berets and tore up Afghanistan looking for this thing," I remarked. "Roslov was dismembered, likely as punishment for losing it. What's so special about that figure?"

I studied Roslov's photo, wondering why so much horror had been perpetrated in pursuit of such a mundane object.

"Keep digging," I suggested. "We must be missing something."

I left Jessie and Mo-bot and headed for the door. Justine followed me and we walked the short distance down the corridor to the forensic science lab. Justine swiped a key card and we stepped inside a laboratory that would have been the envy of any forensics specialist. I'd always invested in cutting-edge technology, and the spacious lab contained everything from a scanning electron microscope to flow cytometers to an X-ray machine. We could conduct most forensic scientific experiments within the confines of the room, and it looked as though Sci had made use of many of the machines. There were discarded consumables all over the workbenches. He stood on the other side of a protective screen, near the X-ray machine, busy studying an image on a monitor. Floyd was standing beside him. Both men turned when we entered.

"I couldn't sleep," Floyd said. "Didn't seem right with Beth and the kids…" His voice trailed off. "Anyway, I wanted to see if I could help."

"Anything?" I asked.

Sci shook his head. "I've treated it with chemicals, put it under the microscope, X-rayed the thing. It's a perfectly normal bronze statue. And I've never hated a thing more."

"Any chance the X-ray missed something?" Justine asked.

"It's solid metal all the way through," Sci replied. "No secret chamber. No concealed surfaces. Nothing abnormal in any of the reactions. It's a copper–tin alloy with traces of other metals. There are no hidden markers..."

He stopped, clearly taken by an idea.

Sci grabbed the bull from the X-ray plate and hurried over to a bench at the back of the lab. "An optical microscope can enlarge the physical structure. We already checked for engravings or concealed codes carved into the bull..."

He went to a white box a little larger than a microwave and opened a door at the front of the device. "We didn't find anything, but maybe we didn't go deep enough."

Sci put the bull inside the device, closed the door, and activated a series of switches. The box was connected to a couple of monitors by a thick tube that looked a little like a high-tech drainpipe.

"This scanning electron microscope can see down to the atomic level. With it we can view each and every one of the copper and tin atoms that make up the surface of this thing." Sci switched on the monitors and operated a roller-ball mouse that seemed to control the resolution of the image onscreen.

An image of a tiny section of the bull filled the monitor. Sci adjusted it to a pin-sharp resolution. "I was on a flight once," he said absently while he made fine tweaks to the machine settings. "I got to talking to the guy sitting next to me, and it turned out we were both due to be speaking at the same conference in Denver. Anyway, this guy was a physicist. He'd trained under Heinrich Kuhn, one of the guys on the Manhattan Project, and he told me how Kuhn had solved the problem of calculating the weight of uranium atoms. 'You use light, my dear boy,' was how he'd put it. Anyway, this physicist was gassing away about how light could be used to read and store data and…"

Sci hesitated and took a deep breath. He gestured at the screen. I saw the tiny craters and formations of an atom. But, more importantly, inscribed around the atom was a series of stripes. Some were thick, others thin, but there appeared to be only two types of mark, and they ran across the atom in a seemingly random pattern.

I gave Sci a puzzled look.

"Is that a form of code?" Justine asked.

"Looks like binary," Sci replied, staring at the screen. "Well, this is quite a thing. Someone has figured out how to store vast quantities of data on real objects."

He shifted the microscope and moved to another atom, where a similar pattern could be seen.

"I can't believe it. This technology alone is worth billions," Sci said excitedly. "But my guess is it's the data they want back."

He turned to Floyd. "You may have unwittingly stolen the most valuable object on the planet."

"So someone has an atomic-scale engraving machine?" Justine asked.

"My guess is they have a box in a lab, probably in SVR headquarters in Yasenevo, that can use beams of single photons to burn data onto the atoms, certainly of metal objects, but why not other substances too? Once the object has been encoded, it is placed into either the same box or another, which acts as a reader to decode the data. Maybe there is even a portable reader you use to scan the object? There might only be a handful of readers in the world, so you can store the most precious secrets and never have to worry about being discovered or losing your data. Unless the object is stolen, of course."

"Everyone just sees a bronze figure," Floyd remarked.

"Exactly, but in reality it's a vast data repository. The ultimate USB drive. How many atoms form the surface of this bull? Billions? Maybe trillions? Effectively limitless storage capacity on just this one object. I'm just…" Sci trailed off. "I'm just blown away. This is revolutionary."

"Can you decode it?" I asked.

"Unlikely without a reader," he replied. "I can capture as many images as I like and try to decipher them, but we're talking about a painstaking process. Imagine trying to reconstruct a photograph from binary. Who knows how this data is parsed?"

"Do your best," I said.

"What are you thinking, Jack?" Justine asked.

She knew me well enough to spot an idea forming.

"I'm thinking it's time to call Victor Andreyev and tell him we've found Captain Floyd."

CHAPTER 85

I DROVE PAST the old factories, their broken windows framed by rusting steel. Towering chimneys reached toward the sky. No longer grand monuments to industry, instead they looked like the fingers of a dead and buried giant trying to claw its way out of the ground.

Andreyev had insisted on meeting somewhere isolated and remote, which was my first red flag. His requirement that I come alone was the second. I knew he had every intention of killing me, but this meeting was the only way we'd have any chance of saving Beth, Maria, and Danny.

I'd chosen the old Baekeland Chemical Plant in

Jersey, about forty minutes' drive from Manhattan, and had agreed a time of 11 a.m. Andreyev was told we'd found Floyd and discovered he'd gone to retrieve the bronze bull. That made the deal very simple: Beth and the children were to be exchanged for it.

The Toyota Sequoia bounced along a neglected concrete service road. A thick covering of snow made it impossible to see the deep potholes, so I bumped and crunched my way toward three SUVs that were parked in the yard between three decaying chemical processing plants. The vehicles were surrounded by a complex network of pipes, tanks, gantries, and metal-and-concrete buildings. The dark gray clouds that brooded above the broken roofs and corroded pipes served to make the setting even more ominous.

Justine had been dead against my plan, and had taken me aside to plead with me not to go. It was a trap, a suicide mission. Why did I have to do the exchange? Could Floyd not go instead? With tears in her eyes, she'd told me she couldn't bear to lose me again. I'd tried to soothe her fears, but didn't think I was successful. I couldn't even convince myself. What I was about to do was dangerous, and the thought of all the things that could go wrong set my heart racing. It was pounding furiously as I parked twenty yards from the other vehicles.

I reminded myself bravery wasn't the absence of fear; it was action taken in the face of it. I grabbed my coat and stepped into the mid-morning chill. The rear doors of all three SUVs opened and two masked men stepped out of each vehicle. Victor Andreyev emerged from the front passenger seat of the center vehicle. He sauntered toward me with the confidence of a feudal king.

"Where is the Bull?" he asked.

"Where are Beth and the children?" I countered.

"Here." He nodded toward the vehicle on my left. "Give me what I want and this problem will be over for both of us."

I studied the man. He was a proven liar and a spy. There wasn't a single reason I should trust him. He sneered at me as if challenging me to disprove how powerless I was. Beth and the children gave him a clear advantage over me, and he knew it.

"Why me?" I asked. "Why did you hire me?"

He smiled. "We needed to find the woman and you are an adequate investigator," he replied, lingering on the word "adequate." "Get the Bull and I will tell you where our interests aligned."

I glowered at him before returning to the Toyota. I opened the driver's door, leaned inside, and grabbed the bronze figure from under the front seat. I left the door open and returned to Andreyev, who eyed the figure greedily.

"Tell me," I pressed. "Why me?"

"There was a certain degree of opportunism involved," Andreyev replied as he took the heavy bronze object. "'Two birds with one stone,' to use one of your American expressions. You see, Mr. Morgan, you made some powerful enemies in Moscow, and for a while they had to play nice, but when this chance came along, well, it was only ever going to end one way. The order for your engagement came directly from the Kremlin. As did this."

He turned abruptly and yelled a command in Russian. As he hurried toward his car, his masked subordinates drew their weapons and stepped forward. I look around fearfully. This ruinous, rusting industrial wasteland was where I was destined to die.

CHAPTER 86

THE MASKED MAN closest to me raised his pistol. I backed toward the open car door. He aimed at my head, but never got the opportunity to pull the trigger. A terrifying rattle tore up the silence as a burst of bullets chewed the concrete directly in front of him and his accomplices. The six masked men were startled, and I took advantage of their shock to run toward the Toyota. The machine gunfire continued and Andreyev barked commands. His masked gunmen turned their weapons on the source of the thunderous volley, but the window on the seventh floor of a warehouse to the east was too far away for an effective pistol shot. Two figures appeared intermittently in the aperture, but only in silhouette, vanishing between every burst of muzzle flash. Their machine guns spat flames and bullets and created chaos. Andreyev's gunmen took cover behind their vehicles as the rounds shredded concrete, drilled through steel, and shattered glass.

I jumped through the Toyota's open door, landed in the driver's seat, threw the car into gear, and stepped on the gas. A couple masked men saw what I was doing and shot wildly at the car as I sped away, but their bullets went wide. As I put distance between me and my would-be killers, I looked in the rearview and saw them scramble into their vehicles, which were being riddled by bullets. The three SUVs fled the scene under a hail of gunfire, which followed them until they disappeared behind a chemical processing facility west of the courtyard.

I turned off the service road and followed a set of fresh tire tracks through the snow. I drove around the warehouse. When I rounded the final corner I saw one of Private's staff cars, a blue Nissan Rogue, parked by the entrance. As I pulled up beside the Nissan, the back door opened and Justine and Mo-bot stepped out.

I joined them in the snow.

"That sounded ugly," Justine said, hugging me.

"It was pretty intense," I replied.

"Didn't mean to get so close," Joshua Floyd said, emerging from the pockmarked old building. Jessie was with him. They each carried a full auto-converted AR-15 over their shoulder.

"You did great," I responded. "Thanks for keeping me alive, yet again."

I turned to Mo-bot.

"How are we doing?" I asked.

She leaned into the Nissan and took a tablet computer from the back seat. She showed me the screen, which displayed a constantly changing map. At the center was the locator beacon representing the tracking device we'd installed inside the bronze figure I'd given Andreyev.

"We're picking up the signal loud and clear," Mo-bot said.

I turned to Floyd. "Let's go get your wife and kids."

CHAPTER 87

WE FOLLOWED ANDREYEV'S convoy along Highway 209, keeping half a mile behind them, so there was less chance of being spotted. No one said much because we all knew the stakes. Floyd was particularly grim-faced, and I wondered how difficult it had been for him not to shoot the men who'd taken his wife and children. But if he had killed Andreyev and his accomplices, there was a good chance we would never have found Beth, Maria, and Danny, so he'd restrained himself in the face of the scorching desire for vengeance that burned bright in his eyes.

I steered the Toyota off the 209 onto the

Glasco Turnpike, a rural road that led toward Overlook Forest. We were in the New York wilderness, a few miles from Mount Marion. We drove through a white landscape, taking care to stay out of sight of the convoy. The road was deserted and the frozen landscape eerily still. I couldn't help but feel the nausea of anticipation as we rolled on, and somehow the silence in the car made it worse. I looked at Justine, who sat next to me, and she gave me a strained smile. Jessie, Mo-bot, and Floyd were in the back, each of them lost in their own world. Floyd caught me looking at him in the rearview and nodded somberly. I recognized his expression; it was that of a warrior ready for action.

Ten miles from the 209, Mo-bot spoke. "They're turning off. Left, in about eight hundred yards. From the satellite imagery, it looks like a farm. There's a trail for about a mile and then some buildings."

I slowed as we approached the turn.

"That's it," Mo-bot said, and I nodded and took a left that led me between two huge stretches of tall trees.

After a while, the forests either side of us

thinned and gave way to rolling farmland. I slowed down, stopping just before the brow of a slope.

"Wait here," I said.

I got out and ran along the icy gravel track to the crest of the hill. I crouched as I approached and peered down into a broad hollow to see the SUVs parked beside a farmhouse. Three large barns flanked a courtyard set a short distance away from the house. I saw two men standing guard outside one barn.

The corrugated-steel building seemed the obvious place to start looking for Beth and the children.

Andreyev stepped out of his SUV. His men did likewise. They removed their ski masks and chatted; some lit cigarettes. Andreyev examined the Bull and said something to the men around him before heading away from the house toward the barns. My heart sank. I hadn't expected things to move this quickly.

He crossed the yard and signaled to the guards standing outside the farthest barn. One of them turned to open the door.

I had hoped we would have more time for

surveillance, but it seemed we would have to act immediately.

I edged back from the brow of the hill, got to my feet, ran to the Toyota, and leaned inside.

"We're going to have to move now," I said. "I think he's going for Beth and the children."

CHAPTER 88

BETH WAS CRYING with exhaustion and the children were weeping as their little hands clawed desperately at the earth. All three of them were digging the hole Beth had started with the broken length of pipe. She felt a growing sense of desperation. Time was not their ally, and she knew escape was their only way of avoiding death. Danny's fingers were raw, Maria's bleeding.

"Please stop," Beth said. "Let me do it."

"No," Maria replied tearfully. "We want to help. We have to get out!"

Danny's face was covered in dirty streaks from where he kept wiping it with his muddy hands.

Fresh tears sprang to Beth's eyes as she looked at her brave children.

"I'm so proud of you both," she choked out. "Let me check it."

The hole was now big enough for the children to escape, but at last attempt it had been too small for Beth. She pushed her head into it, scrabbled under the wall, and tried to force her shoulders through. She could see the snow-covered field on the other side of the steel wall and was invigorated by a blast of cold fresh air. She pushed but the earth would not yield. She couldn't negotiate her way through. It was a matter of centimeters only. She pushed herself back under the wall and inside the barn.

"A little more," she said, and they resumed digging.

She hacked at the ground with the length of pipe, and the children clawed the loose earth clear. Her spirit was almost broken and she longed for sleep, but she couldn't afford to indulge her ruined muscles and broken mind. Her children needed her to keep going.

She stopped suddenly and so did Maria and Danny. They heard the sound of a lock being opened.

"Go!" Beth said, grabbing Danny.

"Not without you," he cried.

"I'm coming," she told him. "Go."

She pushed him into the hole and under the wall then grabbed Maria.

"Take him to the woods," Beth said. "Hide!"

"Mom—" Maria began, but Beth cut her off.

"Go." She kissed her daughter on the head and pushed her into the hole. Maria wriggled through and Beth tried to follow. She threw herself down as she heard the door open behind her. There was a shout in Russian and she heard footsteps pounding across the concrete floor of the barn.

She pushed against the frozen ground and cried with the pain and effort. She could see the snow-covered field and the forest in the distance, but there was no sign of the children.

Please let them be safe, she thought.

She pushed desperately as the footsteps drew closer, but she was stuck half in and half out of the barn. Then she felt hands on her shoulders and turned to see the children either side of her, Danny to her left and Maria to her right. They grabbed her under her arms.

"Push!" Maria yelled. "Come on, Mom. Push!"

Behind her the heavy footsteps were close. She knew she had just seconds. Beth pushed with every remaining ounce of strength. There was a gunshot. Then another. She felt the wall above her shake under the impact of the bullets. Fear and anger surged, but most of all she was propelled by the desire to be with her children.

She strained every fiber and felt the cold earth shift. She elbowed aside a giant clod of soil and wriggled further through the hole. Steely fingers grabbed her ankle, but she kicked out and pulled her leg through. Someone tried to shoot through the wall but the bullets stalled against the tempered steel.

She heard shouts in Russian from inside the barn and knew they were coming for her and the children.

"Run!" Beth yelled.

She grabbed the kids and pulled them forward, aiming for the treeline on the other side of the field. The snow was deep and hard going, and she was bloody, bruised, and battered, but she was free.

And determined to stay that way.

CHAPTER 89

JOSHUA AND I were in the Toyota, watching Jessie take position on the brow of the hill. She lay prone in the snow and set up her AR-15 on a bipod, then checked the magazines of ammunition she had in a small bag beside her.

I glanced in the rearview and saw Justine and Mo-bot heading toward the road. Justine was on the phone, calling the cops as we'd agreed. She looked nervously in my direction.

"She's set," Floyd said. I glanced at Jessie and saw her giving a thumbs-up.

I put the car in gear. "Ready?" I asked.

Floyd patted his AR-15 and nodded.

I stepped on the gas and we lurched forward, spitting icy gravel as the wheels fought for traction. We crested the hill and saw most of Andreyev's men were congregating around the farmhouse. They looked up the moment they heard the engine, and sprang into action when they caught sight of us racing toward them.

My attention was suddenly drawn from the farmhouse by the sight of three figures running away from the far barn. They were heading toward the forest on the other side of the field. I couldn't believe what I was seeing: Beth, Maria, and Danny had somehow managed to escape! I pointed them out to Floyd and a smile began to appear on his face before it quickly hardened to a look of grim resolve.

Andreyev and the two guards who had been stationed outside the barn were running along the exterior wall. They would soon have a line of sight on Beth and the children.

The men by the farmhouse opened fire on us. As bullets thudded into the ground all around the SUV, Jessie replied on our behalf and sprayed the group with bullets. The rattle of machine gunfire sent panic through Andreyev's men. Two of them went down with bloody wounds and were hauled into the farmhouse by their retreating accomplices.

Andreyev stopped in his tracks when he heard the gunfire and yelled something at the two guards before changing direction and running back toward the courtyard. The two guards continued their pursuit of Beth and the children.

I steered off the track and took us around the house and through the thick snow that covered the bumpy hill. We sprayed ice and slush everywhere and bounced around wildly as the engine roared. Above us, Jessie kept laying down covering fire, pinning Andreyev's men inside the farmhouse.

We hit level ground and shot past the house, into the field beside the east barn. One of the guards pursuing Beth turned and opened fire on us. The other shot at her and the kids.

"Stop the car," Floyd said.

I stepped on the brake and we skidded to a halt. Floyd jumped out and raised his AR-15 to his shoulder.

I heard gunfire and looked to my left to see

one of Andreyev's men shooting at us through the back window of the house.

I pulled my Glock from the holster in the center console, opened the door, and returned fire. The man staggered back, wounded, and I turned just in time to see Floyd target the guard who was shooting at us. His pistol could hardly make the distance, but the AR-15 had no such trouble. Floyd squeezed the trigger. The first bullet tore through the man's throat. The second pierced his skull.

Beth and the children were almost at the trees, the second guard not far behind. As his comrade's body tumbled into the snow, Floyd quickly shifted his aim to the guard pursuing his family. He squeezed the trigger and hit his target in the center of his back. The man went down instantly.

An engine roared and I looked left to see a black Porsche Cayenne shoot out of another barn. Andreyev was at the wheel. He raced across the courtyard and out into open countryside away from the farmhouse. He was heading for a track that cut through the woods.

"You go. Look after your family," I told Floyd. "I'll take care of him."

"Thank you, Jack. For everything you've done."

He slung his rifle, shut the car door, and set out at a sprint.

I popped the Toyota in gear and went in pursuit of the fleeing Russian.

CHAPTER 90

BOTH CHILDREN WERE shrieking and Beth was almost hysterical. They were shooting at her babies! These monsters were prepared to slaughter children. They just had to make it to the trees...

Maria was a few paces ahead. Beth saw her daughter glance back.

"I'm with you, baby," she assured her.

Maria stopped suddenly.

"Don't give up. Keep going!" Beth shouted. But Maria stayed where she was and pointed at something behind them. Danny had run on ahead, but he looked back and suddenly stopped as well.

Beth turned to see what they were staring at. Instead of the gunman she expected to see pursuing them, she saw something she couldn't believe. Tears flooded her eyes. They streamed down her face. They fell into the thick snow.

"Daddy," Maria said softly.

Beth shook with relief as she saw Josh running toward them with a rifle slung over his back.

Maria broke free and ran past the two dead gunmen. She sprinted through the snow and leaped into her father's arms. He wept with joy as he showered her with kisses. Danny went next and raced to his father. Josh scooped him up and carried his children to Beth.

He set them down and looked at his wife with all the love in the world.

She threw her arms around him and they kissed until she collapsed against him, exhausted by the ordeal, unable to quite believe it was over.

"I love you," Josh whispered.

"I love you too," Beth just about managed through the choking flood of emotion.

"Come on," Josh said, wiping his eyes. "Let's get out of here."

He held the children's hands and led them away.

Beth took one last look at the place that had nearly broken her and robbed her of her children, before following her family into the trees.

CHAPTER 91

THE TOYOTA'S ENGINE roared and the suspension clattered and clunked as I followed Andreyev along the rutted forest track. His car had more grunt than mine, but we were both pushing our vehicles to the limit. Plumes of smoke belched from the twin exhaust of the Porsche SUV. The Toyota's cabin filled with the stench of overheated metal and I opened the window for a blast of fresh air. Andreyev's Cayenne was churning mud and snow, flinging it everywhere. With the window open I could hear the growl of the engines and every bang and thud as our chassis bounced around violently.

We sped along, winding between the trees. I fought for control of the Toyota at every bend while the snow and ice threatened to send me spinning. Both cars fishtailed wildly, wheels churning, and exhausts burning.

As we came out of a bend, I accelerated and nudged his bumper. He pushed his car faster and opened some distance. I could see the forest thinning ahead, and then clear sky. The track spat us onto a single-lane highway. Andreyev bounced through a bank of slush onto asphalt and skidded around to head south. I narrowly avoided colliding with a mail truck heading north. Ignoring the prolonged sound of the truck's horn, I swung south to chase the Russian.

The forest sped by in a blur on both sides as we shot along the country road. Andreyev overtook a VW Golf on a blind bend and I followed, narrowly missing an oncoming eighteen-wheeler. My heart thundered at the sound of an angry blast from its loud horn. I swung in behind Andreyev and squared up just in the nick of time.

I forced the Toyota down two gears and hit the gas. The car jumped forward and I drew alongside the Porsche. Another truck was heading directly for me. Fast. I must have been doing eighty when I swung the wheel hard and crashed into Andreyev's car. He fought for control, but I held firm and forced him off the road. I swung into the lane as the truck passed by with a roar.

Next to me, Andreyev's car hit a patch of ice, skidded, and came to a crashing stop against a tree. I pulled off the road up ahead of him and jumped out as he emerged from the car. He was dazed but he had a pistol in his hand.

I ran at him. He fired wildly. He tried to adjust but was bleeding into one eye, struggling to focus. I reached him before he corrected his aim, and drove my shoulder into his gut. We both crashed against the back door of the Porsche. He brought the gun down on my neck but I stood firm, instinctively fighting the blank pull of unconsciousness. I swung a punch that connected with his chin.

Another gunshot, this one close to my ear. The world screamed, but I ignored the pain and drove a left cross into his nose. He crumpled and I followed up with a combination of jabs and a hook that sent him to the ground.

He dropped the gun and tried to crawl away

through the snow, whining like a wounded animal. I picked up his pistol and held it against his head.

"It's over, Victor," I said. "It's over."

He rolled onto his back and looked at me with hate-filled eyes.

I kept the gun trained on him as I walked over to the Porsche. I leaned through the open driver's door, reached past the burst airbags, and picked up the Bull from the driver's footwell.

"You traded it all for nothing," I said, walking back toward him. "Your people should never have picked such a common object to store your data. This is a replica I bought on Wall Street first thing this morning."

I tossed the Bull into the snow. Andreyev's face twisted in despair.

"The original is on its way to people who will know how to decode it. People in the US government."

His head dropped. He looked utterly defeated. I leaned against the Porsche and kept the gun on him as I listened to the sound of approaching sirens.

CHAPTER 92

THE SOUND OF the tray crashing to the floor set Beth's heart racing. She hadn't been the same since the abduction, but she was getting better. She looked at Josh, who smiled and reached across the table to take her hand. They were in Al's BBQ Shack, a family restaurant in Shrub Oak that was popular with parents because there was an indoor play area and ball pit. It wasn't Beth's idea of a great restaurant, but the kids loved it and were off playing with some friends they'd bumped into.

Loud chatter filled the air, along with the clatter of cutlery and the sounds of people eating.

Beneath it all, a bedrock of music that never stopped. It was a brash, loud place and all Beth wanted was peace and quiet, but right now she thought the kids deserved every treat they could get.

"My head is ringing," Josh said with a smile.

"Tell me about it," Beth agreed.

"I love you," he said.

Suddenly none of the crashing noise or hustle and bustle seemed quite so bad. The thought of never seeing him again, the memory of what had happened to them, that was true horror. Every day since then had been bliss.

"I love you too."

The kids came running over and pointed out an approaching waiter.

"Is that our food?" Danny asked.

"Looks like it," Josh replied. "Shuffle in."

Maria slid into the booth next to Josh and Danny sat beside Beth. She beamed at her family, feeling the warmth of contentment precisely because she knew how close they'd come to losing everything that mattered.

"Looks good," Josh said, as the waiter served their meals.

"Two burgers, a hickory chicken, and two large ribs."

"Ribs, here," Floyd said. "Beth's having the chicken, and the kids have got the burgers."

"And the last ribs?" the waiter asked.

"Those are mine," Ted Eisner said, sidling up behind him. "Don't you just love it when that happens? You come back from the bathroom and the food is right there. Shift over, youngster."

He nudged Danny along the bench and the waiter set the platter in front of him.

"You've got sauces and wipes, so you should be all set."

"Thanks," Floyd responded as the waiter withdrew. "Dig in, everyone."

"Thanks for inviting me," Ted said. He popped a french fry in his mouth. "I hope I'm not cramping your family outing."

"Not at all," Floyd assured him.

"Besides, you're paying," Beth added with a smile.

"She's kidding," Floyd said. "It's on us. It's the least we can do after—"

"Don't even go there," Ted interrupted. "You'd

have done the same, and the insurance paid out for a brand new car, so we're all square." He sucked at a rib. "This is good."

Beth nodded and smiled at Floyd. "It really is. As good as it gets."

CHAPTER 93

I DIDN'T THINK I'd ever had a highball that tasted this good. I took another sip and relished the peaty undertones of the single malt.

"What time is he coming?" Mo-bot asked.

It didn't matter whether you were grand or low-born: if Mo wasn't in the mood for something, she wouldn't hide it. And right now, all she wanted was to be on a plane to Los Angeles.

"Eight," Jessie replied. "He said he'd be here at eight. Right, Jack?"

I nodded. Jessie had been at my side for much of the past two weeks, helping coordinate our response with federal law enforcement. The implications of what we'd discovered on Roslov's Bull were profound.

The technology alone was priceless, and so, it seemed, were the secrets it contained. Sci had only been able to decipher a tiny fraction of the data stored on the bronze, but it was enough. His refrain for weeks had been "Heck of a thing."

He said it now. "Heck of a thing. I wish I could have had it a little longer."

I'd insisted on handing it to the one man I believed I could trust—the man we were about to meet—Secretary of State Eli Carver.

Justine squeezed my hand and I smiled at her. She responded with a sweet grin. We'd hit some turbulence following the car chase with Andreyev. She felt it was an unnecessary risk— Floyd, Beth, and the children were all safe, and we had the original Bull—why risk my life capturing Andreyev? But I couldn't let him get away, not after all the pain he'd caused. For Roni Alvarez, for Jim Taft, I had to get justice. I think she accepted that I'd never be one of those guys who could sit back and let others deal with problems. I had to get involved, and when I did, I would give it my all.

"He's here," Justine said, and I looked at the door to the Library Bar. A squad of Secret Service agents entered and fanned out as they scoped the place out. Conversation hushed and the patrons of the split-level bar watched to see what would happen next. Moments later, Eli Carver strode in. If he was aware every eye in the place was on him, he seemed unfazed by the attention.

He slid onto the bench seat opposite me.

"Jack Morgan. I just want to shake your hand," he said, leaning across the table.

I took his hand and he wrapped both of his around mine for a warm, clasped shake.

"Where do I begin? This country owes you and your team a great debt. Rick Ferguson led us to two double agents he'd recruited within the Pentagon. You were right to be paranoid, Jack. There were more moles. Victor Andreyev has offered to turn on his former employers. He's probably the highest-value asset we've flipped since Maxim Yenen."

He looked at my team and held their gazes one by one. This guy was a master politician. He knew how to make people feel important.

"And the bull, the Charging Bull. The

technology…I mean, wow! But the data—Roslov was running a huge network. Political interference, financing radical groups, bribing officials, buying influence around the world. We found three senators on his list and the details of every single payment he's ever made to them. No wonder the Russians were prepared to go to such lengths to get it back. We're in the process of dismantling or monitoring what we believe to be somewhere in the region of half their foreign intelligence activity."

Sci whistled.

Carver looked at me squarely.

"So, like I said before, if you ever need anything…"

"I could use a name," I said. "Andreyev told me he'd been instructed to hire me by someone in the Kremlin, that I've made powerful enemies over there."

I sensed Justine shift uncomfortably. Carver was smart enough to pick up on her concern.

"He was probably trying to get inside your head," he replied. "But I'll check it out for you."

"Thank you, Mr. Secretary," I said, and he frowned.

"I've told you, it's Eli."

"And I said I might feel more comfortable with that once we've had a beer together," I countered. "What can I get you?"

He stood. "I'm afraid I can't. Dinner date with some defense contractors. They tell me it's essential for national security, but I'd much rather hang out with you guys."

"Another time then, Mr. Secretary," I said.

He gave a wry smile. "You folks enjoy your evening."

We said our goodbyes and within a few moments, he and his Secret Service detail were gone.

"Heck of a thing," Sci remarked.

"When are you going to stop saying that?" Mo-bot exclaimed. We all chuckled.

"Well, it is," Sci objected.

Mo-bot elbowed him playfully.

"Come on," she said. "I need to grab my stuff. Meet down here in an hour?" she asked me.

I nodded. We'd booked a jet to leave for Los Angeles.

"We'll catch up soon," she said to Jessie.

When she and Sci were gone, Jessie got to her feet.

"I'm going too," she said. "Unless you need anything?"

I shook my head. "You've done more than enough. I'll call you for our regular briefing on Wednesday."

"Thank you," Justine said to Jessie. "For everything."

"Yes," I added. "Thank you. You've been outstanding."

Jessie blushed. "Look after him. He needs watching." She gave a warm smile, then turned and walked away.

Justine lifted my arm and put it over her shoulder. I pulled her toward me, and she settled against my chest.

For a while we didn't say anything, simply watched the other patrons spending a normal evening in the busy hotel bar. True to its name, the place was fitted out like a library in an old English country home and had a comforting atmosphere. It was where Justine and I had flirted with giving our relationship another try, before my trip to Moscow. The place had special significance, at least for me, so I'd chosen it for our last night in New York.

"She's right, you know," Justine said at last. "You do need watching."

"And you think you're the right person to take on the responsibility?" I asked.

"I do," she replied, before leaning in to kiss me.

ACKNOWLEDGMENTS

We'd like to thank our editor, John Sugar, and the team at Cornerstone for their excellent work on this book. We'd also like to thank you, the reader, for coming on another adventure with the Private team, and hope you'll join us for the next one.

Adam would like to thank James Patterson for giving him the opportunity to be part of Private. He'd also like to thank his wife, Amy, and his children, Maya, Elliot, and Thomas, for being such great inspiration, and his agent, Hannah Sheppard, for her continued support.

JAMES
PATTERSON
RECOMMENDS

When the rich and famous
are in trouble, their first call isn't 911.

 NEW YORK TIMES BESTSELLER

JAMES PATTERSON

PRIVATE

NEW YORK · LOS ANGELES · LONDON · PARIS

& MAXINE PAETRO

PRIVATE

I've always been a curious person. It's one of the many reasons why I'm a writer. Something I always asked myself was: "What happens if a 'one percenter' gets into trouble?" The answer: Jack Morgan and PRIVATE. On Jack Morgan's agenda in his debut outing is investigating a multimillion-dollar NFL gambling scandal and solving a series of schoolgirl slayings. Then, the unthinkable—his former lover turned best friend's wife is murdered. One thing you should know about Jack is that beneath his Lamborghini-driving, red-carpet-event-attending surface, he's a very smart guy. And he takes no prisoners. Just wait till you get to the end of PRIVATE. You'll see what I mean.

JACK MORGAN
IS WANTED
FOR MURDER
JAMES PATTERSON
PRIVATE
#1 Suspect
& MAXINE PAETRO

PRIVATE: # 1 SUSPECT

Over the years, I've learned that reputation is everything when it comes to business. While Private's Jack Morgan has a reputation for being effective and discreet, he's also known for being quite the lady killer. But when an ex-lover shows up dead in his bed and all evidence points to him, Jack realizes someone wants to kill more than just his good name. To make things worse, another event threatens Private's stability, and Jack suddenly finds himself with his back against the wall. Characters will do the most shocking things when they have no other options, especially characters like Jack who are used to being in control. I won't tell you what happens, but I will say it'll blow your mind.

THE WORLD'S #1 BESTSELLING WRITER

JAMES PATTERSON

Was Hollywood's most
famous couple kidnapped?
Or murdered?

PRIVATE
L.A.

MARK SULLIVAN

PRIVATE LA

If you've ever wondered what celebrity power couples do behind closed doors, you can stop all of your conjecturing—the answers are all in PRIVATE LA. America's most popular celebrity couple has made an exit...from their lives. No one knows where they went or why, and it's up to Jack and his Private team to breach the walls of security and hordes of paparazzi to find the power couple. But when has anything good ever come from a pile of secrets buried under miles of genius PR? Jack's about to find that out, up close and personal, and he's in for the shock of his life. Because in the city of big dreams, nothing is what it seems. Especially if I'm involved.

PRIVATE UNCOVERS A
SHOCKING PAST AND
A LETHAL CONSPIRACY—
IN MODERN-DAY BERLIN

THE WORLD'S #1 BESTSELLING WRITER
JAMES PATTERSON
MARK SULLIVAN
PRIVATE
BERLIN

PRIVATE BERLIN

Every now and then, I find myself wanting a big change in scenery. Don't get me wrong. Jack Morgan and the Private team are great fun, but sometimes a little taste of the foreign makes life a bit more exciting. And by "exciting," I really mean dangerous. At Private's German headquarters, Chris Schneider—superstar agent—has gone rogue. He's the keeper of quite a few pieces of sensitive information, but one in particular could have earth-shattering consequences. Hang on tight and don't blink. This one is a roller coaster of tension that'll leave you reeling.

photo: David Burnett

JAMES PATTERSON
THE WORLD'S #1 BESTSELLING WRITER

ABOUT THE AUTHORS

JAMES PATTERSON is the most popular storyteller of our time. He is the creator of unforgettable characters and series, including Alex Cross, the Women's Murder Club, Jane Effing Smith, and Maximum Ride, and of breathtaking true stories about the Kennedys, John Lennon, and Princess Diana, as well as our military heroes, police officers, and ER nurses. He has coauthored #1 bestselling novels with Bill Clinton and Dolly Parton, told the story of his own life in James Patterson by James Patterson, and received an Edgar Award, nine Emmy Awards, the Literarian Award from the National Book Foundation, and the National Humanities Medal.

ADAM HAMDY is a bestselling author and screenwriter. His most recent novel, *The Other Side* *of Night*, has been described as ingenious, constantly surprising, and deeply moving. He is the author of the Scott Pearce series of contemporary espionage thrillers, *Black 13* and *Red Wolves*, and the Pendulum trilogy. Keep up to date with his latest books and news at www.adamhamdy.com.

For a complete list of books by
JAMES PATTERSON

VISIT
JamesPatterson.com

 Follow James Patterson on Facebook
@JamesPatterson

 Follow James Patterson on X
X **@JP_Books**

 Follow James Patterson on Instagram
@jamespattersonbooks